T0366145

ENIGMA

(BOOK 1 OF THE PARADOX PROGRESSION)

DAVID PADDIT

PARTRIDGE
A Penguin Random House Company

ISBN: Softcover 978-1-4828-2351-6
eBook 978-1-4828-2352-3

Because of the dynamic nature of the Internet, any web addresses or links contained in this book may have changed since publication and may no longer be valid. The views expressed in this work are solely those of the author and do not necessarily reflect the views of the publisher, and the publisher hereby disclaims any responsibility for them.

To order additional copies of this book, contact
Toll Free 800 101 2657 (Singapore)
Toll Free 1 800 81 7340 (Malaysia)
orders.singapore@partridgepublishing.com

www.partridgepublishing.com/singapore

CONTENTS

To my parents.

"I look into his eyes and see the demons that guzzle and indulge on his secrets . . ."

—LUCY HARLOTTE Hysteria

AUTHOR'S NOTE

Sit down, relax, pop in some music while you're at it, and enjoy *drumroll please* Enigma. (Whatever you read in this book might or might not be real so keep your eyes peeled.) *Cue hysterical laughter*

Prologue

October 09, 2036

I've recently turned eleven years old last May twenty-first.

It's dark outside.

I'm sitting on the couch with my sister Serenity who's one year younger than me, watching TV. I'm eating my red gummy bears.

Serenity always wanted to eat the green ones.

Mom ate the yellow ones.

Crissy ate the rest of the spectrum while we laughed at her.

Dad can't eat because he's an archaeologist in Egypt right now.

I hear the grandfather clock beside the TV talk crazy, "TICK, TOCK." and then the occasional, "DING" marking an hour. Then I hear the doorbell say, "DONG, DONG."

"Just stay here with your little sister and Crissy now. Just call Crissy whenever you need anything." Mom kisses my forehead.

"Haha, there's a lipstick mark on your forehead." Serenity taunts.

I look into an oblate sphere-shaped mirror on a wall located behind me.

There are exactly sixteen mirrors in the whole house and thirty-three windows.

I see a little boy with short curly hair, a round face and a forehead with my Mom's favorite shade of red for lipstick, smudged, and a small hole on its center with the shade of my pale skin.

'Where are you going?" I ask because I know that when she kisses me, wearing her fancy outside clothes, she goes somewhere special.

"I'm going out to the grocery." she replies.

"Can I come?" I hold her hand.

"No, because before the groceries, I need to meet with one of my friends, maybe next time, Damian" she slips her hand in mine.
"Bye, Mommy." Serenity says, kissing her at the cheek.

She goes outside with an automatic umbrella.

I look out the window in front of the main door, see her go in her car and slam the door shut.

Something feels wrong. Usually she goes out with Crissy to help her, but this time she went alone.

The sky starts crying.

Crissy closes all the windows of the house so no water or wind will seep in house and make the floor damp.

All of a sudden I hear a loud bang come from outside. I put my hands on my ears, squishing them to thwart the booming sound entering my ears and collapse on the floor, trembling.

I get on my feet and look out the window, which now looks smudged with droplets.

The shadows of the water droplets are in motion on the floor. They're dancing to the unnecessary sound. How could they?

I see what looks like a grey mushroom cloud form from bottom to top in front of me.

"Nuclear Bomb!" I shout because it's the first thing on my mind.

Crissy out of nowhere drags Serenity and I to the hall that leads to the basement of the house. "Hurry!" she says while I stare at the corner table carrying a nuisance on its back, a vase with a tulip in it. I wonder if there's soil in it. "What's happening?" Serenity asks. "We need to go down to the basement." Crissy opens the door down.

Serenity and I go down first, followed by Crissy who closes the door and switches the light on.

We hurry down. I hear another explosion.

Serenity screams to the top of her voice.

"Cover your ears, Serenity!" I cover my ears. I hope she did.

I tremble under my own skin and I let the tragedy of a feeling sink in me. I'm scared. All my senses are tingling to the rush of my heart. The basement is a dark and cramped-up place full of dust and antiques. I extend my arms to the side to grab hold of something and end up breaking a pot.

Crissy is holding me with one hand and with the other holding Serenity, but Crissy isn't enough to stop the uneasiness I feel. My hands are still searching the walls for something to grab onto and I feel a handle. I grasp it and Crissy as firm as possible. Crissy doesn't react to me squeezing her arm. She doesn't escape the constriction. She recapitulates, "It's okay, it's okay, it's okay."

My ears are deafening to the thunderous sounds equivalent to a million thunderstorms.

The flesh under my skin is an earthquake of heartbeats; I can't slow it down no matter how much I try.

I remember—Mom! Where is she? I hope she's safe . . . and Dad too because he's in Egypt. I hope they're okay.

* * *

5 YEARS LATER

I can still hear the shrilling screams and dreadful shouts after that day of the obliteration of the city. Pandemonium roaming free in the streets, I remember them clearly.

Lives lost, most went missing, at most a couple of hundred thousands to a million, my mom, one of them.

Many things concluded over years. Now that the world's turned into a gigantic archipelago each group of islands were named differently, varying to its conquerors. The nuclear weapons they developed were intended for splitting countries into pieces. One of their reasons of splitting countries into pieces was because they thought it would be easier to invade and overthrow governments. They're right.

My sister, our governess and our dad and I live near a group of islands called Mellous. Mellous is a European-overthrown group of islands. We live in Seattle, one of the only existing independent governments in the whole world.

Everything's been normal, ordinary so far. School can sometimes be so excruciatingly painful that suicide rates grow. Seattle's one of the most sane cities to live in because of many reasons like: independence of government, regulated laws, strong and reliable military capable of scaring potential invaders, urbanized society, cool weather, and technology so advanced, it's possible to do everything in one touch, literally. It all seems a little too perfect for me, but I guess it's something to get used to.

If sanity were a ball it would be a cube now. It doesn't roll, it's stationary, there's just one kind of sanity that keeps us going everyday—the sanity that someday we're going to be able to move on again. We need to be able to accept insanity and chisel it out, but a little insanity is important—that little insanity will be that chisel that will make us roll again someday.

* * *

Chapter 1

5 Years Later

March 16, 2041

The clock ticks against my heartbeat, each second that passes my heart gets faster and faster as exams get closer and closer, I can't fail now. Not now. Not that it's final exams.

The classroom—four walls, one door, a whiteboard in front of me, six rows of seats that stretch to the back of the room, a desk for the teacher and four window panels compressed on one wall that weren't open.

I'm staring at the gaps in between the tiles, which seem like they could go on forever from tile to tile and imagination spewing in my mind, so many thoughts running and jumping enough to make me nauseous.

"Hey, Damian, can I borrow a pen? I left mine at home." someone behind me asks in a voice dipped in honey.

"Yeah, sure." I respond to her soft voice, reaching for my pencil case in my bag. "I have a lot of pens." I say, handing my pencil case to her. "Help yourself."

She grabs the case with her warm fingers on my hand and says, "Thanks!"

I look back to see her. She's someone I didn't recognize.

She smiles with cheeks gushing crimson red, teeth both white and symmetrical, a dimple slightly below her cheekbone, and a round face with a small, but unnoticeable mole under her jawline, a face perfectly matched with light brown hair draped down in between her elbow and shoulder.

I turn to my table and see a couple of papers stacked on top of each other and the first page having to be on the wrong side up. I flip it over and find myself being stared at by half of the class.

"Damian, didn't I say you shouldn't look yet?" Our teacher babbles, giving me a spine-chilling glare that pools with anger.

"Sorry." I say, flipping the paper again, retracting the unwanted attention.

Okay. What we're going to do now is your term finals." Mrs. Garvener says. "This test will make up twenty-five percent of your final grade. I expect that all of you have already reviewed. Besides, this test isn't that difficult." she grins as she looks at me like she was hoping I didn't review, but I did.

That Garvener must be mentally insane—suffering from Schizophrenia. She can be pretty annoying at times, minding other student's business like they're her own, feeling close to them inching closer Just enough for us to want to scream and break down in front of her face.

"One hour starts . . . now!" she says and I look at the clock on top of the whiteboard, "two thirty" it reads.

Everybody flips the papers in synchronized motion, and after that, hushed mouths and fingers writing for their lives.

I get a pen I left earlier in the pocket of my pants for accessible use and look at the test paper. Some of the words were left vague because of the printing making the test difficult to read and my brain hardwired to put more effort.

I fill in some details of the paper like name, date, and teacher and start immediately knowing my time is so limited. It was a multiple choice, so I didn't struggle like the others beside me who by the way didn't review. Breathing in and out, thinking with those retarded brains they don't use, one of them runs his fingers through his hair, feeling nerve-wrecked. They're probably thinking what will happen to them after the test.

I can only imagine what will happen: Their parents will send them to boarding school, or the school will reprimand them.

Anyways, it doesn't matter to me.

It was humid in the room. Sweat dripped from my face to the armchair I sat on. It disrupted me for a second, but it was nothing. I just went on with the test.

The test is easier than I expected, but it could be the lengthiest test I have ever seen and held.

I finish the test, and I stare at the clock. Five minutes to three, but the school bell rings. The school pranksters are at it again, but everyone believed it was dismissal.

I'm surprised I finished it. But again, I reviewed so it wasn't surprising at all.

We leave our test papers in the classroom and rush down the crowded hall, to the school entrance, people pushing and nudging, making me lose my momentum. Before I fall crumble to my knees someone gets my hand. It's Ross, a friend of mine.

He's a heartthrob in our school, the only thing that makes him different from other heartthrobs is his disbelief in the infamous "status quo" which has the ability to physically and emotionally wreck a person. His structure, semi-muscular, dark-brown hair stricken with light, eyes like a dominant tiger, his lips pursing to give a smile that reveals the smallest dimples at the corners of his face.

"Hey, are you alright?" he looks at me like I'm one of his girl victims to fall for him.

"Yeah, thanks for saving me there." I tell him.

Before I know it, not many people are at the halls anymore. I can see each locker forming two rows, opposite sides, left and right, going down the hall of cream white tiles soiled up by the shoe soles of other people.

I find my sister Serenity with her friend, Violet. Serenity's light brown—almost blonde—hair against Violet's raven hair, seems like they're opposites but they're good friends. They're talking about something.

I try to go to her, but I feel someone's hand slip into the collar of my polo and spins it around a fist leaving me to choke for a while. Whoever did this, I'm going to skin him alive if he tries to do something stupid.

"Hey! Where are you going?" I recognize that voice anywhere.

Bronze skin, five piercings on his ear, smells like garbage and one thing that anybody can't miss, his gigantic belly, Nel Gaurad.

"Nowhere" I turn around to get a quick glance at him and raise my eyebrow up.

Everyone stares.

Anxiety is in the air. Nel's stare is nothing but disgust to me and I look away.

He says, "Why don't you look at me?" and then I let my eyes pierce his.

"I don't want to break it to you, but you look filthy and rancid and you don't want my eyes to get damaged just looking at you, right?" I say as a come back to his ignorance.

Nel comes in directly, throws a punch, but I dodge and pull his long, dark, coarse hair with my bare hands downwards to knee his stomach making him jiggle a little. I feel an instant rush in my body. I bet he wasn't expecting much from me.

I fill my lungs with every breath of air I can put in.

He falls down on the concrete ground, face up.

The adrenaline coursing throughout my body's making me want to hit him more and more by the second. He looks at me with a stern look on his face.

Honestly I wasn't expecting him to try to go after me today, but I knew that someday I had to confront him one way or the other.

Spitting at him makes him look retarded for messing with me—correction, more retarded than he looks already.

I could see myself doing it in my mind, but I don't. It will make my public image degrade but I don't really care.

"More, more!"

"C'mon, Damian, get him!"

"That's right, he deserves it!"

Those are the words that I hear from behind.

"Good job, for an amateur fighter like you, Damian!" Ross says pulling me away from Nel. There was a sign of relief afterwards that he pulled me away. I may have lost myself in the moment. I could've dealt more damage to his face if Ross weren't there to stop me. Him being pulled down put me to an advantage of the school's social government.

It was like thunderous silence placed tape on everyone's mouth each time I pass by. People were looking at their phones, the bright lights from them striking their faces.

I look back at Nel to see how much wreck-havoc I've placed on him and see the nerds step at him like he's some kind of rag. They've given me some time to catch my breath before Nel might try to come back at me.

People break silence, finally, by laughing at them. I hear Nel sobbing. I laugh too, blood and snot run down his nose like they did not want to be part of him, to the groove above his lips and into his mouth. I couldn't picture myself in his place but it wouldn't make a difference.

I feel a bruise on my knuckles form, turning dark blue.

The nerds that stepped on Nel pass by us. "Hey, thanks for beating him up. I've always wanted him to taste his own medicine" one of them says, snorting the words out of his mouth. "No problem?" I reply.

Serenity gets my elbow. I can tell. She's the only one that does that.

"Hey! Hasn't dad told you not to get into more trouble than you are now?" she says.

"Yeah, sorry." I say

"Damian?" someone beside me asks. It was a feminine voice that I remembered. It was the girl that asked for a pen. My body becomes hot.

"What is it?" I ask her.

"I forgot to give back your pencil case." she says handing it to me.

"Thanks." I say, trying to mimic the volume of her voice.

"So what's your name?" I suggest.

"My name's Cathy. Cathy Abrahams" she says. Sweat dots my forehead, maybe from how nervous I am, or from the fight with Nel.

A little laugh escapes my mouth; assuming that she knows my name already and I didn't know hers.

"Anyway, my sis and I will be going home now. Bye." I say to her and sweat damped my forehead.

"Damian, let's go already!" Serenity says while I look at the Seattle Space Needle from afar, known as the tallest structure in the world because of the war.

I wipe the sweat away with my arm.

It doesn't take long to walk home. It was something we always did, like a hobby. We learned that the fastest way going there was to talk about the day. It was a fifteen-minute walk, but felt like five.

Serenity and I don't really care about the time wasted to go there. It was fun. We didn't want anything to go between that.

Our usual path going to our house passes a couple of apartment buildings and a smoothie shop we go into for a blueberry crumble smoothie for me and a banana-mango for Serenity and from that point on we have to walk a distance of two blocks and we're home.

The gate's locked from the inside so I ring the doorbell around three to five times. Our maid, Crissy opens the gate.

We go in and Serenity locks the gate.

We go in the house.

The door slams itself against the house.

Crissy's holding an unusual looking letter with my dad's archaeologist crest in her hands, I get nervous.

"I don't know how to break this down, to you two, but . . ." Crissy says. I open up to her, not because I want to, but because of fear. Fear of what she'll say, fear that it will be something bad, I want to remove that fear, I face it head on.

"Your Dad—how should I put this—has been reported missing."

Silence is all I can hear for 7-8-9-10-12-15-16 seconds.

I try not to worry and go to my room as fast as I can.

The words together are like a battery-ram to my heart.

Crissy says, "Wait, Damian!" but I ignore her.

I hear Serenity's cry from downstairs in my room. My Dad, taken away like our mother, all I can do now is hope. Hope he's still alive and surviving, surviving somewhere near civilization, hopefully, hopefully he's okay, surviving, alive, breathing, drinking water, eating, surviving, living, still living, always living.

I set up my laptop on my desk, trying to forget about my Dad for a while, go to Facebook and see a video of me beating up Nel on my wall. I don't play it because I was the one that beat him up. A lot of messages from the public appear. I try not to listen to Serenity's crying.

I remove the watch on my wrist with its cold silver surface skimming my skin and set it on my desk. The watch my Dad gave.

Shut it, Damian. Don't break to tears too. Don't even think of it.

I'm upset with my Dad being reported missing.

Stop thinking about it or you're going to get upset. Don't think of anything. Do not.

I'm trying my best to be strong.

I shut down my laptop and open my window to let in the fresh air.

The cold air ripples throughout my body and my clothes quiver in its movement. My hair soars on the gale getting into the room.

I get my med kit under my drawer and get the elastic bandage. I wrap it around the bruise I got earlier with the fight and lock it in place.

I go out of my room, down the stairs, pass the living room to go to the dining area. I see pieces of chicken wings, salad, and crème brulee at the table, enough for two people. I'm guessing that Crissy ate already.

Serenity is at the very end of the table, where Mom used to sit reminding me of her because of their lookalike. Her eyes are droopy from crying.

"Hey, Serenity, you okay?" I ask.

"Yeah, I just hope Dad isn't dead." and then her tears start flowing again.

She looks down to her lap with her hair covering her face.

I go to her and wrap my arms around her and my eyes water.

I can't keep up this tough façade anymore. I break down with her.

Our sob becomes worst and then my hug tightens with it only getting stronger.

The tears we weep together makes my arms wet beyond comprehension.

My hands turn to fists. I can't feel the bruise. It's too petty to even compare to the pain for our Dad.

Of all days it had to be today that he goes missing.

The word, "missing" in our minds was programmed to mean, "to never come back" after our Mom went missing.

Slowly the tears weaken, enough for me to snap out of this emotional grief that I'm feeling. I think I can handle the burden in my heart now.

I sit at the opposite end of the table and get some salad on one side of my plate, and chicken wings at the other. I eat a leaf of lettuce, then one side of a wing, then a piece of tomato, and then one side of a wing. I'm not chewing, practically I'm just moving the food around my mouth

I repeat the process until all that's left on my plate are splatters of dressing and bones.

Eating didn't feel right to do.

I set aside my plate and get one cup full of crème brulee. I don't know what I'm doing trying to eat like a pig.

I crack the caramelized sugar topping and the cream oozes out. I eat the cream inside slowly and carefully to make the flavors sync into my tongue.

Serenity hasn't eaten.

I finish dinner and say good night to Serenity. She walks to her room in gloom.

I didn't feel like sleeping. I stay at the living room and watch TV.

It's getting dark outside. There's no light passing through the fibers of our curtains except the nightlights of the house that Crissy switches on manually and regularly every night.

* * *

March 17, 2041

It is exactly twelve o'clock. I hear the doorbell sound.

I go outside and open our gate. There's nobody there. I look down. There's an unusual leather parchment cloth wrapping something in it. I pick it up. There is a gust. "What the hell is this?" I ask the wall of the gate. I get out to the streets and look around. Nobody's there.

I lock the gate, get inside the house, lock the door, and go to the couch. The cable is down, so I unplug the wire of the TV that was connected to the socket. I discover some kind of stone with something that looked like a smooth, circular stone with spiral indentions—looks like the way a kindergarten would draw wind, a letter with the crest of the Archaeologist camp

> *To the beloved son and daughter of Mr. Grey,*
>
> *Go to the harbor tomorrow when your vacation starts. There will be a boat waiting for you going to our Archaeologist Camp.*
>
> *In 48 hours that boat shall leave if given that you will not participate in the search for your father.*
>
> *If you are interested to participate please tell the woman on board to go to the island of Egypt. We need your urgent assistance regarding your father.*
>
> *You may bring acquaintances if you think they can be of use.*
>
> *The Manager of Jeremy Grey*

obviously printed, and a map of Mellous on the leather parchment.

I go to my room with all these stuff and go to bed completely tired from everything I've done today. I jump into bed.

I stare at the pale ceiling in silence and let my head skin into the dark blue fabric of the bed. My eyes shift to the walls of the room—two walls having a black and white pattern and the other two as pale as the ceiling.

My eyes slowly close until my vision is completely blacked out like the newest phase of the moon.

The bed swallows me in its cotton fibers. Every last ounce of strength, I used it for adjusting myself to a much relaxing position. I feel like the bed is draining my energy.

* * *

I wake up and stare at the clock. Five forty-seven. I get out of bed and fall flat on the floor. I'm clearly awake now. Today is the day our teachers sign our clearance so we won't go to summer school.

I get the letter, together with the stone and the map.

I go out of my room and walk through the hall passing the masters bedroom, going to Serenity's room. I slowly open her door. She's awake, engulfed into what she was doing in her laptop.

"What are you doing in my room?" she asks.

"I need to show you something." I hand over the things from last night.

"What is this?" Serenity grabs them from my hand and unfolds the odd looking map, then she puts it at the side of her bed and opens the letter.

"So we're going to go to Dad's archaeologist camp?" she asks.

"The doorbell rang last night and found these things on our doorstep" I say. "I'll ask Crissy if we can get going later."

She replies bluntly, "Okay then."

"What's with that look of yours?" I tilt my head and I ready my fingers for a tickling assassination.

"Nothing, it's just that . . ." she says, but I tickle her. She's laughing so hard, "Damian, sto-o-op"

I stop after few seconds.

She stares back at her laptop. She's typing something so fast, I couldn't see. I stare into the laptop.

"You're having a conversation with Violet?" I ask.

"Don't look!" She closes her laptop.

"Just prepare your things. I don't know what kind of things those are but . . . girl things?" I say. "We'll be leaving in the afternoon . . . maybe."

She laughs for her own self-indulgence. Finally.

I'm happy for her. She seems over the fact that our Dad's missing. Or she's trying to keep a tough façade like me, concealing the tears and the pain.

I go back to my room and open my laptop. I click the Safari symbol on the lower left of my laptop. I type in f-a-c-e-b-o-o-k and tap 'enter'. It already goes to my Facebook. I have a lot of notifications on the video of me beating up Nel. First is tagging me, then comments, then likes, then shares.

People make such a big deal out of everything these days.

I look at how many likes. Most of them are the people that actually saw it.

Fifty-seven likes exactly and counting by the minute.

Then I look at the comments. *"That guy totally deserves that!"* says Madley. I didn't want to read the other comments because I was so lazy to do it. Five people shared the video. The first was Ross, then I try to make an effort to read the second one, but I didn't want to.

My eyes widen.

I bring out a suitcase and stuff it with few clothes, black jeans and all the pieces of undergarment I could find in the drawer, because I wasn't sure what was about to happen or how long we would stay in the Camp. These were some pieces I don't usually wear. I get a box of matches at the kitchen, and two sticks of candles, a gun and flare gun just in case something bad happens in the stock room. I go to my Dad's closet. I remember him hiding a survival knife, so I get it for extra security. I'm honestly unsure about this. Maybe I'm just too concerned about my safety.

I go back to my room with the stuff and I put them at the bag. I get the keys to our house and put it in a secret pocket in my bag. I leave my important stuff in my closet so nothing will happen to them while I'm away.

My room looks emptier than before.

It's seven fifteen. I take a bath. It takes me eight minutes to do so.

I change into the clothes that were left in my closet: a black polo, raw denim jeans and a stylish gray sweater. I look at my reflection on the mirror beside the dresser and see a guy with medium length, brown hair, a lean face with slightly defined cheekbones and a light skin tone. I realized just now that I have nice, blue eyes few shades darker than the sky. I wear the watch I left from yesterday on the table. It sends a shiver on my body.

I haven't seen my face in a long time; I almost forgot how I looked like.

I fold my towel in a way that both boarders of it meet and fold it once more. I put it in the suitcase

I go to the dining table and sit down. There are three golden-brown pancakes in each plate, for me and Serenity, a tall glass of milk for me and a tall glass of orange juice for Serenity.

Just the way we like it.

I put a large amount of maple syrup on my pancake. Serenity makes an even coat of it on her pancake. I slice my pancake into quarters then cut the quarters in half. I eat three quarters of the pancake and leave the other quarter behind because of the heaviness of the pancakes all together.

I drink half of the milk that Crissy prepared for me. Serenity isn't able to finish her food, like me. Crissy goes to the table and gets our plates. Before she goes out I tell her about the letter. She leaves the plates on the table and she goes with me in my room. I show her the letter as physical evidence.

"You now what, you can go. I think it's a great idea for them to include you guys in the search." Crissy says.

I walk away from the house with a pumped up fist. Something unusual is going on, but I want to satisfy my curiosity.

It feels like any ordinary day with Serenity walking beside me going to school, staring at the marble streets in front of me.

Just like going home, going to school was a habit.

Serenity wore a dark blue dress with long sleeves that fitted her body perfectly. "Nice dress." I say to her pinching part of the dress. "Thanks." she glances at me for a moment and looks away while I release the dress.

I feel the shivering cold of the wind from the coastline few miles away on my hands. I think about Serenity who didn't wear anything else but the dress. "Do you feel cold—or something?" "Nope . . . this dress was designed for cold weather." she pats it down. "Well, okay. Just please don't give me a lecture about why it's like that. We're not at school." I laugh. She pushes me around. I act like I'm swaying.

People pat my back and give me friendly smiles.

I disgust the feeling in the pit of my stomach afterwards.

I see Nel walking with the crowd. A ray of sunlight hits his face and his swollen eye turns into a dark shade of purple. Nobody seems to care about him, as usual. I think the nerds are bullying him now.

I have the urge to hit him again, knowing that he was weak.

All the lockers of students should have a piece of paper taped to their locker that says "Clearance." and we have to get all the teachers to sign them.

The school-bell rings and I grab my stuff for the classes today – including the Clearance Sheet. I rush to my classroom to avoid trouble.

* * *

It's lunch break. Everybody's is talking about their clearances. All the teachers signed my clearance already. I go to the cafeteria.

They're serving sloppy joe since today is the start of our summer break.

Mrs. Garvener was unusually angry to the whole class today. I wonder what happened to her.

I take a bite from my sloppy joe. Cathy and Ross sit beside me.

It was unusual to find Cathy here all of a sudden.

"What's Cathy Abrahams doing here?" Ross asks me.

"I'm just here because all the tables are full because of the rush hour. You know the sloppy joe's? Yeah, they're really famous now, and people really want to get their hands on them." Cathy tells Ross.

"So, has your clearance been signed by all the teachers yet?" I ask both of them

"Yeah, how 'bout yours?" Ross says.

"Mines been signed by all of them." Cathy says with a voice as smooth as silk.

"Mine's been signed." I say.

I take another bite into my sloppy joe and the filling goes to my plate.

"Alright . . ." Ross comments. "Here, borrow my spoon to scoop it up."

"Thanks." I say, putting the filling in the bun.

I give back the spoon to Ross. "So, anything special that happened today?" I ask either of them, hoping they would talk back.

There was an awkward silence.

"Okay. We don't have to talk about it." I say.

Serenity and Violet sit beside Ross.

"Damian, who's this?" says Serenity. She was referring to Cathy.

"Cathy Abrahams." I reply, playing with my feet under the table.

"Hey, Cathy, this is Serenity. Damian's sister." Ross tells her. They shake hands.

"Nice to meet you." they say together.

* * *

The school-bell rings again.

I rush to the corridor and people are flocking all around me, trying to fight their way out.

I go with the flow out of the school so I don't trip again.

I say my goodbyes to random people who looked drunk and said to me goodbye and look for Serenity, Ross and Violet.

I'm thinking of bringing Ross and Violet at the dock. Ross, because he's my best friend and Violet because I want to surprise Serenity at home. I think this might be fun somehow.

Ross is just beside me!

"Ross! What are you going to do at your summer break?" I ask, scratching my cheek.

"Nothing much, Playing video games, drinking soda, eating potato chips. Why?" he says. I was wondering why I asked that.

"Do you want to go with Serenity and I to our Dad's Archaeologist Camp? Only problem is that we don't know until when we'll come back." I say. "If you're allowed to, go to our front gate as soon as possible."

"Sounds good." he says.

"Okay." I say.

Now I think I'm in so much trouble.

I look for Violet. I tell her the same details like what I told Ross. She's interested too.

* * *

I arrive at home with Serenity. Crissy brought our stuff to the living room. It's four thirty-five and the sun's still high. Serenity's beside me. I say to her, "Serenity, Ross and Violet might join us to the Archaeologist Camp if that's okay with you."

She's ecstatic, jumping up and down and says, "Oh my gosh! Thank you!" and then hugs me.

I go to my room and get the stone, the letter, the map, my phone and my wallet on my desk. I go downstairs and get my stuff. Serenity is already ready.

I hear the doorbell sound. I look out the window beside the door and see Ross and Violet.

"Serenity, Damian, Take care!" Crissy says laughing. She escorts us out of the household.

She goes back in the house.

"You guys ready?" I say.

"Yeah" Ross says.

"Yes" Violet says.

"Let's take a taxi going there." I say.

"Taxi!" Ross shouts. A taxi pulls over and we put our things in the trunk. We go in and slam the door.

The city lights turned on in the middle of the road. It was magnificent. Something I haven't seen before. The bright, street lamp posts, the hundreds of colors beside every block.

The only time I've seen the city this beautiful was before the war.

"Hey, Damian, why are we going to your Dad's Archaeologist Camp?" Violet asks.

"I'm curious" I lie to get rid of the dead air in the taxi.

I bring out my phone and shut it down. I didn't want to waste any battery.

"Same old Damian—curious as ever." she pokes me.

* * *

Chapter 2

Bemused

The taxi stops and we find only one steamboat in the harbor. It's not that big, not that small. Maybe the length and width of our front yard. Probably could fit fifty to one hundred people in it.

It was afternoon. It made the boat look tinted orange.

The sun could fall off from the sky any time now.

There's a girl with a ragged dress and light-brown hair tied to a tail, on the boat. She's holding a cross bow and a quiver of arrows at her back. Her stare is scary, and tempting to get lost into.

This was one warm meeting indeed.

"Who's there!" she shouts.

She aims the cross bow at us.

The arrowhead points in my direction. I can see it flicker with light from the sunset.

"We're not going to harm you!" I shout back.

She revokes her shot and withdraws her arrow into the quiver on her back.

We run to the plank that joined land and the boat. The mysterious girl looks nervous around us. "We're not armed." Violet says.

"Is there a place I should ride you people to?" the mysterious girl says so soothingly and as thin as silk, but has a slightly threatening tone to it.

I think now that this is the boat to our dad's archaeologist camp. "Yes, actually" I say. "Do you know an archaeologist camp near here?" The mysterious girl goes down the plank going in front of us. She stares at Ross, then Violet, then me, then Serenity.

"Is this place a desert? Egypt probably?" she asks.

"Yes," I say. "so do we just get in the boat?"

"What will you offer? I don't accept money." she says and I'm in shock.

"What do you mean by 'offer'?!" I say.

"What I mean is," she walks around us, "If you don't give me something that interests me you're not going in." "Will this do? It's made entirely out of silver." I say, pointing at my watch that my dad gave to me last year, feeling like I'm almost more civilized than her.

"I know what a watch is, now give it!" she says, holding out her hand. I take my watch off and give it to her. She looks excited for no apparent reason at all, smiling and jumping around like a little girl. I put up an eyebrow.

I feel like every day, I'm losing a part of my dad when he's in his archaeologist job, but it's different now. He's missing . . . or worst, dead. I should let go. This day be known, I start off by letting those memories go.

The girl is wearing a red gown that's been torn into strips of cloth bound to each other by threads. It looks like it's about to fall off.

Her cross bow is wooden and sheened with some kind of glossy coating.

Up close her cheeks are blossoming with red and eyes glowing green. Her hair is made up of threads dyed brown and blonde stitched onto her head. "Get in." the mysterious girl says.

We follow her to the deck. "What are we doing here?" Violet whispers in my ear. "I think this is a boat to my dad's archaeologist camp. It's too late to turn back now." I say patting her back.

I feel sorry for dragging them with me, but this could be my last opportunity to see where Dad works. Maybe by chance we get to find his body, or maybe they found it and placed it in a glass pane box or something. I think this ship is a miracle to me. Something about this boat just lures me to go to the workplace of my Dad.

"My name's Damian Grey." I try to talk to the mysterious girl with an enthusiastic approach.

"Am I supposed to tell you my name?" she says in a tone that made with pure anger that flooded her throat.

"If you don't want to, we'll tell our names, and we'll address you as 'that girl'."

"Fine by me." she says.

I try not to say anything back to her. I'm not even sure of what to say to her at first.

"My name's Serenity Grey."

"My name's Ross Hyde."

"My name's Violet Lenn'd." they say.

"Ross is it? Can you put that plank on the boat?" the mysterious girl—or should I say 'that girl' says. Ross, without any words to reply, puts the plank beside the sail so the ship can move. He's taking orders like a pathetic dog.

The sea isn't as harsh as I expected. The waves are slow and steady. The waves are the height of probably a few meters. The wind is strong, which made the boat go faster. The girl goes in a small tower in the ship, maybe to steer the boat.

We arrive at the island in few minutes time.

A mix of coconut and pine trees, and desert sand around us, and the breeze coming from the island was really cold.

Despite the submarines untouched by water, airplane wings that were covered by sand, and the torpedoes that haven't been launched, this place could be a great tourist spot if you were looking for a place with an unusual vibe.

* * *

March 18, 2041

We find the archaeologist camp at somewhere beside the boat. There are still people awake. Some electric powered lamps kindle beside each tent to illuminate the darkness.

The mysterious girl goes to the mast and asks us, "Could you anchor the boat?"

I anchor the boat with Ross to stop it from moving by turning a huge wheel at the corner of the ship.

The girl watches us do it, hoping we don't commit an error

"By the way . . . my name's Isis. Isis Crayon." the mysterious girl—Isis says, and my mind goes, *finally!*

"Isis?" I say.

"Have a problem with my name?" she questions giving me a face with two emotions I can interpret:

Anger

Fear

Both at the same time.

I look at the camp once more and I feel almost unsure about going there without anything to fend for ourselves if we need to. I only have a pathetic, dull dagger and a gun I forgot to load with bullets in my bag.

"No, I was just going to ask you a question!" I look at the floor. "Do you have an arsenal of weapons I can borrow?"

"We have our fists, don't we?" she says.

"Sorry if I wasn't able to learn self-defense in time for this day." I say convicting.

"If you need weapons, there are bows and swords downstairs."

"Thank you for helping us. I'm sorry for the way I acted before." I let down my luggage after holding it the whole trip here.

"It's fine." Isis replies.

Ross comes out of nowhere holding out two swords and bow. A quiver of arrows included of course.

"These are all I could find at the basement of this ship." he says.

Wow Ross, you really know me. My mind says. My heart on the other hand was telling me otherwise, *this is wrong, Damian. You can't handle a sword! Plus you could hurt people.*

I get one of the swords with both hands gripping the handle firmly and nervously. It's slightly heavier than I thought it was. My hands almost drop with the sword. It feels wrong.

Serenity gets the bow and the quiver of arrows.

Violet doesn't get anything, so I give her my dagger from my bag.

"I'm coming with you guys. I might be bored to death here." the mysterious girl says, loading her crossbow.

"Fine" I say.

The people go inside their tents and the lumens of the lamps fade in total blackness.

"So this is what we're going to do, maybe. We ask them where their manager is." I say. "And we're only going to use our weapons if you're in danger—well, just try to survive I guess." I sound like a military dictator telling his troops to survive in a war. It's weird for me to take charge even if mostly because I'm not that type of person who is responsible enough to lead. I feel skeptical for a moment. My body crinkles and shrinks thinking there's a shell behind me hiding me from the shame.

We connect the plank to the boat and the sand. We go down the ship and leave it as is. There are no more lights. Meaning they're asleep

We go to the nearest tent we can find.

Serenity and Isis load their weapons and my eyes roll.

We barge in and point our weapons to the people in the tent. *One, two people inside.* "Could you guys help us? We're lost. We need to find your manager's tent" Serenity says.

"Haha! A bunch of kids with weapons asking for directions, how cute!" someone at the corner of the tent says. He can't stop laughing.

Serenity looks furious. She points her arrow at the man. "Where Is He?" Serenity says angrily, making me scared.

"Just look all over the place, stupid little girl." the guy says. I would regret saying that.

Serenity fires the arrow close to the guy's neck, which is a pretty good effort for someone who has no idea how to shoot an arrow correctly, but it scares me that she's capable of wielding the weapon. He's scared half to death now and I would understand that.

I want to gasp aloud, but that would alert the people in the other tents.

"Don't underestimate us! Tell us where he is!" Serenity says. "This isn't a game. We're not playing a game. Our Dad might be in danger!"

She's doing most of the talking while we stand there waiting for the conversations to end. "Just look for a freaking tent, kid!" another guy says.

"Did You Just Call Me Kid? Hm, Dummy! I'm Fifteen!" Serenity shouts.

I hope nobody heard that. I can think of many scenarios in my mind that would happen if Serenity keeps shouting like this.

"Well sorry if you look too young but—" he says.

"Sorry if those were your last words!" Serenity cuts him, aiming at the guy's chest.

"Serenity, don't. These guys shouldn't die because they don't want to help us." I say.

Bitter silence fills the atmosphere.

"Okay . . ." she says.

She looks at each and every guy in the tent like they're her prey.

"You guys better watch out, if you ever say anything to anyone about us, I swear, you'll die by my hand. No stopping me. No mercy, I will kill you if it's the last thing I do." They're covering their eyes in fear like we're monsters, waiting for us to leave.

"One down, so many tents to go." says Isis.

"We don't want the unnecessary attention! We might be staying here for a long time and people might hold grudges against us." I say.

"Good job, Serenity. You've seriously scared their hearts out!" Ross says beside me.

"My pleasure." Serenity makes it sound like scaring them is an accomplishment.

We go to the tent beside this one and ask the people, "Do you know where your manager's tent is?" I point my sword at him and go closer. I probably look stupid right now.

"Yes I-I k-know where. His t-tent has a buffalo skull above its entrance. Please don't harm me!" he puts a blanket over his head.

"Thank you." Serenity says. The kindest thing she's said since few moments ago. She's beside me, trembling, trying to stop her from launching the crossbow on her hand aiming for his head.

She must be really upset about Dad being reported missing. I can't help her now. She Might Kill Me! But I can try.

I hold her wrist and whisper, "Don't kill him." and she doesn't tremble much anymore.

Her pulse bounces from her skin and at me like it's trying to break free and mangle me. She's more than just mad, but scared. Might because she's scared of what she's doing.

"You won't be able to hurt him. Don't worry." I smile at her but she doesn't look at me.

"Let's get out of here." I say to everyone.

We look for the tent of the so called 'boss', scouring the place from every block, tent, tree, bush, stack of crates.

I find a tent with a buffalo skull at its entrance. That must be the one.

I sneak to the place, but I find a guard at the entrance. I hurry behind a tent hoping they didn't see me. I look back. Isis is behind me. My heart's racing from the adrenaline. I can feel them on my fingertips.

"You stay here while I go to inside the tent. If anything happens to me could you ready your crossbow?" I whisper to her ear.

"Okay" she says in a soft whisper. Isis points her loaded cross bow at the guard to our right. My adrenaline's moving up and down and all over my body. Isis removes the arrow already loaded on the cross bow and replaces it with what I can pick up with my eyes, a tranquilizer, scuffled with fluorescent colored feathers at its bottom

"Why do you have those again?" I ask.

"Always come prepared." Isis says

We're naturals at this, though I knew I was gifted at wielding blades when I stopped a hurdling knife from touching me in our kitchen when Crissy was butchering a thanksgiving turkey . . . or maybe I was just lucky then. Ross in the other hand—the other person with the sword as a weapon—is very clumsy with it. I don't know if he thinks it's too light or too heavy for him.

I hand my sword to Isis and walk directly to the guards.

"I'm here to see your boss." I bring out the letter from my pocket.

"This isn't the Archaeologist Camp crest." one of the guards says. The guard is tall and tanned, his head shaved wearing a slick suit.

The other one stares daggers at me. He's also as tanned as the other one, but shorter. He asks, "Who are you and why are you here?" and I'm bewildered. What's happening?

One of the guards bring out some kind of communication device and talks into it, "There's a strange guy here. Could you get here as quickly as possible?" and my adrenaline starts rushing.

Suddenly I hear a whistle coming from behind and then one of the guards is down. Before I get to look at his body fall down the other one is also down.

"Go inside, Damian!" Isis shouts.

I get inside and see the boss is on his knees with a pillow under him, drinking tea on a wooden table looking all-innocent.

He asks me in a British accent, "What do you want, child?"

He's an anorexic lad, with brown hair, and pale skin.

He looks sick, or he is sick.

"Where's my Dad?" I ask.

"What do you mean 'you Dad'?" he sounds surprised.

Six guards towering me with a huge body mass wearing suits go inside the tent, pointing their guns at me, ready to fire as long as the so called 'boss' says so.

Now there are eight people in the tent, including the skinny lad and me. The tent is larger than I thought. I'm in big trouble.

"My Dad, he's missing. Why do you think we went through the trouble of going here?" I'm searching my pocket for the letter and I hand it to him. His reaction scares me.

"Yes, that's true, but we only sent you one letter saying that he was missing. We didn't write this one though," he stands up and continues hissing, "you're the son of Mr. Grey, aren't you? I can see the resemblance. You two have the same eyes and nose, you even have his face shape." he looks behind me and nods. "I'm sorry, but we have to call the police on you for questioning."

I'm framed. How did all of this happen? What's happening?

Suddenly a tranquilizer hits someone in the back. He falls down in front of me.

I step away.

Another tranquilizer hits another person's back. He falls too, but in the opposite direction. I hear a whistling coming from outside, and a tranquilizer hits another guy.

There are three guards left.

I stand there, scared, afraid, unable to speak, I mutter vowels. My body is paralyzed.

It's weird to know that when you're scared, you'll do anything to survive, reminding me about the nuclear bombing—people have lost their sanity and humanity, people stealing from each other, killing each other, only for one reason which was to survive. The streets were covered in broken glass and blood and oil. Those were the scariest years of my life.

A person headlocks one of the guards and I see his head perch out of the guard's shoulder—Ross.

Another tranquilizer hits the last person standing. He's one of the biggest people I've ever seen. He thuds on the floor with the rest.

All of the guards are laying flat on the floor either head facing on the floor or head staring on the ceiling of the tent.

Violet points the dagger at him. "Where is my Dad?" Serenity says going closer to the boss. I turn around.

"How am I supposed to know? I didn't kill . . ." he says shutting his mouth.

"He's dead?" Serenity says in a frantic voice and the boss goes silent.

A minute of silence passes and the boss finally replies, "Yes. He's dead. We found his body rotting at the side of the island."

Isis gets in the tent and points the tranquilizer at the boss. "Are we done here?"

I turn around and our eyes meet. I shout at her, "Why did you have to tranquilize those guards?"

"Relax," she replies, "they're memory of all of us will be gone by the time they wake up."

I don't know if I'm supposed to be relieved or angry.

"Okay." is all I can say to Isis.

Isis shoots the tranquilizer at the boss and he falls asleep.

"What did you do that for?!" I'm shouting again at Isis.

She gathers all the tranquilizers on the guards and the boss and replies, "You don't want them reporting anything to the police, do you?"

We get out of the tent and I apologize, "I'm sorry, I didn't mean to yell."

"We're going to burn this place until ash surrounds this island. Any of them could have killed our Dad." says Serenity.

"What do we do now?" Ross says, surprised that Serenity's capable of saying something like that.

"We burn them to death! Haven't you been listening to me?" Serenity says.

"Haven't you heard the boss? He said our dad has been there for a long time. He didn't say anything about a fatal wound that could've killed him. He could've just died naturally." I say.

"No, we've done too much damage already." Violet tries to convince her to not do it. "We should just leave everything as is. The police might just think this is some kind of assassination with unknown suspects if we cover our tracks when going to the boat."

Serenity relaxes her body for a moment. Shoulders drop to the ground. Eyelids closed, almost shut, head looks down, knees are shaking, scared of herself.

I doubt dragging everybody here.

She takes deep breaths. "You're right. Sorry." she crosses her arms. "Let's get out of here." Violet says in a soothing voice. "C'mon." I say.

She breaks down in front of me, in front of everybody. Tears start jerking, streaming down her cheeks.

"I didn't want Dad to die." her voice dims to the waves' sound coming from the shoreline

I feel the weak, frail soul of Serenity make contact for the first time. It's reaches me, creeping its way into my ear whispering, "I need help." and then moving on.

I've never seen her in so much despair.

At exactly three hundred forty-five seconds of running, walking, avoiding attention, we arrive at the boat with our footsteps on sand erased while going here. Violet's idea to avoid suspicion.

"So what were you doing in Seattle?" Serenity who's in front of me says, almost like the murder never existed.

"I was just in the city."

Serenity hugs her.

"I need to get something I forgot in my place. I was supposed to go there, until you guys showed up. I'm not saying it's a bad thing, but can I get it first? It's really important." Isis asks for our permission.

"Um . . . sure, we can, right guys?" I say. They all agree because we didn't have anywhere to go except back home.

"I think we better go now, before people see the boat!" Ross says, coughing the words out.

The disk-shaped stone falls out of my pocket and a blast of air pushes the boat farther away from the island. Isis runs to the boat's wheel and steers the boat in the small tower in the ship. I quickly get the stone and keep it in my pocket.

* * *

Chapter 3

Sisterhood

We arrive at a harbor full of what looks like modernized Viking ships. The daylight of morning was bearable to look at. I can see a black outline of the sun that continues to curve down the sphere of the sun.

There's a reserved spot that has a blue flag. Isis goes to it without restriction, excited, with the boat tilting left then right then left again, shaking, we have a personal earthquake.

There are people in front of the reserved spot that wore black suits with frames a little over the top that stood tall with guns on their hands. They look ready to attack us.

I prepare my sword.

I learned my lesson with "the boss" before, but this might threaten my life. I feel like an insurgent.

The people ready a small motorboat where all of us can fit in including the two representatives that go in the boat.

Isis stops the boat and gets out of the control tower to the deck. I can see her from here because the control tower was made of glass. It had to be a sturdy kind, since it hasn't broken itself yet. She runs straight forward, jumps over the railings of the steamboat and plummets straight onto the boat—the only way to get to the boat I guess—as I watch every moment of it like an action movie.

There's only one way to test if it's safe. I draw back my sword, jump off the railings, and plummet into the boat. The people who I thought was going to kill me catch me and put me to my feet. I feel embarrassed to be in this situation. Serenity's in the sky and the guards put their hands up ready to catch her. They did.

Serenity looks like she's having fun, well it doesn't last long because they let her down.

Ross is the last one to jump. The people in black suits catch him. "Violet says she doesn't want to jump so she's staying." Ross says.

Pieces of Isis' dress are on the floor of the boat. I look at her. The dress was nothing more than ruffles and ribbons now.

"Guard the boat. My new friends and I will leave as soon as possible. And when the king asks if I've been here, say nothing." Isis says.

"Yes princess." the guards chorus.

Princess, I thought people from the royal family had restrictions or rules and regulations, to be specific, I thought they weren't allowed to leave their premises.

Maybe she escaped.

I'm not sure what the rules are. I don't know if I'm carrying something illegal, or if I'm doing something illegal. I'm clueless about what's going to happen when I'm going to go to jail here. I'm like a newborn baby trying to learn everything I can in a new environment, not being in the comfort cradled in the womb of the mother. I'm helpless here.

There's a trail leading to this gigantic castle. I've always wondered what it's like in a castle.

Four of the many guards escort Isis on our way to the castle.

The street beside us was a little town that looked like a part of London.

"The princess is going in the castle. I repeat. The princess is going in the castle." a guard behind me says in a dull voice into a microphone attached to his ear. A laugh escapes from my mouth.

"I thought I said I wasn't here." Isis whispers to the guard.

"It was just a test. The king has ordered to double check everything." he says into the microphone and blushes with embarrassment. We laugh at the guard. "Sorry, princess."

"No, it's okay. It's fine." Isis says with a wide smile on her face.

* * *

The castle's being overhauled from the inside, replacing the carpets to replacing the wallpaper, to polishing the precious vases and woodworks. There's wreck-havoc everywhere we stand.

"Follow me." Isis whispers.

I'm not sure who she's talking to.

For a moment, I take a quick glance to their grand living room. There's a gigantic chandelier made by pieces of broken glass with lights that have been arranged that hangs on the ceiling, a rustic design that captured my eyes.

I don't know how a heavy, gigantic thing like that doesn't fall down.

"Good morning princess!" one of the carpenters glances at us and curtsies. He might be referring to Isis.

There's a staircase going to the upper floor.

"Isis" I say. "Where are we going?"

"In my room." she looks behind to find my face looking shaken.

My stomach went from calm to spinning when she said "room". There's something about going to other people's houses that frightens me.

There's a small television beside the carpenter with a news outbreak of a headline in bold, "DEATH IN ARCHAEOLOGIST CAMP"

I call for everybody's attention to look at the television.

The news anchor says, "Archaeologist, Jeremy Grey, is found dead in the outskirts of his camp," and then a picture of our dad flash on the screen, "Doctors have arrived few hours ago to find out the cause of Jeremy Grey's death." the news anchor says.

"Okay, let's go to your room . . . now." I say.

We trail Isis into a large door in front of her.

There's a girl who looks just like Isis, but younger on the left side of the room, but instead of Isis' light, brown, natural hair, she has blonde highlights

"Hey, Isis, what happened to you? And who are these peasants? You know what? You need to . . ." the strange girl says.

"Shut it, Cipher!" Isis cuts before the girl can complete her statement. She walks around the room. "And where's Mom's locket? I remember leaving it here, but I forgot it"

"It's in the drawer beside your bed. Why?"

"Nothing really—I'm just leaving this hideous looking place by the end of the day, you coming with me and my non-peasant friends who are actually more sophisticated than you?" Isis shouts, going to the drawer, taking a black, diamond-shaped locket and positioning it around her neck trying to find both ends of it to connect.

"I don't know—I mean—I need to ask Dad and his fiancée if I can leave." the girl—I mean Cipher says.

"I've been gone for a week and Dad already has a fiancée! That's fast! No matter how many wives Dad will be having, they can't replace our first Mom." Isis laughs with a hint of hysteria.

I look around room.

It's four times as big as mine, a sliding ambry that covered half of the wall in front of me, excellent interior design with the red of the soft, plush carpet I'm stepping on that contrasted great to the black, blues and white in the room, two beds in two opposite sides of the room. I don't know how Isis can call this place, "hideous".

I'd want to live here if the furbishing downstairs were finish.

"I'd be happy if I could help you pack." Cipher says.

This is all happening so fast. But I can still keep up.

"What's happening?" Serenity asks, tugging on the sleeve of my sweater.

"Connard?" Cipher says.

"Yes?" a guard beside her responds.

He's wearing a dark-blue polo, buttoned, ironed and tucked in properly with a sash with the colors red and white in a pattern of white in the middle of two red. His face looks too young. No blemishes, wrinkles, perfect shade of skin. He looks like a teen like us.

"Can you make sure that my Dad won't find out that Isis and I are leaving the island?"

"Of course." Connard answers gallantly.

"You're dismissed, Connard!" Isis says.

Cipher and Isis bring out really old suitcase from under their bed.

They open their ambry and run through the content, examining each and every piece of clothing inside, finding pieces with more worth and purpose and then shoving them into the suitcase, barely emptying the ambry with all the clothes inside.

I just sit down and watch both of them struggle in whatever they were doing across the room. My legs are crossed and my back leaning against the wall, my chin resting on the palm of my hand.

Isis closes her suitcase.

"Do I still need perfume?" Cipher clutches to them with her fingers crisscrossing.

"No!" Isis says.

Cipher closes her suitcase too.

"Are we done, or are we all going to argue about bringing perfume?" Ross says.

"We're done." I say. "Well, I'm done with this place, but I'm not sure about them."

The room looked as empty as my room when I packed my things.

I go to Isis and get her stuff because she's having trouble carrying her luggage.

"Thank you, but you know I can carry that, right?" Isis says.

"You looked like you were struggling." I say.

"Anyways, thanks again." she responds.

Ross is carrying Cipher's luggage, which is heavier because she has three suitcases.

"Hey, Damian, you got lucky for carrying just one suitcase." Ross says, trying to fit the entire luggage in both of his arms, one on the left and two on the right.

* * *

The shipyard is full of crates scattered all over the field. Ships and small boats looked like it was the sea from where I was standing.

"How long will the delivery last?" Cipher asks a guard.

"They're almost done, princess." he says.

Few minutes pass and most of the boats are gone.

"Princess, your boat's ready." A guard says. Other guards get the luggage out of Ross's and my hands. Ross's face turned as red as a tomato. I try not to laugh.

We—including Cipher—ride on the boat we rode earlier to our ship. There's a lever-like contraption on top of us that was used for the crates to carry the things of Cipher and Isis to the boat.

"Cipher, remove your heels! You won't need them, and you can just put on a pair of flats on the ship! We need to climb to the boat." Isis shouts. We go first because Cipher's weak.

All of us are in the ship except Cipher.

"I need help carrying Cipher in, Ross." Isis says.

Once all of us are in the boat, one guard brings up a leather cloth with a bumpy surface.

"Thank you!" Cipher says. "These are weapons specially designed for you guys. I didn't want to disappoint you, Isis, so I brought you all kinds of arrows." she opens the leather cloth and an arsenal of weapons appear at sight. "I don't know you guys, so I got daggers made out of wootz steel for each of you. Sorry if I didn't know what you guys want but in Archaean tradition you need to give weapons to the person that took care of you as a sign of giving your trust to them. Simply meaning you won't kill them with the weapon you gave"

I'm surprised that Cipher already got us something even if we just met. What's more surprising is that she trusts us immediately

"I'm Damian."

"My name's Ross."

"I'm Serenity."

"And I'm Violet. Thanks for the dagger." we say to Cipher.

Isis looks at the arrows that Cipher gave.

There's a dark liquid that was attached to one set of arrows, and a yellow liquid attached to another set. The last two had two entirely different arrowheads.

One with a razor-like head tinted black and one that's like an ordinary arrow, but with tiny jagged lines that I can see from here.

Using my peripheral vision, I see Violet with a fascinated look on her face. I'm just wondering what was special about these daggers compared to the usual ones that are made out of the ordinary steel.

"Thanks for the arrows; I didn't know you got them for me."

Isis finally thanks Cipher after a long pause.

"You're welcome! I got myself a bow so you can teach me." I don't expect Isis to respond after all that I've seen from their sisterhood of hate.

"Where now?" Cipher says.

"If you guys mind, I'm really sleepy." Violet says.

I glance at everyone here one at a time and it's as if our eyelids are weights put on faces.

Maybe except Cipher.

Isis says, "Maybe we can go to the other side of the island and sleep there. I don't want dad to find us here." The look on Cipher's face looks upsetting. It makes her look like she's about to cry. But she doesn't.

Isis starts the boat and yells at the top of her voice at the control room of the ship, "Can somebody go to the basement and feed the flame?"

"Sure!" Ross shouts too.

Cipher keeps her things along with Isis' things at the armory of the ship. I helped her put them there.

* * *

We land on a beach of white sand and clear, blue water.

There are four huts, neighboring each other, made out of stone in the eastern part of this beach.

The huts were things we first noticed when we arrived.

Cipher runs to one of them with a bright yellow seal on its door. The door is made out bamboo; the other huts, blue, green, and red seals have the same architecture. "Where are we supposed to stay?" I ask Isis, holding her shoulder. "In any of the huts, except . . ." she says.

I shiver when she pronounces the word "except".

"Except the one with a red seal."

"Okay." I reply.

I stay with Ross in the hut with a blue seal, which means that Serenity and Violet are sleeping together in the hut with the green seal.

Inside the hut is one queen size bed and a closet full of medium sized clothing for a king and a box on top of all the clothing.

Out of curiosity I get the box and set it on the bed. I sit down and slowly lift the top.

There's a pendant made of gold and rubies, a bracelet with spotted quartz, a tiara with a wreath-like design with a pattern of micro size sapphires, diamonds, and rubies around it, three rings with three unique designs and shape.

When the box is empty after removing all the priceless jewelry I notice a note that was written at the bottom like a secret message.

"To and for my precious Isis and Cipher, with love, Mom"

I put all the content inside the box again and keep it in my bag.

I need Cipher and Isis to see this.

Ross comes in the hut and jumps at the bed, the typical, childish Ross.

I put my bag beside the bed and put the blanket over my legs. I'm amazed that it isn't hot in here. It's actually cold in here.

"Hey, Damian!" Ross whispers. I put my shoes off my feet and on the stone platform and pretend to sleep so I don't have to talk to him.

I close my eyes slowly and everything starts to fade in my field of vision. I lose consciousness all at once.

* * *

When I wake up, the first thing I notice is the smell of gumbo stew. I throw my feet on the floor. Ross isn't on the bed. He left the door open. It's dark outside

An orange light illuminates coming from the outside.

I slowly stand up, rub my eyes with a hand—I'm not sure which one, and gently open the partially closed door with my fingertips.

I didn't bother putting on my shoes because the sand will go in.

The first person I see is Ross slurping down the stew in the bowl and then look around. Everybody else is using a soupspoon to eat.

They've already set up a bonfire and logs around it to sit on.

A pot half filled with the stew rests on top of the fire to keep it warm.

I notice immediately that Isis isn't wearing that rugged dress anymore, instead a white dress with a light brown belt on her waist.

Serenity gives me a spoon and a bowl with the gumbo in it.

"Who cooked this?" I ask.

"Um, I think Isis did—don't worry, tastes great!" Ross says.

"I can see that." I blow the stew for few seconds, take the spoon, sit down on a log, and shove the spoon in my mouth. "Wow, it's really good, Isis!" I say.

She thanks me in a flattery voice

"Are we going to sleep again?" Cipher asks.

"I don't really know with you guys, but I want to stay out here a bit." I say.

Everybody finishes the stew after few minutes.

I get the dagger that Cipher gave me inside my bag and go outside.

The beach looks breathtaking, the moon being reflected by the water. More than that, there's a group of glowing fluorescence coming from the sea. They look like glowing jellyfish.

I sit down on the sand with my legs crossed, still warm because of the sun and press the dagger on it, making it sink a little.

I end up playing with the sand. I'm running my hands through every grain of sand in the area beside me.

I hear footsteps crunching nearer and suddenly it stops.

"What'cha doing?" sounds like Cipher talking.

"I'm just relaxing I guess." I put down my dagger that is now incased in the scabbard and lie down with my hands behind my head and my arms falling lazily on the sand. I yawn.

"So what are you doing here?" I ask.

"Nothing . . . Isis is lying down on her bed she told me not to make a lot of noise and that if I did, I had to stay outside. I'm just waiting for her to fall asleep so I can go back in."

Well that's sad. Having a sister that hates you.

"So tell me, does your sister hate you?"

"Pretty much—yeah, I guess. You can put it that way."

"Do you know why she hates you?" I ask.

"No—I never thought of that ever." she sits down beside me.

"You know what, I'm going to try to figure that out. I'm going to our room right now to check if she's sleeping. If she's not, I'm going to ask her."

"You do that. And I'll be here wishing you the best." I stand up.

"You want me to walk you there? I'm thinking of going back to sleep."

"Sure!" she says while I pat the back of my jeans to remove any sand that's made its way on the fabric.

* * *

Chapter 4

Surprises

March 19, 2026

Last night was one night I might not forget, maybe because of the glowing jellyfish and the gumbo.

The handle of the dagger Cipher gave to me is on my clenched, left hand. Thank God there was a scabbard around it. If not, I would have died.

I tie the scabbard holding the dagger on my belt.

I get out of bed and sit down beside which was the fire, but now is a pile of ashes. There was a farm and a chicken coop behind us that I didn't notice until now.

I go inside the coop and get a basket—which was right beside me when I got in—and a frying pan. Then I get some eggs under the chickens and put them in the basket.

I start a fire outside and put the frying pan on it. "Shoot!" I say. I forgot to get cooking oil. I went back inside the barn, and luckily, I found some.

When I get back to the fire, Isis is already about to cook. She asks me, "Where's the oil?" she stares at my hands. I give it to her. "Don't fuss. I'll just cook."

"Thanks." I say.

While waiting, I get my towel and remove my shoes inside the hut and empty my pockets item by item. My phone, the circular stone, the false letter sent by some anonymous person, the map of Mellous, and my wallet.

I step out of the room with my body anticipating the clear waters beside us.

Isis doesn't seem to look at me, so I remove my sweater not realizing I've put off my shirt with it and put it on shore along with my towel. I remove my jeans and toss it on shore leaving my boxers the only piece of clothing on me. The water was cold. I was shaking.

I throw myself into the water and now my whole body is drenched.

Water dripped from my hair to every part of my body. It felt like I was a cube of butter that melted from top to bottom.

After taking a bath I wrap my towel around the lower half of my body, grab onto my clothes on the sand and go near Isis. I accidentally tickle her.

"Are you done?" I ask.

"Yeah." she giggles. "Why did you do that?"

"I honestly didn't know that was your ticklish spot." I say, looking at her beautiful, green eyes light up.

She pushes me around playfully. "I'm going to put on some clothes on."

"You do that." Isis says.

I smile at her.

I change into a black v neck and a pair of black jeans from my luggage and stuff their pockets with the things I left on the bed

I've placed my wet clothes in a section of my suitcase that hasn't been stuffed.

I go outside and there's still nobody eating.

There are plates made of glass that's stacked, along with spoons and forks on top of the plates. I say, "Hey, let's eat!"

I sit down and Isis gives me a plate, a spoon and a fork.

I get a sunny-side-up egg and put it on Isis' plate. "Here you go." I say.

Isis asks me, "Why are you being so kind to me all of the sudden?"

I wasn't sure myself.

"It's nothing" I respond.

"No, it's something." she says. "C'mon, tell me."

"Can we talk about it later?" I say because of two reasons:

1. I don't know what's gotten into me.

2. I'm afraid of what her answer will be if I tell her that.

"Okay." Isis says and smiles.

I ask her a completely random question, "Why didn't the oil in the chicken coop spoil?"

"Because it's vegetable oil, having a shelf life of one year open or un-open, and the last time we've been here was our yearly Christmas outing." she further explains scientifically how it's possible that vegetable oil can last that long even though not refrigerated or kept in a dry place.

And then I stop her, "Okay then." I laugh. "You didn't have to go that far."

I look at Isis' steamboat and there's someone jumping out of the ship.

Cipher shouts from behind and we're surprised of what's happening, "Connard?!" I didn't realize she was there the whole time.

"Cipher?!" he shouts back. Cipher's wearing a baggy shirt and shorts I barely begin to see.

His clothes are in uniform, just like yesterday—the first time I've seen him.

He should be very hungry, staying the whole night there.

Cipher runs to him and he runs to Cipher.

I look at Isis and ask her, "What's his name?"

"His name's Connard. He's our guard." she replies, taking a bite off her egg.

I look back at Cipher and Connard—I believe that's what is name is, hugging it out in the middle of the beach.

Ross, Serenity and Violet wake up when Isis, Cipher, Connard and I finish our food.

Connard has good eating etiquette. He does not shove his food down his throat like other people do when they're hungry. He chews his food thoroughly every spoonful of egg. He's always polite to Cipher. They look happy together.

Cipher wiped off yoke bright, yellow that was seeping out of the side of his mouth with her thumb and puts the residue on a hanky in her pocket.

I bring out the map of Mellous I've just remembered I've kept in my pocket and show it to her. "Where are we?" I ask. "We're here . . ." She points at the island located at the very center of the map. I nod my head thrice to making sure she was looking at me.

"Hey, we should be heading back to Seattle. Crissy might skin us alive if we don't get back soon." Serenity says. "Oh, so we'll be heading back to Seattle?" Isis asks. "Yeah, I guess." I say.

My head's still wet from taking a bath at the beach. It makes the breeze feel cooler.

I look at the plate with the eggs on it. There are two and a half left.

I go inside the hut dragging my feet on the warm, white sand of the beach and onto the stone platform to get my bag. All at once, there's an earthquake.

I lie down flat on the ground until it stops.

I'm panicking. We're all panicking; I can hear them from outside. I—we don't know what's happening.

My heart wants to burst out of my chest.

There was something unusual about the earthquake. Some kind of skipping pattern was formed somehow. "We need to get out of this island!" Ross shouts from outside.

I get my bag that stood beside the door.

I go out of the hut with the left bag strap of my bag in my hands. "I'll wait for you guys in the boat." I shout, running towards the boat.

The others get their stuff and run to the boat with me. I turn my head one-sixty degrees right. I notice a strange, dark figure that was stalking us.

Our running turned into sprinting.

We reach the boat and the dark figure was far behind.

Ross runs down a flight of stairs as fast as he can and we stare at the water behind the boat.

Isis starts the boat by going to the control room of the ship.

I'm still tired from all the running.

My heart and my breathing raced.

Violet is beside me and I try to start a conversation with her with our lungs still gasping for air.

"Do you think that the dark figure that was behind us caused the earthquake?"

"Not quite." she says. "But considering there was no volcano, there's a slight assurance that it is him, but you know the earth moves too so it might be a natural occurrence of tectonic plates colliding with each other." We're breathing the same air now. "I think he used magic or something like it . . . do you think so too?" I ask.

What was I saying? I sound so silly!

"Well, now that you mentioned it, no. No I do not." This conversation ended as bad as I thought it would

I was never really into talking to people. I'm the type of person that thought friends were a nuisance . . . not until Ross came along. Made me remember the first time we met.

Few months ago, on a Tuesday morning right before our first class started, I was reading one of my favorite books; I can't believe I forgot the title. My bookmark literally flew away, from my table and to the bottom of Ross' right shoe. He asked me if it was mine, and he was right.

We ended up talking until the teacher came.

I disregarded my book. I never actually read what happened next.

I think I should read it once we go back to Seattle.

* * *

I'm getting used to Isis barking out orders to Ross and I in the ship. She's laid off a lot of her alter ego, aka: mean and interrupting.

Isis' taught me some controls in the control room that I just clarified is in a mini building located in the ship, like how to steer and how you should react to a "Titanic" situation. She said to pull a lever tinted red and stop steering. As easy as that was how she said it to me.

We step out of the ship, to a waterfront beside a small, agricultural village with grass even when we go to the harbor, and farms beside every house.

"Where are we?" I ask Isis. "I'm not sure. I left my compass in the island because I didn't know what was going on. I couldn't think straight." she replies. "Sorry. I think we have to stay the night here since it's already in the middle of the afternoon."

Ross hands all of us our luggage with hopes that we can find a place to stay.

The locals were very welcoming to us, maybe a little too welcoming. They greeted us and stayed away just a moment after.

"Do you people have a vacant inn we can use?" Cipher asks an old lady we pass by.

She doesn't respond. For a moment I didn't really think these people could speak like they were all from the same race of people in which they're all mute.

Every person we passed by after the harbor looked scared of us after they greeted us.

"These people give me the creeps." Ross says.

"We don't expect everyone here to like visitors, Ross." Violet says.

"But still, people are people." I argue. "And we're people."

We walk down the lined, cobblestone streets and look around us. Everything here seems so vibrant and colorful. And this place is too big to be a village—it's like a city of its own. On one side of the city is all gardens and plants and crops. On the other side, layers upon layers of homes and little pastry shops and flower carters and meat stands. In between the crops and the domesticity is the cobblestone street. We're in that great divide.

At the end of the cobblestone street is a forest capable of swallowing a person whole. It gave off a strange aroma of lavender, which we followed, hoping there was an inn available, not far and deep in the forest.

We stop walking in front of an old and rundown temple, like the ones with an Aztec feel on it that towers all forms of life in the island, with smoke coming from the entrance. At least we don't get to see those suspicious people from over here.

All of the sudden we can't move. "Who are you?!" a strange person says. He's wearing a black robe with crystals and studs encrusted on it.

He holds a staff made from vines that were intertwined with each other on his left hand. Tattoos of animals and plants printed deep into the skin of his arm, gave me the impression that we shouldn't be messing with him.

A strange aura covers my body.

I couldn't see with my peripheral vision.

My body is stiff. "Why are you here?" he says, pushing the hood of his robe behind.

He has olive skin and a lean face appealing to the eyes, with black hair and tattoos that extend to his right cheek, a wrinkle on his jawline going down to the outer left corner of his mouth casted a shadow on his face.

The only part of my body that I can move was my mouth. "Can you please unfreeze us . . . or something?" I ask.

"I'd like to see all of you try to make me." he taunts me while walking around us.

I feel him bringing something out of my pocket.

The stone with the wind insignia!

"What is this—this stone?"

"Give it back to me!" I shout.

"Answer my question! And how did you get this?"

"I found it outside my house and I'm not sure why I have it, now give it back!" I say at the top of my voice.

He releases us from the strange aura that froze us.

"Thank you . . . now give it back!" I say demandingly. He inserts it in my pocket.

"By the way, my name's Icarus." he says.

"Do you know a place we can stay in?" Cipher asks.

"You guys can stay in the temple with me for a while." Icarus says, gesturing us into the temple.

Taking my first step, and all of the sudden my feet become heavy and I fall down. I stand up watchfully, but my legs feel numb. "Do you need help?" Isis asks. "I'm fine. Thank you for asking." I respond.

I look up and see the tree's branches that overlapped each other, swaying because of the wind. The sunlight passes through the gaps of the leaves.

"Damian, let's go!" Isis says, gesturing me to the temple.

I turn around and Icarus' eyes land on me immediately. I ask, "How in the world are you able to do that?!"

"Well 'that's called magic." he replies.

I don't say anything else. I don't question anything. I'm shocked. I'm bewildered. So there is such thing as magic. My stomach starts spinning hurricanes. My whole world's upside-down. Everything they've told us about magic being fake is now void. I've experienced being casted by a spell so all the, "magic isn't real" crap is just an excuse for humans to make things seem normal . . . but maybe having magic is normal and not having it is "normal" My head is whirling in so many different directions right now. I don't know what to believe.

* * *

We set up a camp inside. Icarus was telling us stories about his travels and how he came to this island.

He told us he could use magic and that he was a traveler of old ruins, like this place. He decided to do research here for a long time before he would go back to the city. He used his magic for finding lost artifacts. He's found seven.

I think I was ready to tell Isis and Cipher about the box of jewelry.

"Isis, Cipher, can I talk to you for a moment?"

"Sure" they say one after the other. I get my bag behind me and unzip it to take out the box and show it to them.

Just maybe they know it.

"What is this?!" Isis says.

"It's your Mom's jewelry box, I think." I say.

Isis immediately grabs the box out of my hands and opens it. I can imagine Isis' childhood in my mind, so lonely after her mother died because I can relate to her. Not allowed to go out of the castle because of her overprotective father.

Tears stream down her face as she picks up her mother's tiara. She makes a sobbing sound that made me feel sorry for her.

"I'm sorry. I never intended this to hap— . . ." I say. Isis hugs me before I could finish my sentence.

She plants her face on my shoulder, making it damp. She asks me, "Where did you get this?" "Inside the hut of your parents." I reply. Isis looks at me and smiles. Her face glistens with her tears.

I wipe them off with my hands. I smile back at her. I feel like smiling at her. Her touch is so warm.

"Thank you for showing this to me." Isis says getting off me, hugging Cipher next. "Isis, look at this." Cipher says, emptying the box. Now they both cry. I can still feel Isis' hug.

Maybe they're reading the note at the bottom.

I feel a sense of relief in me for some reason.

"Damian, what did you do?!" Serenity says angrily.

"I didn't do anything! I just showed them their mother's jewelry box." I reply, putting my hands open on my chest.

I hope she could relate with our mom.

As expected she says in a sad tone, "I miss mom." I get upset too and say, "Me too." I grab her hand and put her close to me so I can hug her.

* * *

March 20, 2041

The sunshine hurts my eyes, and these pillows that Icarus made are really uncomfortable. I put a hand on my face and feel the leaf impressions on it. On the bright side, at least we have pillows.

There was an earthy smell in the air—like a garden.

A moist, damp feeling covered my skin.

Mist came out of my mouth when I tried to exhale.

Icarus comes out of nowhere, drenched with water, wearing the robe he wore yesterday. "Wake up now!" Icarus shouts.

Everybody eventually wakes up after few minutes. "What's happening?" Ross asks. "I need to show you guys something." Icarus says. "We need to get our weapons first, just in case something bad happens." I say, bringing my feet on the ground full of dried leaves, my legs are shaking, trying to adjust to the weight of my upper body.

I get the dagger that Cipher gave me and my dad's survival knife from my bag and put that one on my back pocket and the other one made of wootz in my hands.

Isis gets her cross bow and the quiver of arrows that she placed beside her before she went to bed last night. Serenity gets her bow, borrows an arrow from Isis, loads her bow and puts it in an idle position. She must've left her quiver in the ship.

Ross gets the sword I borrowed from Isis' ship and asks, "Can I borrow this, Damian?" "Sure" I say.

I didn't know I brought it with me. I guess I could have forgotten it.

* * *

We follow him to a gigantic waterfall. None of us know what's going on except Icarus.

There were hidden steps beside it.

Icarus goes to the hidden steps so carefree and without any hesitation the world can throw at him. He didn't care if he was about to slip.

We couldn't stop now. We just followed.

The more steps we have to step on, the nearer they get to the water. Icarus stops at the lowest step, which skimmed the water and showed the reflection of the waterfall.

Another set of steps lead us to the base of the waterfall that went upward.

The base of the waterfall has a huge, steel door.

"Why are we here?" I ask.

"We're here to open this steel door. My magic can't work here, which is why I need your help." Icarus says.

The steel door has a plant-like insignia engraved on it.

All of the sudden there's an earthquake and a dent is created at the edge of the door. The earthquake stops and we fit our hands on the dent and pull as hard as we can.

It budged less than I expected, but it was enough for all of us to fit.

I go in first and bring out the dagger.

Plants surrounded us. Ross comes in and prepares his sword "I think we have a problem, Ross." I say. "There's a lot of work that needs to be done here."

The variety of plants in here was endless. Some plants here I've never even seen.

Blues, reds, greens, purple's, you can find any kind of color in here.

The others come in and Violet looks amazed. She picks up plants around us and stuffs them in her bag. "Can we cut these plants down now?" Ross says. Violet steps aside and says, "Sure" "This is going to be fun." Ross says.

Ross swings his sword left and right, cutting the plants, making green ooze come out of them. "Careful! You might cut us too!" I shout, but he doesn't listen. I've never heard myself shout at Ross like that before.

*　*　*

CHAPTER 5

HARVESTING

It's been few minutes and we haven't seen anything but plant.

I'm still upset about yesterday when Icarus stopped us from our tracks.

"What are we supposed to be looking for?" I ask.

"It's supposed to be a stone with the same insignia like the steel door." Icarus says. Ross suddenly stops cutting down rows of plants and says, "Look down."

There's a gigantic circle glowing green encircling us.

The vegetation's clearing up and going behind us as swift as the difference between the time when lightning strikes before thunder. The plants are connecting and grinding onto each other like magnets, forming what I can only describe as a plant monster. The plant monster is titanic, covered with horns and leaves and vines and roots and flowers.

By the time I gain consciousness I look around me, the place was bigger than I ever imagined.

The glowing circle has the plant insignia on it. There's a sudden attack from behind.

The ground shakes again, only this time stronger. Vines with thorns explode everywhere, slashing me at the elbow.

"Run!" Cipher shouts.

We dash towards the entrance of the cove—the only exit to this place—before we do the monster thinks ahead of us and strikes the ground of the door with thorns as tall as the monster itself.

Icarus points at the thorns and tells us, "I can't pull them out," we look back, "we have no choice but to fight it."

Icarus chants a spell that makes the tips of his fingers light up.

He makes the fire bigger and controls it.

He attacks the giant, but it doesn't take effect. It covers itself with a thick, green liquid that glosses in the sunlight's direction.

"My magic's working!" Icarus says smiling at me.

My dagger becomes a sword; the sword I gave Ross becomes darker in color and Isis' ordinary set of arrow's tips become black, should all be because of Icarus.

Icarus recites something in a different language and a strange aura surrounds Violet. "Violet, you have temporary fire powers. Just use your mind to visualize the fire. The power lasts for an hour." Icarus says. "Okay, I'm going to try to use them." Violet says and a ball of fire appears on her hands.

Ross and I run towards the giant and the vines chase us.

Violet burns the vines into ashes.

"Thanks!" Ross says.

The monster vomits liquid out of its mouth that smokes and tries to dissolve the floor.

We dodge it.

Needle thin, half-inch long thorns ricochet from the walls of the cove to me. Three, four, five, six thorns dig into my skin.

I wonder if this is how my life will end, being darted with thorns that will stick to my skin until my imminent death.

Flaming arrows usher in the monster's eye.

I hear Serenity asking for more arrows.

I look behind my shoulder. I can see Violet hurling blue flames now.

There's another earthquake from the monster. Vines emerge in front of us.

We go our separate ways.

I suddenly turn into five Damian's. I knew this was the work of Icarus. We Damian's surround the monster and start attacking it with our adrenaline working it's magic by giving us superhuman strength and the sword I'm using creates recoil on my arms, but it keeps regenerating itself.

Fire is being shot around the place. It's not long until something explodes—I'm right.

We're on an all-out assault on the monster, attacking him in several different angles, several different directions, several different speeds, several different ways, we're a never-ending onslaught of attacks.

Cipher jumps in and cuts the roots of the monster with a dagger that she should have borrowed from Violet.

I just realized that the roots didn't grow back.

I run back to Icarus and ask him, "Can you make the monster levitate. I think I know how we can kill it."

"Okay." His eyes glint at me.

The other Damian's disappear.

Icarus utters words that I could barely hear and the monster levitates. I run towards the monster and call for Ross' and Cipher's help. I swallow hard.

I'm tired, but it feels like this is the last straw, my blood gushing shades of red around my body.

"Cut the roots." I shout as loud as I can, grasping my sword until my veins find their way up to the tip of my skin, creating humps on my hand.

The roots were larger than I thought. I slash them with my sword.

Roots in every direction, which way I should go, I'm not sure, roots purblind me.

I make my way out of the root maze and the monster timbers its way to the opposite direction from me when I try to look back. It smells earthy.

The plant monster disappears slowly, turning into ashes. The ashes circle around the cove and find their way out. I look in between my feet and see grass peep out of the ground and my feet are suddenly being surrounded by green and growing grass. I look around and everybody is as amazed as I am. The ground sprouts flowers with different colors, I see green pods open and blossom into purples and magentas and blues and yellows and whites.

Another earthquake shakes the ground, but this time the earthquake causes the roof of the cove to collapse.

We duck and put our arms above us expecting shards of the roof to crush us, only to realize they slowly crumble into little bits and pieces and turn into a flock of butterflies.

The ground is slowly being elevated until it reached the roof level.

We we're on top of the waterfall. It's really beautiful. I can see the whole island from here.

I look down and find out all the flowers bloomed already.

Everyone is in awe.

Right when we thought it ended a ray of light pointed at the middle of the meadow.

I run towards it and find the stone with the plant insignia on it.

"Icarus, I got it!" I shout, putting it in my pocket. "But how are we going to get down from here?" "Over here! There's a set of stairs going down!" Icarus says pointing at the waterfall.

I run to the tip of the waterfall, to the stairs that were as wide as an office table.

With the thought of that in my mind, I thought they're about to break.

A rainbow leads us down to where we started. "Do you know where Connard went?" Cipher asks. "I have no clue, Cipher." Isis says.

The sword I was holding turns into a dagger.

All our weapons go back to normal.

I take my sword back from Ross' hands and say, "Thank you for not destroying it."

"No problem!" Ross replies. Cipher has a worried look on her face.

I ask Isis in a soft voice, "Why is Cipher worried about Connard?"

Isis sighs and says, "Those two are secretly dating. My dumb father doesn't even know that they're dating. Once they went on a picnic at our rose garden and I had to stall our dad for a while until they came back."

"I'll just get my bag when we arrive at the temple. I'm going to go to the town. Maybe I can find some interesting things there." I say not realizing we were at the temple already.

I blush with shame.

"Can I come?" Isis asks. "Me too, can I?" Ross asks too. "Don't forget your sister, Damian!" Serenity says. "Don't forget the guy that saved your asses in there." Icarus says. "Sure." I respond to all of them.

"Connard!" Cipher shouts. I look in the temple.

"When I woke up, I saw you guys leave me." he says.

"Aww, I'm sorry." Cipher responds. They hold hands and Connard kisses her cheek.

"I'm going to pretend that never happened." Icarus says with disgust. His face prunes just a little.

I get my bag beside the campfire and leave immediately with the others leaving Connard and Cipher behind to let them do whatsoever it is they do.

"So how do we buy stuff around here? Or is there some other way to purchase here?" I ask Isis.

"You don't buy. Instead, you trade." she says. "They'll only trade if they think your offer is unique."

"Oh, I have a lot of unique things in my bag." I say. Maybe I do. I might've brought something that catches the trader's eyes.

"Good luck. These people take trading seriously. Never attempt to buy things; it's illegal around these parts of Mellous. And trust me when I say this. The jail here is almost resembles a torture chamber" Isis says. I wondered why she knew.

"So how'd you know we should trade here?" I blurt out. "It's something we've done in Archaea for a long time." she replies. "Just a comment, the government official's renamed London to Archaea ever since the war split the world's exterior into several, petty, pieces and plenty of cultures collided."

I feel the parts of my body with thorns that the monster launched in me throb with pain.

"Are you okay?" Isis asks me.

I collapse at the wet grass road to the town.

"I can help." Icarus says. "I just need to see where the wounds or whatever it is."

I look at him and he looks at me. He's scanning me from my feet to my head. "Okay." he pulls out a thorn from my ankle with an aura that surrounds my body.

I pant; I cry for the pain to stop

Two in my left arm, one on my right leg, one on my right hand, and two on my chest, they're bleeding. I'm in so much pain. I feel like one big wound.

I stare into the wounds and the aura goes into them.

I feel so much better. The pain subsides.

I stand up tall, but embarrassed because of the wounds.

"Here are the thorns that were in your body." Icarus hands them to me, coated with blood. I'm impaled.

Serenity slaps them out of his hands and asks, "Can we go now?"

"Yeah, sure." Icarus removes his robe and holds it with half an arm.

He wore a pair of tattered jeans and a white t-shirt that was spotless.

"Okay." I say.

I look around me and we're at the middle of a forest on a road to the weird village that's just up ahead.

We start walking.

I see a squirrel pass by us, followed by another, and another. "What's going on with the squirrels here?" I ask. "I think they and the other animals are going to the meadow." Icarus replies.

I hate Icarus less now. My temper is just enough to make it seem like he's friendly-annoying me. He's been so helpful.

I glance at Icarus and tell him, "Thank you. For everything."

"No problem!" he says with a smile.

* * *

Chapter 6

Not So Normal

"So, what happened to your Mom?" I ask Isis.

Her face is scarred with pain. "Um, it's okay if you don't want to tell me. It's your business, not mine." I say. "No it's okay . . . I can tell." she looks at the dirt and rubble under our feet.

"She died because of cancer. The doctors didn't specify what kind of cancer it was. It was unusual, like they wanted to keep something important from me," Isis looks sadder that I've ever seen her. Her eyes look almost bloodshot for a moment, "but I guess they told my stupid dad and he could've told the doctors not to tell me no matter how demanding I was, thinking 'it's for my own good and or safety' because I'm supposed to be this fragile flower in his eyes, but I know that I am the spear to his heart because I'm supposed to be the rightful heir to the throne. I could replace him, but the law states I 'have to be beyond eighteen years of age to rule the kingdom' so my father took advantage of my age and kicked me out at my annual ball. My mom was the one who had royal blood in her veins, my dad didn't until he married her so I think now that my father's too power-hungry so he would do anything to get the monarchy in his hands."

I shouldn't have asked in the first place. I feel terrible. Regret heaves my lungs in a desperate attempt to get out, stomach grumbling magnitudes of uncertainty.

"Sorry." I apologize. "I shouldn't have asked."

"It's fine really. You even asked for my permission to know about it anyways, and my mom's death was five years ago," just like mine, but her body was missing, "so it's just a distant memory now."

I look around the area for a moment and realize now, we've lost the others while talking!

We're lost.

Lost in a sea of mini structures called "houses" and thriving vegetation.

We better just make the best of things and look around. I know in my gut that they'll come looking for us.

We end up at an entrance to a small, item shop made from a simple, rectangular structure that was closest to the boat of Isis. Not really eye-catching.

"Can I help you with anything?" the owner of the shop gestures us in. Something catches my attention in the shop, a black coat that was long enough to cover three fourths of my body.

I look in my bag and find the gun. "Can I trade this gun with that coat over there?" I ask the shop owner. "Give me another one and I'll accept your offer." he says.

What would he want with another gun?

I grab the flare gun in my bag and give both guns to him. He puts the black coat near my reach and looks at the guns. "Now I can melt these guns at the blacksmith and make a pendant." he whispers. "What was that?" I ask, getting the coat from him. "Oh nothing—nice doing business with you, I guess."

I wear the black coat.

It's warmer than it looks, and it's made out of leather. The leather wears me in a way that I feel comfortable.

"I told you trading here was serious. You lost two things for the price of one, and the gun cost more than that stupid coat. That kind of trading is a rip-off." Isis says like it's a crime. "But it was worth it." I reply, patting the coat down. "This is how to trade!" she says.

She's bluffing.

She walks to the owner and points at a blue, two-piece swimsuit.

I couldn't hear the conversation, but the guy gives her the swimsuit and she walks back at me. "How'd you get it for free?" I ask. "I didn't see you give anything back "He just gave it to me." she says. "Hey, you're not trading, and why do you need that?" I try to make my face look puzzled. "I'm going to swim at the waterfall tonight." she says. I smirk

It's good to see her happy again.

I'm relieved.

Damian, note to yourself, don't ever ask about her mother ever again.

I put the thought at the back of my mind.

"Let's look for the others." I say. "Okay." she says. "But first, how does this look on me?" She puts the top on. "I—it l—looks g—good on y—you." I put my hand over my eyes and sneak a small hole on my hands to peek. I couldn't resist, but to actually look at what she was doing.

"You can look now." she says taking my hands off. "Please don't tell me you're going to change here, are you?" I say with my face supposed to look disgusted by squinting my eyes and showing a half smile. "Of course I'm not . . . now you were saying something about finding the others? I remember we left them in the blacksmith's shop." Isis cheeks are blush-red.

"Then let's go!" I say.

I start walking and then I find Isis pulling my arm and she says, "I almost forgot, we need to find a compass."

I turn around.

"I need to replace the one I left in Archaea." she looks at the floor with her face drooping. "And I'm also tired."

I say, "Do you perhaps, want to take a break? We have a lot of time to waste anyways, and it's not like we can find the others in an instant."

We stop in a pastry shop adjacent to the trader's shop where I bought the coat, and not to mention where Isis got her bikini.

"So how the heck are we going to trade stuff for pastries?!" I ask Isis.

"Well, there's a currency for trading too ya' know most especially in these cases where you have to buy something cheap like bread. It would be complete nonsense to trade a million-dollar watch for bread. It's just absurd. Not unless you think poop is something you can trade." she replies.

"Well, you're one of a kind, Isis, to be able to think that poop is something that you can trade." I tease her.

She pushes me and says offended, "Hey!"

"Hello there." the cashier of the place says. "What would you like to have?" she prepares a brown bag for the bread we'll be picking.

Isis points at a sugar coated ball of bread from the glass pane that stops us from touching the food.

"How many would you like, ma'am?" the cashier tries her best to sound polite. She opens the pane of glass and picks up a pair of tongs.

"Ten please." Isis says.

In a swift motion the cashier is able to put in ten of the pastries in the bag in less than seven seconds not taking her time, like she's in a rush.

She folds the paper bag to lock and hands over the pastries.

"How would you like to purchase that? Through trade or through currency?" she asks.

"Currency." Isis puts her hand in the pocket of her skirt and brings out what I can make out, a Pound, and hands it to the lady.

She reaches her pocket in search for change. I hear the coins jingle in her hands. She finally brings out the change and gives it to Isis.

"Thank you very much, come back again." she says.

I turn to Isis and tell her, "We really need to get that compass soon."

The sun starts dipping on the sea covering the island in a blanket of orange hues. The sea glitters in each wave cresting that creates a din of melody.

A gentle breeze passes by and Isis closes her eyes. I ask her, "What are you doing?"

She replies after a few seconds, "I'm being reincarnated by the wind if you don't mind." I chuckle.

"What? Is there something wrong?" she complains and opens her eyes.

"No. There's absolutely nothing wrong . . . except the idea of reincarnation to me." I say.

"Further explain to me how the idea of reincarnation is wrong." Isis requests.

"To your request I shall explain." I say. "It's weird for a soul to just suddenly drift into a random body or thing. Yes the body is a medium in which the soul exists in but if the soul would like to escape the medium because it's unsatisfied with its medium shouldn't it have all means to escape just like when the body dies it has all the right to escape?"

Isis nods and says, "Fair point."

We've already tunneled through most of the shops in the island and all I can say are five very disappointing words: No Compass Around The Area

* * *

"Damian, Isis! Why'd you guys leave us here?" someone shouts at our direction few meters away . . . what I can make up—Ross!

I turn to get Isis' arm and I'm dragging her with me. "Damian, slow down! There's no need to rush!" Isis says clamoring.

My feet tiptoe to stop myself from running and to avoid bumping into Ross.

I look at Ross' hand, and he's holding his dagger. "Why do you need your dagger?" I ask.

"Touché. I'm trading it for an axe. Now answer my question."

"Isis and I were trading. Well, Isis—um, let me put it this way . . ." I say, but before I completed what I was saying Isis cuts my sentence from being told by nudging me. "Isis traded for a bikini. And I got this coat for two of my guns."

"What did Isis trade to get the bikini?" Ross asks, tilting his head to my right just a few degrees from the right. Isis responds to the body language by crossing her arms around her chest.

"Oh, I get it now! The guy's seduced!" Ross says figuring it out on his own. His head tilts left to recover the normal stature of his head, and suddenly I'm blushing with the thought of Isis putting on the swimsuit

"How'd you know?" Isis asks.

"I have people smarts." he says putting one of his eyebrows up.

I hear some kind of metal being smitten by a hammer in the shack beside us.

"So what happened to Icarus?" I ask, looking around for him and then back at Ross. His eyebrow drops "He left a moment ago."

"So what's taking the blacksmith so long?" Ross says with a silly smile with the corners of his lips going side-wards.

He barges in the shop and gasps. "You control water?!" he shouts and my eyes widen.

We all go inside. "It's true." the blacksmith says. "I do control water. Please don't tell anyone and I'll give you your axe for free."

He controls the water to go around the glowing red axe. "My name's Shun. Shun Wren." the blacksmith says. The glowing red axe slowly turns into a black axe.

The blacksmith stares at us weirdly. He looks one or two years younger than me, with light brown hair flapping hundreds of directions, pale skin, dark circles under his eyes that make him look restless for someone his age, eyes glitzy blue. His face is round with cheekbones chiseled on each cheek. He's almost as tall as me and I'm not necessarily tall, wearing shorts a little bit over the knees and a dark green long sleeve shirt.

He puts the water at a wooden bucket beside him.

He attaches the handle at the end of the axe and hammers it down and puts a glossy, quick hardening liquid on it so it's not loose. "Thank you!" Ross says snatching the now complete axe from Shun in such a way that Shun falls to his knees.

I'm in total shock, and yet I'm not.

It might be because I've seen crazier things than this.

We walk away from the shop and all I could think of was how controlling water was possible.

"That was really weird." Ross says. "I don't want to go to that place ever again."

"And why not?" I ask.

"He took so long for a guy who can control liquid." he replies.

"Hey, Damian, did you forget something?!" Isis says. "We still need to buy a compass!"

"Isis, we can just go back to town tomorrow." Ross says.

She replies, "What if there's no tomorrow. Like tomorrow will turn into an endless fathom and we can only survive through the things we have—and we can't because we don't have the compass. What if."

"A tad overboard, Isis, you don't have to brag about your intelligence." I say.

"You're my gauge of intelligence, if I'm smart then you're smart." she replies.

"Except that I'm smarter than you." I reply.

Isis pushes me enough for me to almost trip.

* * *

Chapter 7

Troubled Waters

It's early in the afternoon. We're approaching the temple now. The ground is transforming into marble with every step we take.

"Hey, Isis, can I go with you, tonight . . . at the waterfall?" Serenity asks Isis. "Sure!" she responds. They both smile at each other.

I'm head-over-heels with this idea.

I'm about to ask if I can come too, but Ross interrupts. "Can I come." he says. "Sure." Isis is now looking at all of us. "You all can come if you like."

We're at the temple now. I've just noticed a bunch of good-smelling plants and flowers that were taken cared of by hand.

They were placed individually in handmade pots of wood that's been tempered to be made more durable.

Everybody rushes in like a stampede of wild beasts trying to catch the only meal they can afford to get. They hold up their towels. Ross is holding a bottle with a rich dark green color labeled . . . "Clairette de Die, Vins de Bourgogne de France" and if I remember anything from French class, "Vins de Bourgogne" it means bubbly wine.

"Where'd you get that?" I'm pointing at the bottle with my index finger.

"Oh this, I got it in my Dad's wine cellar." Ross puts an emphasis on the word "wine".

"That's just great." I feel guilty he brought that. I didn't know he would bring a bottle of wine in the harbor.

"Damian, are you okay? You look sick." Ross pokes me with the end of the bottle.

"I'm not sick. I'm just . . ." I'm thinking of an excuse. "Um . . ." I'm nervous. "Let's go." I end up saying.

"But the girls are changing." Ross says. "I don't know why they have swimsuits in their bags."

"Always come prepared with any scenario. And in the scenario you told us that we were going to the harbor. You know, beside the beach so I told Serenity to bring hers" Violet says going near us. She's wearing a brown swimsuit.

Serenity comes in too wearing navy blue and a skirt. "Are we going?" she asks.

"Is Isis done?" I ask.

"Yeah, but I don't know where she went." she replies.

"I'm here!" I hear Isis shout. She's running to trail to the waterfall wearing the swimsuit she bought—or should I say 'got for free'—with a white towel dangling from her shoulder. The other girls get their face towels while Ross, Icarus, Connard and I catch up to her.

"Wait up!" Serenity shouts from behind.

The trail is made of stones and pebbles with grass peeping out of them. There are trees swaying in the wind against us. A flurry of orange and green leaves fall down and go the opposite direction we were running. I can't find Isis in front of me. I suddenly hear a splash of water and a scream of enjoyment. We're in front of the waterfall. I see Isis already in the water. Her towel is at one side of the place.

"The water's warm!" Isis says, trying to swim.

I remove my shirt and jeans and catapult myself in the rippling water. I feel my feet touch the pavement of the waterfalls. Rocks, pebbles, water.

The water isn't deep, but deep enough to make me drown. The thought of that makes me scare my heart out.

The water's warm like a blanket early in the morning after sleeping.

Ross jumps in shirt off and grabs my leg in the water, pulling me in for a moment until his head emerges out of the water. His body is buff and just the right tint of skin. It's no wonder girls in our school like him. He tells me he doesn't like it but I know for sure he secretly does. He enjoys the luscious stare of girls but acts like he disgusts it.

I feel insecure about my body.

I'm moving my feet around to float.

Icarus and Connard arrive momentarily with their bare skin of the top of his body showing, both just showing enough to make them look physically inclined.

Serenity, Violet and Cipher finally arrive.

They jump in at the same time and Serenity pulls my shoulders down with her.

There's something wrong with almost everybody today, like they want to drag me down with them.

Ross presses his hands on the ground and gets the bottle of wine that I didn't know was there.

He splashes on the water and says, "To us." Icarus sends the cork of the bottle flying, hitting the water then floating. "For good friendships and defeating that plant monster." he completes his statement.

"What is that?!" Isis asks.

"Wine! Drink up!" Ross says, passing the wine to Isis.

"Well, okay. I guess it wouldn't hurt if I drank a little." she says putting the bottle on her lips to drink. "I love this wine!" she passes it to Serenity, but she says, "I'm not a drinker."

"Where did you get this?" she asks Ross.

"I just randomly got it in my Dad's wine cellar." he says.

Serenity passes it to me. I take a sip and pass it to Icarus.

I'm surprised the wine tastes sweeter than the usual wine, but it still has that bitter taste in the end.

He passes it to Shun, but his reaction after tasting was dissatisfaction.

He passes it to Cipher, then we continue passing it until the bottle was empty.

I don't notice until now that the wound from the plant monster stains the water around me red, but then fades with every ripple of water that makes its way around the pond of the waterfall. It didn't hurt.

I can see the falling sun bending, curving with the ripples of the water, glaring my eyes one by one starting with the right, then the left with the reflection of the water.

I didn't want to say anything about the blood because they would make a big deal out of it.

"So what now?" Ross says.

"Why don't we play truth-or-dare?" Serenity suggests.

"Yeah, I guess that could be fun." Violet says.

We go out of the water and form a circle around the bottle and sit down. The bottle spins around and around. I couldn't see who spun it.

The tip of the bottle lands on me.

"Damian, truth or dare?" Ross asks.

"Truth."

"Hmmm . . . do you know Nel's crush?" he replies.

"No! Wait, why are you asking me this?!" I ask.

"Because he has a crush on your little sis!"

I didn't want to respond in any way. *Someone just slice my throat out. I don't need it to speak for the moment.*

I look at Serenity who was in front of me looking acerbic. "Ross!" she shouts, going berserk on Ross, hitting him repeatedly with her fist, and then pushing him in the water.

"You promised me you wouldn't tell him!" Serenity says to Ross.

"It's not like you like him anyways." Ross responds.

I chuckle. "I don't, but it's embarrassing." Serenity argues.

The bottle lands on me again and again.

Ross asks me "Truth or dare?" "Truth." I say. "What's your most embarrassing thing you've ever done."

Come to think of it, I didn't know.

I've always avoided anything that would make me embarrassed.

I sat there, stared at everyone and scratched my neck. "I don't know." is all I can manage to say with a slight pause on every word. "Why does the bottle always land on me?" I say.

"Oops." Violet says, partially drunk.

I've never seen her like this.

"You figured it out."

"Found out what?" I question.

"We always stopped it on you every time you looked away." Isis says laughing.

"It was just a practical joke." Ross says.

"So all those truths I told, and the dares I've done was a practical joke?" I say.

"We should really be getting back." Icarus says. "There are robbers around this time of night"

We leave the bottle behind and put on our clothes on our way back to the temple.

* * *

I lie down outside the temple for a change of scenery and look at the stars.

I feel less tensed.

I find the stone with the plant insignia in my pocket and put it in my bag beside me.

The moonlight was bright, but it wasn't a nuisance to my eyes.

The smell of lavender filled the area.

I look around me to see that the others are lighting up the essence of the flower in a pot.

I couldn't help to think what Crissy was doing right now because her favorite flower is the lavender. I bet she's worried about us.

I can imagine the look on her face.

Her face is filled with gloom.

The trees swayed because of the wind.

Some of the leaves go to me.

The aftertaste of the wine is taking its effects on my tongue.

I'm lying down on grass.

I'm using my sweater as a blanket.

Everything is okay now.

I'm becoming sleepy and sleepy.

I wish it could be like this every night.

My vision becomes blurring.

I'm almost asleep.

Conversations beside me, I can barely hear them.

The sky is a slushy of inky blue and gray clouds, colors competing for space. I would give them space if I could, but I can't. It's strange how the clouds are so far from us even if it seems so near. Sometimes when it seemed so close I would extend my arms as far as I could possibly stretch them and try to clutch onto it but fail unsurprised. Sometimes I imagine how it feels to touch clouds, they look so bubbly and fluffy I imagine touching the softest cotton on earth, but if clouds were cotton I would rather sleep up there than down here on dirt.

Violet gets up, passes through me, and runs behind the temple.

I quickly get up and trail her.

She stops on a tree, bends down and I hear her gagging.

I walk up to her and ask, "Are you okay?"

"I'm never drinking alcohol ever again." she spews.

"Are you promising that to me?" I rub her back and she asks me, "Do you have a mint or water?"

I tell her to wait at the same spot and run to Icarus to ask him how to get water. He tells me, half-asleep, that there's water in the temple in a water jug. I get in the temple look around for the water jug—it hides behind Icarus' luggage. I open it and pour it in a cup I find on the ground and hurry back to Violet.

"Here's the water. I don't think we have any mints with us though." I hand Violet the cup. She drinks it voraciously and emptying it in three seconds after receiving it.

"Seriously, never drink alcohol ever again." I say.

"Don't tell anyone about this, Damian." Violet points the empty cup at me like a threat.

"I won't"

"You better not." Violet walks away to leave me alone in the dark.

* * *

Chapter 8

Sickness and Health

March 21, 2041

I get the day going by testing the dagger I got from Cipher. Suddenly, the blacksmith from yesterday appears from nowhere with all of his things clinging from his back. "Why are you here?" I ask.

He saps out the liquid in the plants around us.

I point my dagger at him.

"I'd just like to be part of your team." he says, restoring the moisture of the plants.

I stop pointing my dagger at him.

I get in the temple.

I look back and he's not there. "Come in." I shout and look back.

He runs inside the temple and sits down at the corner trying to distance himself from us. After what has happened—us running into his shop, finding out he can control water, his own secrets threatening him, Ross talking about him like he's filth—I don't expect him to feel as welcome.

* * *

"What good will this guy bring to the group?! He's just going to be deadweight." Isis replies to my offer of him joining us.

"He controls water! You don't see people born with that talent every day," I argue, "anyways we can just drop him off somewhere in Seattle." "The more the merrier." Icarus says. The conversation ended to the conclusion of keeping him. "Hey, come here!" Ross invites Shun to the group, completely contrast to how he treated him yesterday.

He drops all his things on the floor and slowly walks towards us.

There's a voice that's beckoning to me out of nowhere, "Put the nature stone in the altar. Put the nature stone in the altar." that belonged to a little girl. It's strange. She repeats it until I decide to ask Icarus, "Hey, Icarus, is there an altar for the nature stone?"

"Yeah, I recall there is one, deep inside this very temple." he says.

"Can we go there now?" I ask.

"Yeah, we can. Just in case, bring your daggers."

I get the nature stone and my daggers out of my bag and follow Icarus in the temple. I feel an uneasiness stirring in my stomach like butterflies clashing their wings on the walls of it.

Icarus walks deeper into the temple. "Put your hands on the walls." he says. I do as he says, my arms are searching the darkness and then I feel an icy, numbing tip on my fingers. I bring my hand to get hold of it.

"Illuminate!" he says. The tips of his fingers create a bright lumen bright enough to cover the field in front of us.

Spider webs filled every corner and crevice of the place.

I hear rats squeaking from the wall beside me. "So this temple's bigger than it looks?" I ask Icarus. "Yeah, I don't go down here much." he responds.

We continue walking

A staircase led us down. We see the altar from the staircase. "Be careful. I can't go down. Only the person with the stone can go in." Icarus says.

He's stuck in the staircase.

The staircase is slippery, so it's difficult for me to keep my momentum stable.

A force field doesn't allow Icarus to pass.

I get down and put the stone in the altar. It and the stone go down. I get nervous.

A ray of light pierces through the wall on the altar, a door opens beside me and the light becomes bigger, brighter.

The force field weakens and Icarus goes in the room.

I go inside the stone door in front me. It's a whole different world. I see flowers dangling on walls stricken with sunlight. I'm almost blind by how much sunlight is in this room, the sunlight's leaping off the walls and into my eyes, I need to squint them just to be able to see what's in front of me. That weird voice just lead Icarus and I into nowhere. I'm questioning what that weird voice was.

I see a stone griffin at the end of the room.

All at once my arm starts burning like white-hot steel on my arm and the griffin comes to life, breaking the bits of stone on its body.

I rip the sleeve of the burning arm. I'm howling for help.

A strange tattoo is being drawn on my skin, a tattoo that takes form of a teardrop.

The griffin runs straight into the tattoo. I feel weak and strong at the same time, the griffin howls in me. I'm gasping for air.

"Damian!" Icarus shouts. The eerie sound of Icarus fades in my ear. I collapse on the ground and my eyes shut. My body's paralyzed on the ground and I can't move. I still hear Icarus' voice shouting my name in a fuzzy tone it makes my ears itch and then my body shuts down on me.

* * *

I wake up on a wool bed with an emerald in my hands with an intricate design. Each and every stroke of green resembles a teardrop on my hands. I shove the gemstone in my pocket. I'm inside the temple.

"I'm awake!" I shout.

I hear a scream, which belonged to Violet. Isis, in front of me, shoots an arrow to a mysterious person taking Violet as hostage.

He's wearing a mask and a black coat holding a dagger with the same material of the dagger Cipher gave. The arrow passes through his face.

I grab the sword beside me and charge straight at him.

"Give me the stone!" he says.

I stab him, but it doesn't affect him. Fire balls, arrows, even Ross' axe passes through.

"What stone?" I ask.

"I know you have it! The circular stone!" he shouts.

"I'm going to kill this girl!" he says putting the tip of the dagger on Violet's neck, making a dent on her skin.

Violet's screaming, "Help, help!" I have no choice but to give it.

I get the stone in my pocket and throw it to him. He snatches the stone from the ground and leaves a cut on Violet's arm.

I catch a glimpse of the mysterious guys face. A cold look in both of his eyes, a smile on his face that could rip the whole world apart and black hair slicked back behind his ears. *Evil, sinful, beastly, corrupt, wicked.*

I'm suddenly blind.

I fall on my back as the sounds of the people around me become loud, then soft, then loud, then unclear in my ears. All I hear is complete jabbering. My head is pounding in thousands of corners in my mind. I just want it to stop. I just want it to stop. It hurts too much. I want it to end.

It feels like I'm dying and there's nobody who can save me.

* * *

March 22, 2041

I wake up on the same pile of wool. Isis is beside me treating my wounds. I'm burning a hundred degrees.

The heat I feel is relaxing, and then annoying to the point that I just can't take it, but I also feel cold, ice cold, the skin under my hand is freezing and I don't know if I should wrap myself with blankets or not.

My fingers feel numb, my limbs feel numb, my body is numb.

My fingers run through the other side of the pile of wool and it's cold. I flip my body to the other side of the wool.

I didn't know what time of day it is, or how long I've been out.

It feels like a morning.

The time of day when the sun shined just right, when the windows of my room usually fog up.

I close my eyes when Isis tries puts a wet cloth on my forehead.

My body's throbbing with the pain from every injury in and on my body.

I look like a sheep—wounded from dull sheers, lying down at my own wool.

Isis wipes a wound on my left shoulder. "Ow!" I gasp.

I finally open my eyes. The first thing I see is Isis' rosy-red cheek with a lock of hair curling down to her neck.

"Are you okay?" Isis asks.

"I'm fine." I say. "But you don't have to do this."

"It's the least I can do. The others are preparing for our leave, but we can't leave without you." Isis says.

Emotions in me were making me nervous and the air around me constricts my throat.

I choke a little. I stare into Isis' green eyes and see my reflection. "Thank you for doing this." I say.

Isis closes her eyes and exhales. I stroke her hair with my hand and she pulls back. "Umm I'm going to get your lunch." she says anxiously.

I sit up straight and stare out of the temple waiting for Isis. I couldn't stop thinking of her. From the way she smiles to the color of her hair . . . she made me feel so vulnerable, yet so safe at the same time. Maybe I'm just obsessing over her.

Isis comes back with a bowl of stew.

"What kind of stew is it?" I ask, holding a hand and twisting it counterclockwise.

"Chickpea, tamarind, It's good for you." Isis smiles. "You sound like my mom." I say with a short-lived laugh that escapes my mouth.

"Hey, just eat your stew!" Isis says joyously. "Or do I have to spoon-feed you?"

"Umm—no—that's not—um—I mean—please don't do that, please!" I'm not in the mood for laughing.

"I'm just joking; you don't have to make such a big fuss about it." Now Isis laughs.

"Haha, very funny." I say.

"So what's Serenity doing?" I ask.

"Serenity is helping Ross look for food, Cipher's braiding rope and Violet's looking for ingredients in the meadow for your meds. She said she saw some ingredients for it yesterday in the meadow to mix with some of the plants she got in the cove where we defeated the monster." Isis replies. "I just remembered . . . I need to check on Violet," Isis waves, "Bye."

I look at the bowl of stew. It's a mushy, yellow water with chickpeas with few pieces of carrots. Surprisingly, it tastes really good. It tasted like chicken soup with a slight tangy taste, must be because of the tamarind.

Violet and Isis come back immediately after one spoonful of eating the stew with green liquid incased in a small jar with the circumference of her hand.

"Is that the medicine?" I say coughing each and every syllable.

“Drink it every two hours and you’ll be better by tomorrow.” Violet hands the jar to me.

“Thanks, Violet” I fit the jar in my hands trying to compare how long her hand is. My hand overlapped by a couple of inches.

I hold the jar with my fingertips on the lid and shake it with the only strength I have left to check the consistency of the liquid. I get tired.

It’s very skim.

I hold it by the sides before it drops. “I’m going to take it from here.” Isis says to Violet.

“I don’t have anything to do, so I’m going to start the fire for tonight.” Violet replies and I see the wound of the dagger on Violet’s neck.

I billow at myself, mostly because I’m disappointed at myself. If I were awake yesterday I could’ve stopped him from leaving without a cut on Violet. I wish I had more time. Time management isn’t my forte, but my weakness. If I had a genie I would waste one of my wishes on time . . . time to fix my errors, time to relive short- lived moments of my life, have so much time on my watch that I die at the age of one hundred twenty and in my lifespan marry a beautiful woman and attend dozens of colleges to become one of the most successful human beings on earth and have kids who become more successful than me.

“So what happened to the guy who attacked Violet yesterday?” I ask, handing the jar to Isis. “He almost killed you actually.” Isis stares at me. “He threw a dagger and Icarus blocked it with his magic. Somehow his magic scared him away.”

“Do you know why I have these scars then?”

“Yeah, you fell down on some sharp stones near the temple.” Isis looks away from me.

I smell the smoke of the burning wood.

It’s mellow and fragrant.

I’m staring at a medium-sized bowl tinted copper with water stained with blood and rocks sitting at the very bottom.

I see a replica of the bowl beside it with a small towel drowned on bloody water.

I lie down soundly to avoid disturbing them. Isis damps the cloth again and puts it on my forehead. Isis has already done enough for me to recover.

I just wish she would stop making a fuss over me.

I hear footsteps getting nearer and nearer to me.

I open my eyes. Ross and Serenity are here, along with Shun and Icarus. Ross is carrying a live, tied up chicken with his right hand and Serenity's carrying twigs and branches on both of her arms.

"Hey, how are you, Damian?" Ross puts down the chickens.

"Nice chickens?" I reply.

"Yup, you're okay to have the strength to talk," Ross laughs. "the chickens are nice, aren't they?"

"Yes they are." I nod.

My back falls on the wool and fall asleep.

My body's starting to get warmer and warmer after I drinking the medicine.

I open my eyes and see Isis trying to make the cloth damp, but when she tries to put it on my forehead she starts screaming.

I couldn't hear anything anybody was trying to say.

I can only see and feel what she was doing. Isis is trying to shake me like I'm dead.

Everyone appears in my field of vision. Ross, Serenity, Shun, Icarus, Connard and Violet. They're all in awe, some of them covering their mouths from shock. Their faces are filled with tragedy. I can't move. I don't know what to do.

I wake up and my back rises from bed almost immediately after.

My heart beats strong enough that I feel them coarse on my fingertips.

I look to my right and find out that Isis is still where she was few minutes or hours ago. I'm not so sure.

"Are you okay? I tried to wake you up because you've been acting strange in your sleep." Isis says.

"I'm fine." I say followed by a cough.

"D-Damian!? Your eyes! They turned blue!" Isis sounds shocked. But my eyes are blue.

"But my eye color's blue?!" I argue.

"No, it's green. Isn't it?" I didn't know how to respond to what she just said.

"Whatever you saw, please just don't worry. You need to rest, Isis. Good night." I say, putting my hand on her cheek.

She hugs me and says, "I just don't want to see you sick."

Does she really care about me? "C'mon, please rest Isis, for me." I say, removing the hand on her cheek to let her know that I wanted her to rest.

* * *

March 23, 2041

I look to my right again, Isis' sleeping soundly, face down.

I'm glad she slept.

Sleep.

The thing we do every day to rest the body from its long, hard work. The good about it.

The thing we do too much and become lazy. The bad about it.

The same lock of hair's still curled down her neck.

I feel so much better thanks to Violet's medicine which I drunk all the way to the bottom.

The medicine tasted like a bitterer version of oolong tea.

"Damian, you're awake!" Isis says in a weak tone of voice, barely opening her eyes to adjust to the sunlight that strikes the temple's entrance.

"Yeah, I am. And I'm not sick anymore" I say. "Thank you for taking care of me, Isis."

She closes her eyes and turns to me.

I stroke her hair with my right hand.

My heart's pulse is getting faster and faster for every second that passes when I stroke Isis' hair.

Isis opens her eyes and says, "You're the only guy that has ever attempted to get to know me. Thank you for doing so." I feel like exploding after what Isis said.

My pulse has now officially reached its limit.

Body temperature rising, irregular heart beat? Are these normal?

I just smile.

* * *

We prepare the things for our leave today. Wood for the furnace of the ship, our luggage, even we need to prepare.

I put my dagger in the pocket of my black coat. Isis loads her cross bow. Serenity holds her bow. Ross doesn't have much of a choice but to carry his axe.

Icarus leads us to a cramped up tunnel that he calls, "The shortcut going to the harbor". You can already see the end of the tunnel, the sunlight piercing through the thick darkness. Each step we take the end gets bigger and bigger.

Inside the cave I have my face get stuck onto cobwebs and spiders crawling all over my body and I'm left trying to fend myself from their tiny bites, not to mention it was dark inside so it was difficult to know what you're doing or what others are doing or what things you might end up holding and have no clue whatsoever on what it is you're holding. Icarus says that this is the only way to go to the harbor without attracting any attention.

We're finally at the end and Icarus rushes out of the tunnel to drop the lumber.

"That was exhausting to levitate." Icarus sighs out loud.

Stepping out of the tunnel, I'm blinded for a moment and then everything gets its own definite color and shape and I can see again. The boat is few meters away from where I'm standing.

"That's one nice boat you've got there, Isis." Icarus sounds amazed.

"Thanks!" Isis replies.

"So it operates with heat?" Icarus asks.

"It operates with fuel too, but since there isn't much fuel available I use lumber to create heat." Isis explains.

We toss our things into the ship and Icarus discretely tosses the lumber in using his magic while he and Isis talk about how the ship is a hybrid of a yacht, a steamboat, and a sail boat, having the luxury feel of a yacht with its interior and it can be fueled with diesel and oil or heat and can be moved using the sail while we get into the hybrid boat and wait for their conversation to die.

I put the wood they chopped up yesterday in the furnace room.

The furnace room's full of dust and ashes, which make the floor a bit slippery.

A box beside the furnace was labeled 'Charcoal'. Beside it was dozens of small boxes of matches.

I put some charcoal in the furnace and pile some wood on top of the coal.

Ashes from the last fire go around the room.

I feel the boat rocking left and right.

I open the door for fresh air and cough out what I thought was ashes in my mouth, but instead just my saliva.

I wave my arms around and get a box of matches and start a fire at the charcoal. In a flash, the wood goes to flames. The wood that Serenity and Ross got is really flammable meaning I have to frequently go down here to put in more wood.

I put the box of matches on top of the charcoal box before I walk up the stairs that lead to the deck of the ship. We were already out of the land.

I go to the control tower and tell Isis, "We should really get back to Seattle."

"Oh yeah, okay." she replies, "But I still don't have a compass."

I'm looking around the place, only to find out that the ship has a built in compass and I'm pointing at it. "Isis, that's a compass, right?"

She stares at it long enough to react, "Oh . . . My . . . God . . . There's a compass in here all along."

I cover my mouth so that she won't see me giggle, but then I burst to laughter.

"Stop laughing at me!" Isis shouts with her face boiling red.

I get out of the tower and to the deck quickly.

* * *

Chapter 9

Another Danger

The boat crashes onto something. I wonder what, but I feel like I'm in a scene of titanic.

I see Isis get out of the control tower and she says, "There's something wrong." she walks towards us. "Apparently there's a huge layer of ice blocking our way to the next island."

Shun goes in front of the boat and tries to break the ice with his water controlling ability. Unfortunately it doesn't work.

"Yup, there's a problem. The sea surrounding the route going to Seattle is frozen, from rock bottom to the sea's surface." Shun drops his hands forcibly.

Icarus goes in front as well and creates fireballs to melt the ice.

Everyone goes in front to see.

The water starts to contract to its original form, which was ice.

"This is no ordinary ice. This is the legendary Moving Ice City of Atlantis." Icarus says shockingly.

It wasn't surprising hearing that after what had happened these few days.

An arctic wind ripples throughout my hands.

It was a good thing I wore my black coat before we left.

I rub my hands together to eventually create heat, but the wind is too much to bear.

I button the button nearest to my neck. "We should go in the furnace room of the ship and think of a plan to go to get to the other side." Isis says. "Good Idea." Icarus says.

* * *

"Any idea on how we're going anywhere with this kind of obstacle?" Shun asks.

Icarus grits his teeth.

He's always had a problem with Shun ever since Shun joined the team. Icarus always wanted to do a better job than Shun. I wonder if he's jealous of him because of all the attention he's getting. I wonder if Shun's jealous of him too.

"We can just split up into teams and search the land if there's a body of water that will lead us away from here." Ross says.

I never thought of Ross as a thinker, but more of a fighter. There must be some things I just don't know about people. I couldn't think of the plan he had in stored for us.

We exchange looks and we all agree. Well, all except Cipher. "What will happen to us if we get caught by a snowstorm?" Cipher says.

That was actually a good point, but doesn't she remember we have Icarus? He can just make some kind of force field. So I wouldn't worry about that.

We cover our mouths to stop our laughs from coming out.

Ross gets a leather jacket from his bag, along with Violet with her leather jacket. Isis and Cipher are getting their coats from their bags.

I'm already wearing my black coat anyways.

I look at Isis wearing a really striking, yet beautiful crimson red coat.

She pushes her hair out of her coat. Then I look at everyone else.

Cipher wore an aquamarine coat. The opposite color of Isis'

Violet's trying hard to zip her coat up. Serenity beside her helps by pushing it down and then up again.

Connard is . . . astonishingly fine with what he's wearing.

Icarus wears his robe.

Ross opens the door and Icarus goes out first, then Ross then Isis then Cipher then Violet then Connard then Serenity then me. I close the door and head up to the deck.

He ignites a fire at the center of his palms and makes it bigger and bigger until the flames meet. All at once, an ice volley flies toward us. Icarus makes a split second decision and throws the flame that consumes the ice volley.

The flame is scorching; nothing was left from the volley.

Mermaids jump their way to the boat. I start counting, five, eight, eleven, until the mermaids become uncountable.

The mermaids are pale in color, they're just like humans, and only their legs are fins, fins with scales dyed on a spectrum of colors. They wear blue cloth along their chest, their skin color varies, along with their hair color.

I try not to look, but then I see Ross looking at them maliciously. Cipher slaps him at the face. "What was that for?!" Ross says. Cipher ignores him.

"Why are you people here?" a mermaid with blonde hair and tan skin demands for an answer.

"Why are you mermaids here?" I ask angrily.

"Glad you asked, but you all are under arrest!" she says.

That was one thing I didn't expect a mermaid to say, but it happens.

Icarus chants in languages unknown. The mermaids turn into stone starting from the tip of their fins to the tips of their hair.

"Destroy them before they come back to life!" Icarus shouts.

I kick one of them and they create a domino effect. A row of them breaks. Shun uses his water power to destroy half of them. Ross, he still looks at them maliciously. Isis kicks them just like what I did. Three-fourths of them are destroyed. Mermaid shards scattered around the deck.

"We're running out of time! Let's run!" Icarus says. "We can run now and when the field is wide open, we can use that to our advantage and kill them."

We make a get-away by jumping off the boat. Before I do I wince back at the ship and see crimson liquid spewing all around and then I start jumping after realizing that those that didn't break returned to color.

The others that didn't break run after us. It they're running after us and we're trying our best to run away from them.

They're out numbering us.

A fleet of mermaids spring from the ground in front of our eyes, as if they appeared from nowhere. I eventually slip because of the ice. It was really difficult to keep my balance.

We were surrounded by the mermaid troops.

They carried spears and swords made of steel and iron. Some of them carried shackles.

"What do you want from us?" Icarus says.

"Nothing really, but this place is mermaid territory."

"By the way, we killed most of the troops you've sent earlier. It's a bloodbath there." Ross tries to taunt them.

A mermaid behind me put shackles on my legs and other mermaids puts shackles on everybody else.

They get me from my elbow like I was nothing.

"Get up, human!" the mermaid says.

"Shut up!" I reply. These guys are getting on my nerve.

They tie our arms with a rope.

The mermaid ties my wrists with a rope.

"Go to hell!" I hear somebody say from behind me. A mermaid kicks my thigh. Now I have to limp my way to their headquarters!

* * *

A spiral staircase in front of us lead us to a hidden ice metropolis under the unmeltable ice. The buildings are as high as the ones in Seattle and homes with architectural design, even for mermaids. It's too bad we're their hostages. But not for long I hope.

Mermaids with different ethics swarmed the area, staring at us like we were their meal. "You all are pests!" Ross says.

I hear a conversation from behind me.

"What do you think they'll do to them?"

"I think they're going to be our little pets."

"Or get tortured till the point of their death."

I grit my teeth.

"Or even get cooked. I'd like to get a thigh this time."

It's terrible here! Eating humans, getting tortured till the point of death?! My palms start sweating and adrenaline surging to try to fight off the mermaids staring at us.

* * *

I read a sign, which says, "Stadium this way." I'm getting terrified. My legs are shaking.

I look at Isis, keeping her cool as ever. I wish I could do too.

It's the right time to sweat right now from all the anxiety, but I couldn't. It was freezing in here.

"Where are we going?" I ask, trying to get my legs out of these shackles.

"If you should know, we're taking you to the Kings Quarters. The king will decide on keeping you people as hostages, of set you free, which I doubt he'll do." a mermaid with a tattoo on his neck says.

* * *

As much as I hate to say, I'm in prison right now. I'm in prison with my friends. Technically, we're in a waiting cell waiting for orders from the so-called 'King', sitting down on the cold, crystalized ice floor.

"Isis, we have to think of some way to get out of here." I say to Isis who's beside me.

"Damian, after we're done with this island, we need to go home." Ross says. "Um . . . okay." I say.

Why did that fake letter end up in our house that night?

Why did the stone with the gale insignia wrapped with the leather parchment map end up on my house?

I have some suspicions. There might be someone out there who set this all up. I don't want to think of it right now.

My life is now in the brink of being eaten.

"Damian!?" Isis says shaking me until the upper half of my body drops on the cold floor.

"Yeah?" I respond trying to get myself sitting again.

"While you've been deep in thought, your eyes have been turning green and blue." Isis helps me up.

I roll my eyes around the room thinking that statement was just a practical joke.

Violet hands me a mirror from her pocket to see my reflection.

My eyes actually turned green and blue!

I noticed a difference in my facial features.

More defined than before, or I haven't seen it in a long time.

I was speechless.

I look at the mirror again and my eyes stayed blue.

"Why did it do that?" Shun asks. Before I make a statement, a mermaid puts us in chains.

Once they were locked on our legs it made some sort of 'click' sound. The mermaid kicks me at the leg.

These mermaids really love to kick!

I get up on my feet and look at the mermaid at the eyes. He didn't look very friendly with the blue scales on his face covering his nose.

I hear more clicking noises coming from beside me.

I look to my right and onto the cold, glass floor, a foot with a chain laced around it.

I look up and see Isis. She's in agony.

I feel the chains around my foot prickling me, making my foot go numb. I groan. “All of you will be next to be judged by your actions.” the mermaid says. “Just shut up!” Ross says. “Start walking!” the mermaid demands.

One by one, each of us go out of the cell starting with the mermaid that locked in chains on us. The chains were interconnected with one another.

I go out of the cell and into a hall made of ice and glass, leading to a sun lit room. The others follow.

The mermaids beside us held our weapons in their hands, teasing us that they have them. It looks like they were about to let them fall, but they grab them.

* * *

Chapter 10

The Epiphany

Rattling noises bounce off the walls of the hall making me feel nauseous.

"Damian." Isis whispers to my ears. "Damian." she says again. "Once we meet the king, Icarus will make the chains break, run as fast as you possibly can outside the stadium when I say 'now'."

I turn to Isis and say, "Do you think this is a full proof plan?"

"Of course, why do you think I'm telling you this?" she replies.

I look at the guard in front of me. He doesn't seem to be listening. "No reason whatsoever . . . I'm just confirming." I say, taking deep breaths.

"Don't worry. We'll get out of here." she says.

The sunlit room was nothing more than a gigantic courthouse made to look sunlit with the bright, fluorescent lights I recognize.

They must be the glowing jellyfish from when we were in the huts of Isis and Cipher, meaning they could have traveled here because by the sea current.

"So what are these humans doing here?" someone wearing a crown in the courtroom says with nothingness in his expression, smiting the gavel. I get the impression he's the king.

I feel more nauseous than before.

It felt like my throat just fell to my stomach, being consumed by the gastric acids.

I couldn't talk for a moment because I was terrified of the king.

He has literal black pits in his eyes.

The court has beams that looked like they could surface the ice that keeps this metropolis of a city hidden from outsiders. There are columns of beams on both my sides, left and right, meters away from me that reach the raised; elevated desks for the judges. There is no jury. The floor extends half a kilometer from where I am to the desks of the judges.

I'm seeing an open stairway leading all the way to the floor above us beside the bench.

"These are the people who sailed to our territory!" the mermaid beside me replies to the king.

"It's completely rare for humans to land on our territory." the king hisses at us.

The king looks human like us. He has long, brown hair that he fixes every minute that passes by.

"What's your business here?" he asks.

I hear an intense sound of slithering coming from behind.

I try to look back and see a group of mermaid troops coming toward us. They must be for extra precaution on guarding the king.

The atmosphere is extreme and quiet. I don't want to break silence.

"Now!" Isis shouts. I get ready to run.

Icarus makes all the mermaid's eyes burn.

I turn my back and see Ross get my dagger from the mermaid beside him. "Catch!" Ross says tossing my dagger in midair. It spins around.

I catch the blade cutting my left hand and I desperately grab the handle with my right.

My left hand's bleeding uncontrollably.

I wrap it around my t-shirt and look around me at the same time.

Isis gets her bow from the mermaid beside her.

I swing my sword around hitting the mermaid in front of me.

The mermaids beside the others are dead.

"I think it's time to run now before it's too late!" Icarus shouts, and the shackles from our feet snaps like a twig.

Violet runs toward a huge door behind us. We follow.

The mermaid troops fall down, chasing us to the gigantic door, but we close it and lock it before any of them could reach us.

That was close.

* * *

We end up outside the courtroom, none of the mermaids out here don't notice us.

I get the feeling Icarus turned us invisible. I can see the others follow Icarus into a window of a house made of obscure glass and ice that linked them together.

I'm getting dizzy. Everything is twisting. Could be because my loss of blood. I shouldn't faint now. I keep going

A mermaid family of four can see us. They're frightened.

Icarus chants a spell in some kind of ancient language of a sort.

The spell steals ice shards from the crevices of the room and clash into each other to form ice soldiers.

"Trap them!" Icarus commands the soldiers.

The soldiers cover each family member's mouth including the little children with a hand and the other to grab their arms and put it behind their backs in unison.

I feel a sudden pain on the palm of my left hand.

I unravel the section of my t-shirt with my clenched hand that is now painted with a deep, crimson red color and stare at the hand. I've been bleed a lot, but it barely healed. I sigh in a way that I sound like I'm in pain.

"Damian, why do you always get hurt?" Violet says bringing out a thick, red liquid incased in a jar in her bag. I don't know if she's trying to sound mean or empathetic. "Here, put this on your wound." she says handing the jar to me. "It's an antiseptic."

"When did you get to make an antiseptic?" I ask.

"When you were sick." Violet runs her thin fingers through her dark, raven hair. "I figured someone might get hurt, so I made some."

I unscrew the lid of the jar avoiding it to make contact to my cut and a horrid smell goes into my nose.

I put the jar on a round, glass table beside me to breathe with the lid free and the jar open.

I put my index and middle fingers in the antiseptic and smear it on my wound.

It feels a lot better than it did few moments ago.

A soothing, cooling sensation takes over the wounds pain, like menthol you just pop into your mouth, or a wind that passes through your body. It was a relief.

I breathe in and out. My body wishes to just put that cooling sensation all over.

"Thanks." I say to Violet.

I put the lid on the jar and twist it to lock the lid in place.

I look at the mermaid family and almost feel sorry for them.

The ice soldiers sit down with the family on their laps. The same time, I hear a large group of mermaid troops slither and hiss boisterously around the streets of sleet. I stare out the window to see how many they are, an endless onslaught of troops that slithered through the ice streets like running water.

"Everybody, get down!" I whisper-shout.

We all get down to our knees.

"What's happening?!" Serenity asks.

"The mermaid troops are looking for us!" I reply

* * *

Few minutes pass and I don't hear the slithering anymore. I sneak a peek on the window and see no sign of the troops anywhere. I look back at everyone and say, "No sign of them."

Icarus fills the window with ice shards to replicate obscure glass just in case the troops come back. “That was close.” Icarus says.

We all take a breather and take our time to relax for a while and release tension that constantly builds up.

“I’ll check the living room!” Isis says.

“I’ll check their bedrooms upstairs to look for bed sheets for us to sleep in or something.” Serenity says.

“I’ll go to the kitchen.” Shun says. I feel left out of the group.

Violet tries to negotiate with the mermaids to live with us for a while. They nod their heads. “Release!” Icarus says. The ice soldiers melt, creating a puddle.

I go in the living room to look for Isis. “Isis?” I utter in dead silence.

I look around and see a huge block of ice in front of me. I notice a red cloth stand out from all the blue behind a glacier and from all the blue hues coming from the glass and ice.

I walk around the glacier and see Isis lying down on the cold, glass floor.

I yawn out of the blue.

I lie down beside her and ask her, “Are you still awake?” she comes nearer to me almost like she wanted me go nearer too.

I put off my coat and put it on top of us like a blanket, keeping us warm, but not warm enough, so I wrap my arms around her waist.

I hope she wouldn’t get angry. It wasn’t how I intended to sleep, but I was afraid she would get frostbite in the middle of the night.

Her delicate body comes nearer and nearer.

My cheeks burn with anxiety.

* * *

March 24, 2041

"Damian, wake up." a masculine voice says followed by a howl of an eagle.

I open my eyes to see if I was delusional.

I don't see who or what that masculine voice was coming from.

I guess I am delusional.

Isis is gone from my arms, though I can still feel her presence in them.

I wear my coat and go to the kitchen. *What's happening to you, Damian*? My arm suddenly gives me a shock.

I put a hand on the arm.

"Hey, Damian!" Shun says.

I try to look for him.

He's in front of some kind of floating fire roasting some squid on skewers with Connard.

"Yeah?" I ask.

"The others are in the room beside the kitchen." Shun says.

A delightful smell doses the room with lemon fragrance. I don't mind but to take in as much of the fragrance in me.

I look beside me and notice Serenity sitting on a glass table with two of the mermaid family's children playing together in the room beside me.

I walk in and sit down beside Serenity.

"Oh, hi Damian." Serenity says with a small, pretty smile developing its way to a wide, enthusiastic smile "There's calamari at the table if you like to eat now."

I take a look at the table beside me and find a plate full of the squid on skewers that Shun was cooking.

I grab one skewer and bite off a tentacle.

The others walk in the room with the mermaid parents.

"Thank you for giving us a tour of your wonderful house," Violet says to them. "and we're sorry again for keeping you hostage last night."

"You're welcome dear, and don't worry, we understand if you were paranoid, so you had to just for security." the mother says.

"Oh, look! There's squid!" the father says while I still chew on the squid tentacle.

"So how are you guys able to get fruits and vegetables like lemon?" Violet asks. "Oh, we have a system that works here in the city. The King usually sends the best hunters out to land when the metropolis moves near a city to gather essentials for food, other than fish which is a protein. We need more than protein to survive in this earth you know?" the mother says.

"Hi Damian." says Isis, still wearing the crimson red coat from yesterday. I swallow. "Hi." I smile.

She goes nearer to me and leans on the table avoiding eye contact.

"Can you come with me?" she asks me nervously.

"Yeah, but what for?" I ask. She grabs my arm making me drop the squid, dragging me to the place we slept last night and my temperature rises intensely.

She lets go of my arm and lets me sit down with my back straight on the glacier. "Okay, why?" I ask.

"I can't take it." she says. "Why are you being so kind to me?"

I wonder what the problem with being so kind is.

I have a flashback of that very same question when we were in Cipher and Isis' island.

"Ugh, I don't know what's wrong with me today. I should be thanking you."

Isis blushes and looks down on me.

She sits down beside me.

She's so close. Close enough that I can feel her breath go through my eyelashes.

I push the hair that covered her face behind her ears with the back of my hand and look at her lips. She looks me in the eyes.

Breathing was something I desperately needed right now because I held it for quite some time now

Her eyes, they flicker in much motion, the lights of the seabed make them look like stars embedded on her face. I got lost in the greenness them. I was enchanted in a forest that compels me to get deeper and deeper in adoration.

My heart quivers in thousands of untold emotions.

"If it weren't f-f-for you . . ." Isis' voice tumbles.

My face tilts and I feel the tip of her nose touch mine.

My lips pressed so gently, so delicately on Isis'.

Her face is a bed of silk I'm dying to lie on. Her lips as soft and warm as cotton.

My heart's crying out for her, pleading for her to love me back.

The unbelievable feeling of it was something I didn't know could feel.

Her presence tears me nearer and nearer to her

I don't want this to end.

I decided. I Want Her. I adore her.

Her eyelashes tickle my face with its bristles.

I'm breathing into her and she's breathing into me, and with each breath my soul is renewed.

She runs both of her hands with her thin fingers through my brown curly hair and tangles her hand on my head.

The kisses became more and more desperate and demanding every round of a second.

I hold her hand and she uses her other hand to press on my chest.

I love you, I love you, I love you. Was the only thing in my mind. I wish she would be able to hear my soul yearning for her.

My free hand slips into the hem of her shirt. Her lips smile on mine.

Isis' figure falls down with my lips still on hers somehow.

I'm on top of her now.

I open my eyes for a moment now our lips are apart.

Her arms sway carelessly on the floor and I laugh.

I don't want to be in control. I want the flame in my heart to incinerate anything in its path.

I close my eyes and let her feel me.

I'm feeling the small on her back.

I don't know how long we've been kissing, but it feels like we could do this forever.

Gravity isn't holding me to the ground; it feels like I'm fluctuating in the void emptiness of the universe.

I kiss her again but she pulls back to breathe.

"I love you, Isis." I say to her.

She gives me one of those smiles like she was about to cry, with her cheeks blush red. She goes into my arms and the hand on the small of her back drops dead on the floor.

"I love you . . . I love you . . . I love you . . . I love you" she whispers in my ear.

It was the kind of reply I wanted from her right now.

Her hug is so delicate. Her arms barely touch my hips.

I put my hands around her too.

"Do you mind keeping this a secret from the others?" Isis' request is soft in the ears like an indescribable melody.

We're both facing the ceiling glittering like sapphires.

"Sure." I answer back, carrying her from the waist and stand up.

We start laughing and Isis says, "That was . . . weird."

We don't know what to do except laugh.

She gets back on her feet so gracefully.

She really is a princess. "Let's go back to the dining room." I say, prying Isis' hand.

"Don't do that!" Isis puts her hand behind her back in an instant. "Why?" I ask. "It's awkward." she says.

I look at her face one more time before we go to the dining room.

She looks frazzled.

Her cheeks gushed with redness.

I try to think of ways to comfort her, even just a little, but nothing comes to mind besides kissing her again.

I feel myself getting scorching with heat.

I sit down at the table with Serenity beside me and look at her still playing with the mermaid children. Suddenly, Serenity turns to me and asks, "What did you and Isis talk about?" in such a way that we were about to trade secrets to one another. "Not much." I reply. "I know you're hiding something." she babbles.

I cross my arms and tell her, "That's none of your business."

She nudges me.

Out of nowhere Violet pokes me at the back relentlessly.

"Where did you put the antiseptic?" she asks.

"I think I left it on a round glass table somewhere around this house."

I can't concentrate. I can still feel Isis on me like a magnet.

I see Icarus go in the room with the jar of antiseptic cradled in his arms. "Forget what I said earlier about it on the round table." I say. "It's with Icarus"

Violet stops poking me and goes to Icarus. I get this feeling they're about to fight.

I look away.

"Damian?" Isis beside me asks.

"What is it?" I scratch my back.

"I think I know how to melt the ice." I get excited and my eyes open wide.

"Then do tell!" I shout with excitement.

"We need to put some kind of stone in an altar. The stone is on the necklace of the king." she says.

I then wonder how she knows "How do you know this?" I ask.

"I don't mean to sound silly, but something tells me it's the only way to melt the ice." she says bringing back the memory of the voice that beckoned to me to put the nature stone on the altar in the temple.

I don't tell her anything about it.

"Damian, your eyes again!" Isis says.

"Maybe you have two souls." Icarus says.

"What do you mean 'two souls'?" I ask looking at him.

"There's something in my spell book about it." he says, bringing out an old looking book from his robe.

He tosses it into the air and it floats at the mid-section of his body.

He flips pages of the book and stops at a certain page half way of the book.

He reads aloud, "Those who have two souls, often called an 'Amalgamate' are humans or any creature that have two actual souls in their body." I remember the masculine voice.

"Symptom/s: Irregular attitude and/or body parts." I think about the eye color changing.

"That's all it says." Icarus says closing the book and putting it back in his robe.

"How do you get it out of me?" I demand, destroying the table with my fist.

"There isn't anything about getting out." he replies fixing the destroyed table. "Relax; there isn't anything it can do to harm you. It only changes your eye color."

"Hey guys, were you listening to me?" Serenity says at the backdrop. "I want to go home."

The truth hit me in the head like a pebble. Saying *Hey there, I'm taking to you.* I was living a fantasy.

I feel sick to the pit of my stomach.

Almost like I was about to hurl after what Serenity said.

"You're right, Serenity." I say with guilt. "We should be going home, and I'll take full responsibility for dragging you here."

"Then we need to melt the ice!" Isis says.

Connard comes in the room, from the kitchen and says with an enthusiasm I've never seen from him, "Melt the ice?!"

"I guess we can try to melt the ice. There's no way to say Isis' assumptions are false until proven false." I say to both of them. "Yeah, after all, we've been through a lot so why does ice have to stop us?" Ross says coming in the room from the kitchen. "Let's do this!" Icarus shouts.

I feel motivated again. "Okay, all hands in!" Ross puts his hand in front of us.

"Not me!" Icarus replies.

We all laugh with hysteria.

"Not funny." Icarus walks around.

* * *

"If you're looking for the king, he's on the top floor of the court." says the mermaid mom.

"Please save us from his reign." the mermaid dad says.

"We'll kill him." Ross says, holding out his axe.

I bring out my dagger made of wootz steel from my back pocket and put it on the hand I injured yesterday to check if it still hurt.

There's a mild stinging sensation coming from the hand that was bearable I find the pain relaxing – not that I'm a masochist, but I just do

I turn around to see the others preparing their weapons. Icarus reading his spell book, Serenity loading her bow and Isis loading her crossbow, Violet testing her temporary powers Icarus gave just like the time we defeated the monster. "Okay, I'm going to turn us and our weapons invisible now." says Icarus. "Good luck." the mermaid mother says, giving me a shell with a deep blue color. "Purblind" Icarus and Violet say at the same time.

I keep the shell in my pocket. "Just remember that anyone who can't see us can still feel and hear us." Icarus says. "And we can see each other."

I open the door and see mermaids and mermaid troops with different ideals mixed around the crowd.

I sneak at the sidelines of the street with the others behind me, avoiding the touch of people, making our way to the gigantic door that was opened by a dumpster boy.

We slip in without touching the door to make it seem normal from the outside.

* * *

Chapter 11

Melt the City

The difficult part coming here is yet to come. Looking for the king and killing him.

We end up finding a flight of stairs in front of us.

The silence in the court made me feel sleepy.

We go up one floor and another set of stairs beside us was heavily guarded by five higher ranking troops because of their uniforms.

Isis fires an arrow at them but they deflect because of some kind of force field. They're alarmed.

Icarus makes a small fireball and makes it bigger. Violet coats it with a purple aura making the orange fire black.

"Fire!" Icarus shouts and the mermaids burn to a crisp along with the force field. "We're not invisible anymore." Icarus says while running to the top of the stairs.

"So what happened to the force field?" I ask.

"The purple aura that Violet coated is made so it can penetrate through most things." he says while we make it to the third floor of the court. "Now she can't use much of her powers anymore. She needs to rest for few minutes."

"Okay, so where's the Kings room?" I ask Icarus. "I've scanned the place with my magic before we went here. Move to the left from here, to the nearest door you can find." Icarus replies.

"Thanks." Isis says running to the left.

We follow her and find an obscure glass door. "Unlock!" Icarus says and the door opens.

From the moment we step in, I knew that we were in trouble.

"What a surprise." the king says, almost like was waiting for us.

He wears an exact replica of Icarus' robe and has some of the same facial features as Icarus does.

Isis fires an arrow, making the bristles of the feathers brush through his face. "So close!" she comments.

The king sends his furniture flying across the room, to us.

We eventually dodge it.

"Brother?!" Icarus says aloud.

"What do you mean by 'brother'?!" Ross says.

"The king is my brother." Icarus breaks the force field. "How did you end up like this?" Icarus asks the king and blackness fills the pupils of his eyes.

He tosses Icarus halfway across the room like a doll with his magic making Icarus' forehead bead with blood.

"I'll take care of him." Connard says trying to aid Icarus back to consciousness.

"Get the stone around his neck." Isis fires another arrow that goes straight to his hand.

He doesn't react. "What's up with this guy?" I whisper to myself.

"You don't know what you're up against, Soul-Sentinel." the king says in a lifeless tone.

I wonder who he was referring to as 'Soul-Sentinel'.

The hand of the king that Isis dug an arrow into bleeds, made a puddle of blood beside his feet.

I look back at Icarus and see Connard cleaning his wounded head. "He's conscious!" Connard shouts.

I turn around and suddenly I'm being pushed by Ross, avoiding both of us from being hit by a fireball that passed us in a blink of an eye.

I look at the king next and he says, "You can't keep dodging my attacks, Soul-Sentinel."

I get the feeling he was talking to me.

He makes me curious why he was calling me that.

I throw the dagger from my hand and slash the king's face. No feeling, but he bleeds, yet again.

"You can't kill a necromancer with any kind of knowledge you know, Damian." I hear Icarus' voice from a distance. "You can only kill a necromancer by stopping him from casting spells." I hear Icarus going nearer to me. "He can regenerate lost blood, skin cells, put more calcium in his body to make his bones stronger than ordinary bones. These are just some things that he can do that make him invincible. He isn't himself. Please make him snap out of it." Icarus clutches onto my shoulder from behind.

The hunch that he was under hypnosis was absurd, but it was the only option I had to let him snap out of it. I was sure what I was going to do now. If it fails, we end up dying. I can imagine how we would each die if I pass this opportunity. I've bitten off more than I can chew.

I remember Cipher braiding rope. "Cipher, you braided rope when I was sick right?" I ask. "Yeah, but what do you need it for?" she replies. "I just need it right now." I turn around and get the rope—more like a thick piece of string I didn't actually expect, but it's long enough for me to tie around the hand of the king—in her pocket and tosses it into the air. I get it.

I tell the others, "Distract the king. I have a plan." "Okay." Ross, Isis and Connard say, nodding their heads at once.

Connard starts attacking first by drawing out a sword from a scabbard tied around his waist, almost letting it run through some of Ross' short, brown hair.

"Sorry." Connard says with his voice fades as he charges to the king's chest, but Ross charges in a different approach, by going around him.

Before they could attack, Icarus' brother saps out water that melted from the ceilings and walls of the room and freezes their weapons making it difficult to carry their weapons.

Isis took that opportunity to hit his leg. He falls down, breaking his glass crown, still no reaction. "Icarus, do you know a spell that can reverse any kind of hypnosis?" I ask. "Yes there is, but it will take me eight seconds to do so." I was sure of myself that this could be a full-proof plan. "That's all I'll need." I reply.

I count down from *eight*, running to Icarus' brother.

Seven, I reach him.

Six, I get his hands and go behind him.

Five, I clamp his hands together and start tying the rope from his wrists.

Four, I wrap the rope around his flattened hands.

Three, I look at Icarus in front of us and a glowing force surrounds him.

Two, I finish the knot but he struggles free.

One, the glowing force that surrounded Icarus goes into his brother's eyes.

The wonders of the "adrenaline rush" are still on my side.

"Get off me!" Icarus' brother says. "Ah, why does my body hurt?" he asks, groaning, asking for help now.

"I'll help in any way possible." I say to Icarus. A red aura that Icarus' brother makes goes into his wound. "Much better." he says and the deep wounds on his body stitch together from the deepest part going all the way up to the bare skin like a spider web pulling the two sides together.

I untie him and we get to know each other. "By the way, you can call me Brien." he introduces himself to us. It's time for me to ask Brien why he was calling me 'Soul-Sentinel'.

"So why did you call me Soul-Sentinel before?" I ask.

"Are you joking?" he laughs at me. I look at him seriously.

"You're not joking, are you?" Brien says.

"No I'm not."

"Do you even know the legend of the Soul-Sentinels?" he asks me.

"No, now tell me why you . . ." I say, but he finishes the sentence. "—why I called you a Soul-Sentinel? I'm not sure. I was hypnotized by something. Someone. I'm not sure who."

"Okay, just tell me the legend." I say.

He started the legend, "It all started not so long ago, maybe a couple of decades ago when Icarus and I were still kids." "Mother and Father used tell us stories of clans.

"One of the clans had powerful objects that could rule the world. Isn't that right?" Icarus says.

"Yup, and the other clan was completely jealous of the other and could control souls with a series of secret spells that nobody could acquire," Brien says, "also known as the Grey's."

Grey—the surname of Serenity and I.

I ask, "Is 'Grey' a surname?" just to make sure I'm NOT one of those clans.

"Yes it is." Brien breaks me. I plant my face on my hands and sigh and shake my head trying to deny what I might possibly be.

Icarus says, "It's no wonder I feel a magic presence when I'm around you guys."

"What magic presence? You've only told this to us now." I say, getting an arrow beside me that Isis launched.

"All kinds of magic users can sense magic. It's complicated." Brien's voice becomes mellow in my ears.

"Damian, don't listen to this guy, he's nuts." the masculine voice from this morning says.

My ears go fuzzy for a moment.

I wonder if that's the second soul in me.

I just want all of this information to sync in for a moment, my mind is a sponge soaked with so much information, I shout out, "Everybody just keep quiet for a while." and everyone goes silent.

I close my eyes and put my thumb and index finger on my nose bridge. "Damian, are you okay?" Isis asks.

I open my eyes to see her.

She takes her arrow from my hands and puts it in her quiver.

"Yeah, I'm just having a hard time taking-in all of this new information." I say. "Okay, let's just continue the legend without any reactions." I go up to Brien who towered me by a few inches.

"Okay . . . The objects that could rule the world were stones that seem to have the power over the elements. And I have one of them that can turn things into ice." he says, putting off his necklace. "It's not as efficient as my magic, I don't really know why or how this thing can rule the world."

The altar pops up in my head. "Have you ever considered putting it in an altar somewhere?" I ask, bringing out the emerald with the plant insignia in my pocket and show it to Brien.

"Where'd you get that?" Icarus asks, getting it from my hands.

"So this is what happened after you placed the stone with the plant insignia in the altar?" Brien asks.

"Yeah, I think." I say.

"Can I borrow that for a moment?" Brien says, while Icarus hands it to him. "This gem has magical properties." he grows a plant beside him and the stone glows, but then it shrivels up and disappears in the wind. "Can you put this stone in the wall where I sit down in the court room? There's the same insignia engraved on it." Brien removes his necklace and gives it to me. The necklace has a diamond shaped stone on it.

"You got it!" I say.

"In the meantime, I have to finish what my hypnosis has done to this city. Good luck."

"Brien, how did you even end up here?" Icarus asks.

"Long story short, I snuck into a ship, got arrested by those mermaids, and in the prison cell some strange guy walked up to me with strange magic and hypnotized me. After the hypnosis I can't remember anything beyond that."

"Thanks for everything!" I say.

We go out of his room and we hear him shout, "Be careful." and go two floors down to the courtroom.

I go to the seat of the king and find the same ice stalactite on it.

I put the stone in and all at once the walls start melting and Isis faints, but I catch her, making my wound open again.

I put her arms around my neck and carry her.

I look around me and the floor was covered with water.

I begin to wonder why.

All of a sudden the walls crack and seawater springs out.

The ice cold water touches our feet. Icarus speaks an unknown language and a transparent platform goes under our feet, making us float.

I just realize Brien didn't finish the legend.

The water rises quickly and the platform floats us outside the court.

I'm still carrying Isis, but I'm losing balance. "Icarus, can you make the platform bigger?" I shout. "I can't, but Violet can." Icarus says, and Violet chants something in a really strange language and the platform becomes as big as a room, so I lay Isis down and hold her elbow so she won't fall off the platform. "Do you know where we are?" I ask Icarus, looking down at the transparent platform. Icarus turns the platform into a literal room.

I don't see much ice anymore, except a layer on top of us, meaning we were already submerged in water.

We float to the layer of ice, and because of the water pressure, it breaks, making us see Isis' steamboat from afar.

The sun is still high, so it's either late morning or early afternoon.

*   *   *

Chapter 12

Home At Last

Icarus floats all of us to the ship.

Isis' still unconscious and in my arms. There's a sapphire that's in her hands. Light blue lines forming a diamond shape with part of the ice stalactite melting.

I get it and keep it in my pocket.

I get freaked out when I see a half human with a lower torso of multicolored, slender, coiling serpent with wings, holding a bow and arrow beside Isis after putting her down at the cold, metal flooring of the ship.

"What are you looking at?" the creature says, guarding Isis.

"Do you guys see what that thing is?" I ask aloud hoping everyone can hear me.

"Damian, what are you talking about?" Serenity asks me. I point at it and she thinks I'm crazy.

"Hey Lil, this is my guardian, Damian." I hear the masculine voice talking to me. All of a sudden a griffin comes out of nowhere and goes to my side like it was guarding me.

"Who are you?" I whisper, hoping nobody could hear me.

"You know you can use your mind to communicate with me, right?" the griffin says going through me.

"What are you doing in me anyways?" I ask him.

"I'm the Elemental of Nature. And please stop overthinking things in your head. It's giving me a headache." he replies going back in me.

"Am I supposed to believe you?" I look at Isis while trying to ask the griffin.

"Hey, don't look at her you human!" the beast says. I recall the griffin calling her Lil.

"Is your name Lil?"

"Yeah, it's short for lillend, the creature that I am. Now stop looking at my master." she replies in a threatening tone.

"Master?" I ask, not realizing I've asked too many questions over the past few minutes

"I'm the Elemental of Frost."

"What's with this 'Elemental' thing? It's really weird."

"This 'Elemental thing' only happens when an Elemental Spirit chooses its owner." Lil replies.

I get confused

"Don't be. It's simple if you paid some attention to everything that's happening around you." the griffin says.

"Then explain to me you dimwit!" I respond.

"This is how it goes. Put the stones with the elemental insignias in their corresponding places, the spirit of the element goes in you, Nature, Frost, Inferno, Void, Lumen, Motion, and Time."

"The person who controls the element guardian can control the element, but there's a cache. You get at least one characteristic of the elemental guardian, like for you example. You have the eyes of the griffin. You may not have noticed, but you can use it for extending your vision limits. My guardian, I believe her name's Isis has the hands of a lillend. In time, you can control these characteristics through practice so you can be normal around humans who don't know this thing." Lil says.

"Can you listen to my thoughts?" I ask Lil.

"That all depends on you, if you're open minded then Elemental Spirits can hear you loud and clear like telepathy." the griffin answers me.

"Hey Damian, you've been staring at the floor for a while now, what are you thinking?" says Serenity. I look at her feet going up to her face like I was scanning her.

She's wearing a light blue shirt and white shorts that was few inches higher than her knees.

Her hair was tied into a ponytail. Something she almost never did. I liked it that way.

"What is it?" I say, looking back at Isis.

The griffin and lillend are gone in my sight. "We're thinking about letting Isis wake up first so we can go home, if that's okay with you." she responds. "Yeah, it's okay with me." I tell her. "Damian, can we relax here for a bit before we go back to reality?" "What do you mean by that?" I say. "I mean, all of this was really fun and all, but it's like we live in a dream, it doesn't last long. Do you know what I'm saying?"

I understood very well what she was saying, but I didn't feel like telling her.

I just sat there looking at Isis feeling guilty bringing all of them here.

I press my thumb on Isis' cheek to comfort myself. I don't know how it comforts me, but it does somehow.

I look back at Serenity and walk up to her. "Sorry, for bringing you guys here. Sorry for not being the big brother you wanted me to be." I say to her.

She hugs me.

"You were always the big brother I wanted you to be. This trip was one of the best things that has ever happened to me. Well except the death of our father though. I just hate the fact that he's dead."

I let go of her.

Lil's voice beckons behind me, "I forgot to say one more thing. If you already have an Elemental Spirit in you, then another Spirit has a choice to go into another person."

"Damain?" says Isis.

I turn to her. She's still pale in color.

I run to her and whisper to her, "Did you see a creature that looks like a human with the body of a snake and has wings?"

"Whoa, slow down, I just woke up!"

"Okay." I reply, looking at her face. It slowly turns to its normal color.

"Stop looking at me like that!" she shouts.

I look away, worried that she'll slap me. "Sorry. I didn't mean to shout." she says.

I look at her, but this time with caution. She's standing up. "Hey, relax." I help her up. "Are you guys . . ." Serenity says, but the wind breaks her sentence. "What?" I look at her. "Nothing!" she replies. I sit down beside her.

Isis removes her coat. It was getting hot around here. I remove mine too.

Her hair fell from the coat to her shoulders. She pushes them back.

I'm wearing the same black v-neck and jeans I've been wearing for the past few days. Isis in the other hand was wearing a white short-sleeve shirt with a slim fit that reached her thighs and white shorts I thought was part of the shirt, long enough to reach her knees.

Isis looks at me confused. She didn't know what was going on. I knew how it was like to not know. "How long was I unconscious?" she asks a couple of times.

"Honestly, I think I lost track of time." I handle her wrist with my left hand and find my way to the back of her soft, warm hand. I pry her fingers. "Are you hurt?" I ask Isis.

She shakes her head from left to right, making her hair sway the opposite directions and says, "I'm fine."

Footsteps come nearer and nearer. I recognize them, Serenity's footsteps. "I knew it, I knew it!" she says.

"Knew what exactly?" Isis slowly untangles her fingers from my hand.

"Are you guys—together?" Serenity gives us a chance to tell the truth.

"Okay, yeah we're together, but you have to promise me that you won't tell anyone." I keep my hand to myself.

"Yeah, sure." Serenity replies.

"DAMIAN?!" Cipher shouts, but I can't find her anywhere. She comes out of nowhere. "Where's the matches in the furnace room?" she crosses her arms. I was sure there were extra boxes of them. I stare at her blankly.

"CIPHER, I FOUND THEM!" I hear Icarus' voice coming from the furnace room.

Good timing. I thought I was going to get yelled at by her.

"That reminds me, Isis, what are we going to do or where are we going from here?" Cipher plays with her feet and stares at the floor.

"We can go to Seattle." I tell both of them. "Oh yeah, we have a lot of vacant rooms in our house."

"I'm sure Crissy wouldn't mind if you guys stayed with us." Serenity adds.

"I've never been to Seattle before. Are you sure we can stay at your house?" Cipher complains instead of thanks us for inviting them. "Cipher, I obviously came prepared. I brought millions of Pounds from Archaea and two credit cards with each the limit of money you can put in them." Isis replies.

She's incredibly, undeniably rich, richer than I thought she would be. Along with Cipher, I'm not sure I can count the money they have.

I adjust my sitting arrangement and hug my knees. "Wait, why do you have money if you trade?" I ask.

"Well, there are still lots of parts of the world that still uses cash you know." Isis says.

"Anyways, I have to help Icarus start the fire for our leave." Cipher looks at the water.

"Why do you need to? Can't Icarus ignite the wood with his powers?" Serenity says.

"He and Violet can't, they've used the last of their powers for 'teleporting' logs since we ran out." Cipher looks behind.

"So meaning Violet can use more than fire magic?" Serenity walks around.

"I'm not really so sure about this magic thing. It's kinda new to me." Cipher says while her voice diminishes as goes to the stairs leading to the furnace room.

I was getting used to the magic and all.

It made life very interesting that there are people who can use magic.

I wonder if mythical creatures were real too because of the elemental spirits.

"I think I'm going to prepare for our leave in the control room." Isis says. I help her stand up and notice a strange mark on her arm, like the one on my arm.

* * *

The sun's setting and we see a heap of grey and green up ahead, few jagged lines resembling buildings, the city of Seattle.

I've never been so excited to see such a sight, and yet so sad because of the great times we had for the last few days. I'm not sure how everybody will react to our return. Maybe Crissy will be furious or think we've arrived too early. Maybe she'll even feel happy we're safe.

"There it is!" Serenity points out.

Violet and Serenity sat together at the deck. Icarus and Shun seem to be getting along together.

I heard he learned how to make water freeze, and make tidal waves that was both used to make the boat even faster. I sat beside them so I was listening to their conversations.

I asked Icarus how he controls or uses magic. He said he needed to visualize what he should do. He told me more things about magic too; like they have a specific limit to your magic called a "magic summit" and that limit can cause you to collapse, or even die in severe cases. It was because magic used all the body's senses.

It tired the user which is why he and Violet only "teleported" the wood.

I couldn't stop thinking about Isis who wasn't here at the deck.

I wondered why she could captain a boat and why she escaped her place.

I laugh a little every time I think of Isis. Shun and Icarus thought I was psychotic.

A horn coming from the boat sounds. We must be already here.

Cipher stayed in the armory of the ship hugging, kissing, and missing her stuff because she thought the mermaids stole them.

We're at the harbor and no boat is here except ours. I remember the last time we went to the harbor. We didn't know who Isis was, but now we know who she is.

So much can happen in a week, new friends, new capabilities, so much experience.

It starts to rain cats and dogs, but before the raindrops go to the ship, some kind of barrier forms in front of us and turns them into condensation. "Icarus, did you make that barrier?" I ask.

"No. But why is it there?" he replies. His eyes widen and he shouts, "Warn Isis not to go any further!"

I start to run. The way Icarus said it was alarming, like it was a threat. I run up the stairs, to the control room and see Isis steering the boat.

"Stop the boat!" I grab her feeble arm.

"Why? Shouldn't we be going to Seattle?" she sounds mad.

"Icarus says 'stop'. I'm not sure why."

"I know why. There's a magical barrier that can burn anything to a crisp and we're heading right through it!" the lillend's voice says.

"Trust me, Isis, and trust the lillend. We don't know what we're up against."

"Okay!" Isis pulls down a lever from the controls. "But what was that voice?" Isis asks.

"Nevermind that now . . . I think Icarus needs to tell us something." I say to her, dragging her all the way to the deck of the ship.

"Okay good." Icarus says.

I look at the barrier and it burns a bird that passes by. "What's going on?!" Serenity asks. She and Violet go near to us. Cipher comes up the stairs and to us and asks the same question.

"First of all, that barrier isn't mine. Secondly, that barrier is above my magic skill so it's completely dangerous to just pass through it." he replies. "What are we going to do then?" Isis removes my hand from her arm.

A message lights up at the barrier,

> If you ever want to go back to your homes, collect the stones.
>
> Put them at their rightful places.
>
> Gather all the Elemental Gemstones and come back to this very spot. The force field will fade when it detects all the stone—J

The light fades.

I'm suddenly I'm on the floor and I see everyone knocked out.

My eyes are chattering.

I see a black impression come to me and carry me to a corner of the deck and injects a needle in my arm, putting some kind of fluid in my system, making it shut down almost rapidly.

I'm out cold.

I don't know what's going to happen to me next.

I can see but I don't dare to do it because of fear.

*   *   *

Chapter 13

Washed Up

March 25, 2041

I wake to a slight pounding in my head.

I'm still in the boat, tired, I haven't had much sleep. I was either too scared of sleeping, or too sleepy to get scared. My mind is clueless. I don't know what just happened to me.

My muscles inflict pain.

I try to yawn and my throat aches.

I could've shouted yesterday but never realized it.

A black impression, needle in my arm, fell down.

Isis and the others are down. Is all I remember.

It's pretty early in the morning.

I stand up and whisper-shout, "Wake up!" Serenity reacts.

She rubs her squinting eyes with her arm and adjusts to the daylight. "Where are we?" I help her up.

I stare at her blankly, emotionless. I'm not sure how I'm supposed to feel right now.

Her eyes suddenly widen with a red glowing reflection in her eyes that obviously came from behind me.

I glance and see an active volcano with molten lava streaming down the volcano like it was crying.

I then turn my back to look more at the island we just ended up on.

People should be crazy to even try to live here. No trees, no animals that I couldn't live here.

What looked like a sea of tar was obsidian rock that connected to the volcano.

I see its rough surface flaking.

I wonder why we ended up here.

"Damian?" Isis' voice beckons to me from a distance of few feet from where I'm standing.

"Yeah, what is it?" I turn to her.

"Where are we?" she stands up on her own, but it didn't really matter if I helped her. She's a tough girl from what I've seen her do.

"I can tell you one thing. We aren't in paradise." Serenity says.

"Do you want to check this place out?" I ask.

"Yeah, sure." Serenity and Isis chorus, staring at each other, and then laugh. I giggle just a little.

Isis comes to me. I slip a hand around her waist. She doesn't seem to mind.

Serenity comes too, but doesn't make any physical contact.

We jump off the railings of the boat and to the dark, hard, obsidian that chisel and brittle under my feet. *Scary*

"You guys are new to this relationship thing aren't you?" Serenity asks.

"Yeah, is there a problem?" I ask her.

"Well, now that you mentioned it, you guys are staying few inches away from each other, meaning you two aren't really comfortable with each other." Serenity starts walking.

I look at the space between Isis and I . . . It was socially acceptable.

"Are you comfortable with the way I'm handling you?" I ask Isis. I stare at her face.

She bites her lower lip and says in such a vulnerable voice, "I actually wanted you to stay nearer to me." My eyes open wider.

My cheeks burn, I think my heart skipped a beat.

I push myself nearer to her. I hope she's satisfied. "Better?" I ask with a voice coated with sugar.

Her head leans on me.

Her warm fingers find their way to my hand fitting perfectly like Isis' set of hands were designed for me.

I was honored she would open up to me, and that she would try different things with me that was out of her comfort zone.

"Let's go." she tells me with a smile. "Okay."

* * *

We've seen bears, some birds and trees, meaning things could actually live here, but not many things. We've reacted to the bears by running and making loud noises to scare them away. I'm surprised how much my legs can withstand run away from danger ever since we arrived on the island. It should be a feat.

I'm sitting down at the obsidian rock with Isis and Serenity, breathing heavily, trying to catch our breath.

We're not far from the ship. Maybe few meters ahead.

"This was a bad idea." Serenity says, still tired from running.

"Then why did you come with?" I breathe with every other word launched into the air, creating vibrations, making us hear what I'm saying.

"I just thought it would be nice to see both of you together." she tells me and I stare at her intimidatingly.

"Is that a complement or an insult?" I ask.

Serenity glances at me and then turns her head hundred-eighty degrees away from my face.

We're breathing normally now.

"C'mon . . ." Isis says. "Let's go back to the ship." I stand up without having to breathe so heavily.

"You're making me dizzy here, Damian." I hear the griffin.

"Shush it, I'm trying to rest." I hear the Lil's voice in Isis' distance.

"What was that?" Isis gets scared.

"This is what I was trying to ask you yesterday, if you saw a half—human, half-serpent with wings and holding a bow." I reply.

"Then yes, I saw one," she stands up, "I saw one after you placed that stone in the altar."

"Isis, don't worry. It's not a bad thing really. It took Damian here a while to coop with us guardian spirits." the griffin says.

"What's going on?" Serenity asks.

"Wait a moment, Serenity. Isis and I are talking." I complain to her. "And Isis, please try to communicate with me with your mind. Nobody can hear us if we do, except the guardian spirits." I say to Isis.

"Okay. Let's just go to the ship first and then we'll talk about this." Isis' voice is now in my mind.

"This is getting creepy. I think I'll go to the ship now." says Serenity walking away from us.

"Wait up." I get Isis' hand and start walking. I turn back and carry her from her legs and put her in my arms. She wraps her arms around my neck. I run to Serenity who is just now few feet away from the boat.

"Hey, are you angry?" I ask.

"No, I'm just a little mind-boggled because of what you two were just doing few moments ago." "I wish you could understand." I say. "Do you remember what Icarus told us yesterday in the kitchen of the mermaid's house, the thing about the two souls?"

"Yeah, why are you bringing this up now?" Serenity crosses her arms.

"Somehow, Isis has two souls in her too. The souls in us told me when Isis was unconscious. The souls go in us or something after we put the 'stones' in their 'altar'. I don't really know" I say. "I really wish you can understand."

"Serenity!" I hear Violet's voice coming from the ship. "Are you there?"

"Yes, I'm here! Can you get us up there?" says Serenity.

"Us? Are you with Damian and Isis?" Violet asks.

"We're here!" I say. "Maybe you can ask Icarus to float us up there?" Isis says.

"Sure!" Violet shouts.

I see Icarus and Violet stick their heads out of the ship.

We're stuck in an aura. Icarus is using his magic. We end up at the deck of the ship standing.

"Hey, thank you." I say.

"Why are you carrying Isis?" Icarus asks.

I put her down as quickly as I can and say, "Um . . . nothing, well we were running away from animals in the island and Isis got tired, so I carried her."

"Exactly!" Isis adds.

"Okay." Violet says with devastation. "We need to talk about something. Icarus and I found partially empty syringes few inches away from where we were knocked out."

I wonder why I haven't noticed them.

"We've filled one syringe with all the content left from all the others and used it on Ross, who was by the way awake when we found them, and he's now asleep."

"So meaning there's someone who did all of this to us?" says Isis.

"Yes, there could be someone responsible for this. We're in the middle of investigating the boat right now to check if there are any more suspicious things the person could've left."

"Have you guys found anything in the island?" Violet asks from behind me.

"We've found lots of bears and birds and trees." Serenity says.

"Oh . . . I think I can make food out of seagulls." Shun says in a soft tone.

I haven't seen him in a while.

"Where were you when we had the conversation?" I ask, turning around.

"I was at the furnace room. Seems that we've ran out of wood." he goes to Ross who's asleep face down and gets his axe collapsed on the floor. "We need to get some wood."

"I can help you find the wood." Serenity smiles at him. "I'm going to help because I think I heard screams and yells that might have come from you guys when you were gone." Icarus goes near Shun.

I feel embarrassed.

"I'm going to moor the ship to a more convenient position." says Isis walking to the control room.

"I guess I'm going to stay here and watch over Ross." I say to myself because nobody was paying attention to me.

I go to the railings of the boat watching the whites and the blues of the swirling waters below forming waves because of the wind.

I'm alone for now with Violet investigating.

Everybody is busy doing something, even Ross.

Isis is steering the boat side to side until suddenly it stops. I hear Isis' voice saying from a speaker in the ship, "Can you anchor the boat!" and I have a grin twisting on my face.

I make my way to the wheel I'm supposed to turn to let the anchor free and turn it counterclockwise from where I'm see it. It hits the seafloor creating recoil on the ship.

My legs shake a little.

"Damian, are you okay?" I hear Isis in my mind, could be because of the elemental spirits.

"Yes, I'm fine. How is it at your end?" I run up to the control room.

"I'm fine, thank you for asking." she replies. "Did you know that we can feel each other's presence from far away?"

"No, I didn't know—wait, how do you know that?"

"Lil told me a lot of things about the power of Elemental Spirits. Now I can read your mind if you're not careful guarding it." Isis taunts.

"So how do you guard your mind and read it?" I swallow hard.

"I think it needs to be developed somehow. I think I was just lucky.

"You need to transmit ions in the air and look for ions similar to it." she says "People with the elemental spirits in them have specific ions in the part of their brains that allows you to think and turn it into sound waves that can only be noticed with ions similar to it.

Now, the person who transmitted the ions will have the ions notice the sound waves and put it in the part of the brain of the person that allows you to hear. That's mind reading"

I understood everything she said. It was weird I did.

"So how about stopping you from reading it?" I ask.

"Again, with the ions you can use them to block the passage way in the part of the brain that allows you to think so no ions similar to it can penetrate."

Isis grabs my hands and clamp them together like I'm about to pray. She puts hers around mine and closes her eyes. I can feel an unusual, fuzzy feeling that comes from my hands going up to my head.

"Can you hear me?" I hear Isis' voice echo in my mind.

I look her in the eyes and tell her, "I hear you."

"Your eyes, they're glowing with green." she says it with fascination and not with fear. Maybe she knows about my power.

Isis shakes her head, gets serious and says, "Okay, now you're going to try to stop me from reading your mind." She sends what feels like electricity running through my veins. I detach my hand from Isis. "You're not even trying. I'm going to do this again, but this time I want you to visualize particles that will fill your ears." she holds my hands again, but this time, I turn them into fists.

I imagine dull, gray particles filling the inside of my ears.

Isis sends the fuzzy feeling again, but before it goes to my head, it stops. "See, you did it." she releases her hands.

"Thanks?" I tell her. "Do you know anything else about the Elemental Spirits' powers?"

"Sadly, no—I don't know much of anything. Lil said she would teach me how to control my power."

"That sounds like something that Lil would really do." the griffin says.

"So this is the famous Elemental of Nature that Lil keeps telling me about." Isis says.

It seems to me that Isis is more enlightened about the Elemental Spirits than me

The griffin appears in front of me and looks at Isis. Now Lil appears in front of Isis and looks at me.

"It's amazing how fast this girl learns. Maybe she'll learn something new with the powers of Elemental Spirits." Lil says, disappearing in the air. "Hey, Damian, maybe I'll teach you how to control your powers too." the griffin walks around and then disappearing like Lil. I laugh uncontrollably after the griffin tells me that he'll teach me.

I walk around the little control room's cramped-up space.

"How do you work here? It's so tight." I tell Isis.

"It's only tight because you're here!" she replies, pushing me out of the control room. "And I can't focus if you're here so please leave."

Suddenly, I'm hearing screams and shout calling out and repeating my name in distress, "Damian, Damian, Damian!" until my name doesn't sound like my name.

I hurry down the stairs of the mini building—the control room—and check the railings of the ship that are supposed to keep us from falling down. Both my hands clutch on and I lean against it.

Icarus, Serenity, Shun and Cipher. They're the ones calling for me—running away from what seems to be white-gray, fuzzy fragments of the clouds.

I put all my weight on my hands and launch myself off the boat and to the obsidian with my right, then with my left feet. I'm lucky to be standing up.

I see the fragments clearly now—they're—they're wolves, and a full pack of them—more than a pack of wolves, an army of them. No wonder they're shouting.

I feel a strange, immense power running through my veins. The power is luring me to rip the throats of the wolves out in one piece.

I'm breathing heavily now.

Icarus, Serenity, Shun and Cipher now run behind me. "Get to the ship!" I shout. "Icarus, I'm counting on you get them safe." I've never sounded so brave before.

"Damian, what are you doing, you're going to kill yourself and you know that! Are you that insane now that you know your powers?" The griffin comes out of me.

That's right. I have my powers.

I am consumed with rage. My body's trembling with intense emotion.

I feel the ground shaking. Large roots sprout out of the ground in front of me sending pieces of the obsidian flying all over the place.

I see the wolves in the gaps of the dark-brown roots that are now just few feet away from me.

Before they reach me, the roots get each and every wolf out there and constrict them to death.

Blood splatters.

I don't know if I've done all of this.

The roots rot and turn into soil that fills the potholes they make.

"Damian, we can go now." Serenity says from behind.

They haven't moved from this spot ever since I was in front of them.

"Thank you, Icarus for saving us." Serenity adds.

Icarus suddenly interrupts while I was trying to say something, "I didn't do that. I've used up all my energy. I'm exhausted. Even if I did do that I would be dead by now." he pauses. "Did you do that, Damian?" and I'm paralyzed

I turn around and Icarus grabs my shoulder. "I don't know—wait just a moment," I say, "so you didn't do that?" "You're dang right I didn't, but I felt an incredible amount of magic leaking out of you just a moment ago when you said 'get to the ship'." Icarus is now holding both my shoulders.

He looks at my right arm and puts up its sleeve.

I look at it too and see the tattoo glowing dark green and then slowly fading.

We look at it stop glowing.

"What is that?" he asks, slowly rolling up his eyes to meet mine. *I don't know! You tell me!* Is what I wanted say, but nothing comes out. I also wanted to say, *It's all the Elemental Spirit's fault,* but I can't because it's the thing that saved us. "Oh—so that's what it was. It's the second soul in you." he says.

I'm laughing.

"I don't know, Icarus." I'm laughing hysterically. "I don't know." I insist. "I don't know what it is."

He puts down my sleeve and says, "That's it isn't it. That was really powerful. It sent chills down my spine. God, I'm so jealous. I haven't met someone who has reached my level of magic since my brother."

Now he's laughing.

Why is he laughing? I don't know

Did I do something wrong? No, of course not.

Why is he jealous? It could be because of the immense power that was 'leaking out' of me.

He punches me out of no reason.

It didn't hurt.

I think it wasn't meant for me to be hurt. Maybe it was a friendly punch.

Was it me who actually did that all of that?

I'm desperate for answers. Answers that will help me reach the full extent of my powers and help me control them before it's too late.

I feel dangerous.

I don't want to be dangerous, but I am dangerous.

I'm twitching out of fear and excitement.

I can't tell the difference between the two.

They feel like the exact rush of emotion.

I'm pondering my head out without realizing it.

I take deep breaths.

With all the power I have now, am I good or evil?

Isis, maybe Icarus and Shun—because they have powers like I do—will be the only ones who will understand me and understand what I'm going through right now. I wish Ross, Serenity, Violet, Cipher and Connard can learn how to understand us.

I wonder if there are others like us—people with Elemental Spirits in them—in other parts of the world.

I'm constantly staring at an obsidian field. I haven't realized Icarus was talking to me. His lips are moving but I don't hear anything

"What was that?" I ask.

"It's nothing really. I was just talking non-sense to get your attention. I hope it worked, or are you talking unconsciously?" he says in front of my face.

"I don't think I'm talking unconsciously so yeah, you got my attention." I say. "Now let's go back to the ship." I put on a dull face at Icarus and then to the other behind me.

A rope ladder was put from the railings to down here to bring us up. Serenity says Isis was the one who did it.

* * *

I'm chewing on a piece of seagull meat that Shun cooked.

Ross is finally awake.

It's late at night.

I only notice now that the seagull is too salty for me. "This is disgusting." I spit it out with the flavor of the salt still lingering in my mouth.

"Is that so?" he says. "I guess my pallet is too salty for you." Everybody puts down their food.

They're luck.

I was the first one who ate.

"I'm not hungry anymore." Isis says.

"Me too, and I just woke up from a twenty hour sleep." Ross says.

"Sorry, Shun" Serenity says sounding sweet.

"It was a bad idea to put salt on a seagull since it's been eating and digesting fish from the salty sea. EMPHASIS: SALTY." All I can say is that Violet is very truthful.

"It's okay for me." Connard says. "I eat this kind of stuff in the castle."

There's nothing but harsh comments to Shun. I feel sorry for him.

"Okay, we all need to make a curfew you guys. We will never know if you're missing or not." Isis says.

I agree in an instant.

"So the curfew time will be when the sun is completely down." she says. "That's not such a bad idea you know." I say.

Everybody nods their heads.

A light and heat source came from the active volcano.

It should be cold, but it isn't because of it.

* * *

Everybody's sleeping at the deck of the ship with some old blankets we found at the basement while Isis and I are still awake. Currently we're lying down together trying to sleep.

"Damian." I feel Isis' face on our pillow adjust to me.

From looking at the moon, I look to her direction. "What is it?" I'm asking.

"I thought you died today—when you were fending off the wolf attack." she starts sitting down.

"Wait—how?" I sit too.

"I couldn't sense you after you did that uproot thing." she replies.

"Is it an Elemental magic thing?" I hear the sound of my own voice reverb around the deck.

"You could say that." Isis crawls beside me. "And you don't know how much I felt like crying a while ago." she laughs. I have no choice but to laugh with her to make her seem less insane. "So many things has gone down these past few days. It's getting tiring trying to catch up with all the information overload."

"Amen!" I exclaim.

"I want to lie down with a TV in front of me to watch a dumb soap opera and forget everything." Isis lies down on the floor. "I want to be unconscious for a while."

"Isn't that what sleep is for?" I clarify.

Isis doesn't reply. I poke her with my index finger to check if she's conscious—she's fast asleep.

* * *

Chapter 14

Trapped

March 26, 2041

My mindset of the world is different now.

Knowing that I have a power like this is pretty amazing, yet frightening.

You feel invincible, unstoppable. Nobody can tell you what to do.

I've attained a power that people will have to get scared of, and because of that I need to control it before it goes into a rampage. It's trapped like a tiger, but it does not give up trying to free itself. The lock is cracked and it isn't long until the voracious animal realizes it. The tiger is growling at the person containing it in—me—warning me that when it gets out, it will maul me until I'm shreds of flesh and mangled bones. I need to know how to tell people that I am just like them, only with supernatural powers, but how?

I don't know if I'm a threat to civilization along with Isis who has similar powers like mine—only she controls frost because that's what Lil said to me before she woke up.

I remember Brien telling us that "these stones can rule the world."

This makes no sense whatsoever now, but I hope I know what I need to know in the next coming days ahead of us.

I'm constantly in the eyes of Isis.

I've allowed her to read my mind. She's also allowed me read hers.

There's a reason why Isis is reading my mind, because no matter how far we are, we can always contact, but the response is slower than when nearer.

Her feelings are very delicate when she's in love. That's what I believe because she wasn't this vulnerable when we first met, so I told her that she should be strong.

I'm currently eating seagull sunny-side ups. I hope they weren't cooked by Shun after what happened yesterday.

They actually taste good.

It's early in the morning.

We're thinking of going hunting today, now that all the wolves are gone. Now the only threats are the bears.

"So when we're going hunting today, we should bring something that we can use to make loud noises to scare of the bears." I say to all of them, taking a micro bite off the egg.

I cut the egg in half, the yolk isn't runny, it held together in the egg white.

I'm still chewing on the micro bit in my mouth. I'm just playing with it, pushing it on the walls of my mouth with my tongue and chewing it slowly.

"How about we tap our weapons on the obsidian and create weird noises?" Ross says. "Okay, so it's settled. We're going to do that." Icarus takes a bite off his egg.

"Okay." I say.

Connard says, "We don't have water. Mineral water, distilled water, any water for us to drink."

Without water Icarus should be weak.
He can't use his magic then.

*   *   *

We finish eating and we set up our weapons.

I'm holding my bag with the few pieces of clothing just waiting to be dirtied up.

I search my pocket and realize I brought my phone with me.

I take out my phone, a long rectangle supersizing my hand. I need to hold it with both of my hands.

The back and corners of the phone are tinted black, the way I wanted the design of my phone to be.

I remember turning it off when we were at the taxi, so I turn it on by pressing a button at the top of it once with my right-index finger and it lights up.

"Slide to unlock" it says with an arrow beside it. I slide it with the same finger.

All my apps appear in a rapid pace.

I look at the upper-right corner and read the time, "10:38"

I go to the settings and put down the brightness and turn the phone mute to consume less battery.

I look at the icon beside the time that looks like a battery with a bright green filling it.

It's still 83% charged.

Lots of the phones these days have superior battery span.

I try to call Crissy to assure her we're okay but a voice message replies back, "Server unattended due to low signal strength. Server unattended due to low signal strength. Server unattended due to low signal strength."

I suddenly hear ruckus coming from behind my back. I hear "*Serenity!*" and "*No, that's—no, that's not right.*"

I turn around and see them arguing about a bow.

"What's happening?" I ask.

"Damian, it's my fault." Isis says. They're handling a bow with an untied string. "Hey, Serenity—that bow was bound to get broken someday." Isis starts. "Don't worry. That's my practice bow when I was young."

"That just adds to the pressure of loosening the strings!" Serenity's face is confusing. One of the hardest faces I've ever tried to interpret. Her facial expressions are very random. She's smiling when she's angry, or even if she's nervous.

I can read a lot of other people's but there are some like her I simply just can't make out.

"I have a secret stash of bows at the basement if you like." Isis creates a circle with her hands and cups them on Serenity's ears and suddenly I'm hearing Isis too. "It's below the tile of the armory that is right, to the nearest tile of the door." She stares at me and un-cups her hands.

"Oh—I'm going to get one now." Serenity runs down the ship while saying, "Wait for me!" and her voice gets tipsy when she says me. I hear her pronounce "me" as "mie."

Icarus in front of me turns his head counterclockwise and says, "Are we going yet?" He's wearing dark khaki pants and a shirt with thin fabric. I don't know if the color is supposed to be white or blue.

The thin fabric made him look paler than his natural skin color—olive. It looks nice and decent to me.

His tattoos are more defined and darker in color, straying from behind his neck to his bicep.

Serenity comes back with what looks like a silver or titanium bow and a fine set of arrows in an expensive looking quiver. They all glared with a natural shine.

"Hey, you picked my favorite one!" Isis says gladly. She turns to Cipher and says to her, "I can teach both of you how to use a bow and with just a quiver of arrows properly." then she looks at Serenity.

Cipher screams to the top of her voice and replies, "Thank you, thank you, thank you!" in a squeaky voice, I have to cover my ears just to hear what she's saying.

"As long as you don't do that ever again." Isis adds.

Connard is holding 2, 5, 8 leather water canteens stuffed in the spaces of both his hands, each with a sling for us to hang on our shoulders. He hands us one each. "Wait here, there's still more in the basement." he's carrying one, but hands it to me and runs quickly to the stairs going down.

He comes back with two, big, empty jugs with a round circumference at the bottom on his hands. "If you could just hold this . . ." he gives one jug to Ross. "Now let's go."

I give back the water carrier to Connard.

We're jumping yet again, crashing on the hard, rough obsidian ground making me almost drop my dagger. My legs are shaking from the drop.

We don't know where we're supposed to go for hunting.

My throat is dry. Our throats are dry. Dry from the lack of water ever since yesterday morning.

"Let's go." Isis who is in front of all of us turns to look. "But first we need to split into split into teams of two to make the search more efficient."

"I'm going with Violet, Damian and Serenity." Ross pulls me near him while my feet scrape the obsidian. I don't hesitate.

"Okay." Violet gets nearer to us.

"So how about the others? Are they all another group?" Serenity goes to Violet.

"Wait just a moment; I want Icarus on our team." I say, clutching on his right shoulder like a desperate attempt to stop him from moving. "We might need your powers."

"Okay, but please just remove your hand on my arm." he's laughing. Why is he laughing at a time like this? "I'm going to be with the rest of you who aren't in Ross' team." Isis heeds my advice. Her voice is unbreakable. She sounds tough, and yet it isn't rude. My hand is slipping from the shoulder of Icarus.

Connard grabs the handle of his sword and brings it out of the leather incasing it, trapping it from suddenly squirming its way out when he runs.

I notice now that he's wearing a silver pin on the chest of his polo, which was buttoned on the wrong buttonholes and draping carelessly with a message engraved, "Chief of Unit 5" and his name in uppercase letters just under the message. I read aloud, "Connard X. Maison" He stares at me with eyes always alert and asks the question, "Yes?" He has a bit of an English accent mixed with a little American.

"That's your name, right?" I'm staring straight into the strange color in his eyes, dark-green.

"Is there something wrong?" he sends the question flying.

"There's nothing wrong. It's actually a nice name." I complement, but I wonder what 'X." means. Maybe if I get a chance to ask Cipher, she would tell me. "Thank you." he replies with a smile.

His voice is soft and loud, somewhere in the middle of both, it's also very deep, but not too deep. It's just right. The way he talks is graceful. I want to mimic it.

Isis is still staring daggers at us. She tells us, "We should all be back here thirty minutes to one hour tops." I'm looking at the wootz dagger and snap; I know the difference between wootz steel daggers and normal steel daggers. Every time I've cut something with the wootz, it was always smooth cutting. Normal steel on the other hand is rough and difficult.

"If you're not back here by then we know that you are missing." her voice is devastating.

"Okay. We'll take the lead from here." Ross says pouncing forward into action. Serenity, Icarus, Violet and I try to catch up to him, but he's too fast. His knees are arching, his muscles contract then expand.

I'm ahead of everyone except Ross. He's still on the lead.

My legs spread forward and I'm sprinting, trying to fill my lungs with all the air going by me. Inhale, exhale, inhale, exhale, Ross slows down and pushes out a word from his chest, something like "woo" or "boo". We need to slow down. Our lack of water is making our tongues rough and dry. Prickles of sweat appear on my forehead, slowly turning into larger amounts of water stream down my face, or at least that's what I expected from running that fast and that long. Behind me is the team that Ross made including him down to the ground, laying lazily and tired. Their chests are lifting and going down.

"Have you suddenly become athletic?" Ross' face prunes and breathes heavily.

"No." but I remember me joining the track and field team of our school. We haven't made regionals for three years straight so I quit, that's all I remember. "Let's get back to hunting, but if we should look for water first. "There's an awkward silence just waiting to be broken and boom, it's there.

"Okay." Ross helps up my little sister, then Icarus.

"Hey, how about me?" Violet is lying down there waiting with her elbows on the crackling floor.

"Just please be patient, please." Ross then helps her up on her feet.

"Let's just walk." I comment.

* * *

We're beside a small stream with water casting shadows with movement and light glaring into our eyes. This is perfect.

Icarus begins to suck up water and fill his cheeks. I think he's ready to use his magic now that he has the strength to do it.

I haven't seen any bears come by us. Something feels off about this place.

I bend down near the water with one knee creating a right angle and open the nozzle of the water canteen by twisting it and put it straight in the gushing water creating bubbles. And suddenly it stops, and the water canteen is full.

Now for the large jug.

"Ross, can you give me the jug?" I ask.

"Sure thing." He hands me its end. I put it on the ground.

"I can fill it." Icarus says with water floating above us and dripping on our faces. I pop open its lid and the water coming, going in with the water's end thinning at the opening. I hear the weird contained sounds in the jug of water splashing and colliding on each other's end. My arms are getting damp. Then the ground starts flooding. "You can stop it now!" the words come out of my mouth and the water flow stops. I secure the lid back to the top to make sure nothing will happen to the water on our way back to the ship. "Hey, you need to fill your water canteens." I say. "You'll never know we might need the water."

"Why? It's not like you did." Ross says. Sometimes I just want to smack him at the face for being blind.

"Actually . . ." I get my water carrier hanging from my shoulder. "I did." I put it in front of his face.

"Fine." he opens the nozzle of his. I look at Icarus "Save the nagging for later, I already filled mine." he says. "Mine too." Violet after Icarus.

Ross is beside me on his knees collecting water. "I'm going to carry the water jug." I get a firm hold at the bottom. "Okay, I'm done filling my water canteen." Ross' voice is fuzzy in my ears.

I start carrying the water jug weighing a ton on my hands. I quickly put it down before my fingers snap. "Here, I'll help." Ross hangs his water canteen on his neck.

"Thanks." I try lifting the jug again, only this time Ross is at the opposite radius of the jug from where I'm standing. There was still weight, but not as heavy as before. I think I'm lucky to have Ross as a friend. I couldn't wish for a better one.

"Do you really need my help?" and the fuzzy feeling I was getting from him is gone in instant. *How could I have the strength to carry this?* I'm not as surprised as before.

"Ow, ow! I need a little help here." I'm faking. Ross believes and he carries half of the weight, while on my side it feels like carrying a stuffed toy.

"You shouldn't push yourself." he replies. My capabilities have grown tremendously. I try to overlook things.

First, I can bring out roots from the ground.

Second, I don't tire as easily as before.

Third, I have the strength of an elephant.

Whatever's next, I won't be surprised.

Are these all powers of an elemental guardian?

*　*　*

On our way to the ship, all we could see is bear cubs wining—calling out for their mothers—biting their nails, licking their fur. The first thing I wonder is *Where are the mothers?* Then I realize there are other bears, huge sleeping ones, but only some of them. *Are those the fathers?* But the next question to ask is why the place feels so off to be teeming with life, and how can there be trees here. Seeds can't just fly with wings and suddenly plant themselves into the ground.

I know for sure that spots near the volcano have rich soil, but I realize that the obsidian ground we're stepping on is full of that type of dark, rich soil.

Someone should have placed them manually, scattering them around this island—no, I mean to say volcano.

Someone should have kept the bears' mothers captive somewhere, but what's their goal trying to do so? What kind of knowledge can they attain by doing all this? Why create life in this island?

I know it's not a bad thing, but it just doesn't seem right to do all of this, not right here exactly.

We're currently with Isis' group beside the steamboat. They didn't find water, but they found crops—tropical fruits, grains and vegetables (The green stuff)—got them and placed them in a shirt. Going back to the question *Why is this place teeming with life?*

"Let's go back to the ship." Connard says. "I'm completely tired from today. I want to kick back, relax and eat food. I'm starving."

Icarus creates a staircase made from his aura going up to the ship to make it easier for us to transport the things we've got in our hands.

Magic is really vacant.

Walking through the staircase is a rollercoaster ride. It's scary because you can see the swirling waters of the sea under your feet. My feet are wobbling when I stand on the ships' platform. I try to stand on them as steady as possible before walking. Honestly, I'm scared of heights.

'I'm going to the kitchen of the ship." Isis says.

"You have a kitchen?!" I sound surprised.

"Yeah. You should really explore the ship more often rather than being useless and stare at the water." she replies. I choke down on a laugh, but I'm smiling.

She asks, "Do you want to help me cook?"

"Sure, but trust me when I say this . . . I'm not good at cooking."

"It's not like you'll be the one cooking you know."

"Sorry."

"What do we do with the water?" Ross asks. I forgot all about the water jug. I guess he was the one who carried it to the ship.

"You can leave it at the corner." Isis says.

"Then my work here is done." then he drops the jug perfectly on the floor.

I pat Ross at the back and apologize.

I remove the sling of my water canteen and put it beside the dropped jug.

"Let's get cooking." I say.

Isis starts walking, I follow going down the stairs of the ship, to an odd looking door located beside the furnace room. She opens a set of lights lighting up the dark hall of the basement of the ship. Metal, bolts and a crate at the end of the hall is all I can see. Isis opens the door and enters with a slight creek. I enter too and I see lights flicker on. Isis is at my chest for some reason.

Her heartbeat is steady and fast, yet she's so calm.

"So what do you think we're supposed to cook?" Isis turns to me with a face full of pink. She's sweating. No wonder her heart's beating fast.

"The only things I know how to cook are pasta and noodles." I feel dumb around her.

I look around the kitchen. I'm amazed at how much it feels like a kitchen at home if you cancel out the teeter-totter of the ship.

Then I see an isle table in the middle of everything surrounded by a ground of bamboo flooring. The ceiling is dark blue with twinkling LED lights that reflect on the floor.

The walls are a light shade of mahogany red with one wall located beside me with light piercing out as if something is glowing from behind.

The pans and pots are all the same color, copper, that was hung from several cords on the ceiling, going down and up like a wave. Ladles, strainers, technically every kitchen tool you can find—excluding those for cutting—is in a cylindrical casing with holes on the sides for air circulation. The ones for cutting were inserted in a royal white, marble-like case.

The stove for cooking is silver with streaks of gold following a pattern of a flag I've seen before—the Archaean flag. "Wow." Is all I can manage to say right now. I could have been mumbling, but I didn't.

I grab the shirt-wrapped crops from her and ask, "What are we going to cook?"

"I'm thinking a pasta." she looks me right in the eyes.

"Really, you're not saying that just to tease me?" I laugh out of the dead silence in the kitchen.

"No, I'm serious. Do you think I'll just joke around with food?" she puts her face nearer and nearer until I say, "We have to cook first." she pulls back and slaps my chest.

"Fine." she's so cute when she's angry. She walks away from me, but I get her hand before she does.

"Wait, I'm sorry." I sound sincere. Then I peck her at the cheek with my lips and run behind the isle table and put the crops atop.

She runs to me with green eyes turning into shivering blue. "God, Damian, don't do that!" and she hugs me.

I don't mind that Isis' eyes turn blue, I like it that way, and it makes us less different. My blue eyes turn green and her green eyes turn blue. That's fine.

We suddenly slip on the floor with our lips aligned perfectly, and then I hear the door open. "Damian?!" I hear Serenity. "What the hell are you both doing on the floor? I was just going to check if you guys started cooking because we're hungry." We stand up in an instant we hear the words come out.

"We weren't doing anything, promise. We just fell on the floor because I think I might have pushed Damian down." Isis says.

"Oh, that's actually good to hear." Serenity's voice is relief.

"Actually, we were just about to start if you want to help us." Isis goes to her and gets my sister's hand.

"Wow, you sure I won't ruin anything?" she asks.

"Yeah, it's just pasta dough." Isis assures.

"Damian, there's flour at the cabinet in the isle table." Isis tells me. I locate a round shaped handle under me and pull it to reveal the cabinet.

I bring out just the right airtight container. "Flour." it's labeled in the italicized letters. The container is gigantic. The container has half of the flour left.

I put the flour on top of the table beside the crops. I accidentally untangle the delicate knot. Four vibrant red tomatoes the size of my palm, ripened pineapples, two of them, a bundle of long green rods of celery are the things I can only see. "What are we going to do with these?" I ask Isis.

"We're going to combine the pasta with shrimp we caught just this morning, tomato relish we're going to make now, pieces of pineapple to give it a balanced flavor and celery." Isis says like a culinary teacher.

"Oh right, you caught shrimp this morning with Shun." Serenity adds. "You jealous?" she looks at my direction. I roll my eyes.

"Let's make the dough for the pasta." Isis goes beside me, wipes the table top clean with a sponge and puts three cups of flour. "Can you wash the vegetables?" Isis asks Serenity.

"Sure." she gets the vegetables out of the cloth.

"By the way, who owns the shirt?" I ask.

"Connard. He lent it to us." Isis gets some eggs somewhere beside us. I don't know where and puts them at the middle of the flour.

* * *

Chapter 15

Their Past, My Present

I left the kitchen and went to the mast before I saw how Isis made the pasta that she's now making with my sister. I'm with the others drinking cupfuls of water, emptying three water canteens.

Shun puts a new meaning to playing with water. We laugh while he controls the water in all kinds of directions and shapes and puts it in his mouth.

Connard seems to be relaxed. His body lies down on the floor with his arms and legs stretching out to try to meet the mast's corners.

I'm leaning on the railings with a paper cup filled with water on my fingertips as if it's weightless, but that's how it feels like to me.

"So tell me, when did you learn how to use your powers?" Icarus turns his head clockwise to my direction and tilts just enough for him to look curious.

"Truthfully I'm not quite sure when, but the moment you were attacked by those wolves the other day . . ." my voice trembles. "I felt a sudden urge to kill them."

"Damian, I think it's my fault." The griffin says.

"Why would it be your fault?" I ask.

"There's something disrupting the balance of nature in this island, I've must've taken my anger out of you and then out of them." he says.

"Well, that's magic for you." Icarus says. "Suppressing that will of your overpowering emotions you feel, instantly is impossible." he leans to my ear. "Well, close to impossible, but it's possible." And I'm interested in where this conversation is leading to—words that tingle my senses.

I might be able to suppress my powers for good and not worry. Just the thought of it makes me laugh out of excitement welling up in me. "Why are you laughing?" Violet asks.

"It's nothing." I turn to Icarus and our eyes meet at the same time.

"You were saying something about suppressing it?" It's hard to believe nobody is reacting to what was known as nonsense few days ago before we met Icarus. They must be used to the fact that there's such thing as magic.

"It's possible if you have a bipolar disorder—you know, the sudden change in emotion." he straightens his back.

"So meaning to say," I begin to ask, "that you need to shift emotions?" "Seems easy enough." I put my hand on my chin.

My eagerness to know is disappearing slowly into the makeshift of my mind, into the empty corners of my mind but it leaves me a question in my mind that makes me irritated. *Why did Icarus say, "It's close to impossible"?*

He interrupts my thoughts, "It's impossible, is what I meant to say—my words got jumbled up in my mind—because you need to shift your emotions instantly and when I mean instantly I mean almost meeting the speed of light. You might have not known this but no matter how much humans want to shift their emotions to that instant . . . my point is, basically you can't, not unless you can shift your emotions as quick as whatever is fast."

I'm sick of the word "can't" to the point that "can't" doesn't even sound like a word

"Example: When you get angry and you want to be that jolly, happiness will take time to develop. Your chances of succeeding are zero. No chance at all. And don't think I haven't tried because I have and in my case it seems hopeless. I've never heard anyone being able to successfully perform it. Never" He puts emphasis on the word "Never". My hope of achieving suppression it is depleted. "Just be careful and think about the magic first before casting it." Icarus adds.

"Oh I forgot to say to you." Icarus sounds very optimistic. "I've come cross a whole section of Second Souls or 'Offerings of the Beast' in my spell book hidden from both Humans and Magic-users. I used a reveal spell on the book when we were preparing to fight our brother in the ice metropolis because I noticed some of my spells were incomplete. And then I came across a whole chapter of it stating the complete story of the legendary "Soul Sentinels" or the 'Grey's'" Icarus leaves an echo of his voice in my ears. I feel I'm putting on a weird face.

"And it appears that they've kept the souls of powerful magic-users in corpses of mythical creatures that are capable of keeping their power at bay. Specifically seven corpses of mythical creatures bringing them to life because of the living souls, but they still had to contain it. They have to put them in objects—seven of them—sparkling gemstones that represents the color of the element of the powerful magic-users element. This is the part where my brother gets wrong in his version of the 'Grey's'" Icarus pauses and everybody's eyes fall on him.

"Because of the carelessness of the Grey's the gemstones have been stolen by a notorious group of necromancers known as The Dyers."

I feel disappointed. My family's careless. I sigh out loud.

"The Grey's aren't jealous of them, but instead they're angry at them. The Dyers hid them in places people least expect to look, and if ever somebody finds the place they've heavily guarded it." his eyes glitter. "If memory serves right we fought a plant monster to get the stone with the plant insignia to get the emerald—aka the Nature Gemstone—in the temple before. The book does not say anything about what you will be encountering to get the stones for opening an entrance to getting the gemstones with the powerful magic-users souls. The book also does not state anything about the entrance to those gemstones." Icarus starts creeping me out. "I think I may be silly, but I have a weird feeling a sprite is responsible for giving you direction." Icarus says.

For some reason I'm relieved that the Grey's aren't the ones that stole the gemstones, but how does the gemstones affect me? And what's Icarus talking about, a sprite?

"Damian, you asked me that question if there was some kind of altar to put the stone with the plant insignia. Almost the same situation happened with Isis, but she suddenly knew about the stone with the stalactite and that it was the necklace my brother was wearing." Icarus sends his aura dispersed in the air.

Some kind of miniature female human being wearing nothing but a dark blue skirt and a strap of cloth on her chest with a set of white bird wings tries to flap away the aura. She's trapped in it. She's trying to struggle free. She's helpless.

"Fine." her voice so tired and so restless. "I admit. I told them." she confesses.

"I didn't think you guys were smart enough to know about the stones and their powers. Please don't kill me!" she's in tears.

I look at Icarus. His lips dance with emotion. "These humans are going into a path they can't handle themselves. Their future might be decided by the Regales. Whatever you do, magic-user don't hand them over to them." she says.

"I will never hand them over to the Evil Ones." Icarus says. I feel left out in the conversation. Things are starting to get weird. "Right now you pose a threat to us. The Regales will find out soon if you're not dead."

"Kill me now. Promise me you'll protect them for me, the Soul-Sentinels. They're all the Regales need after finding all the Elemental Gemstones" she doesn't have the power to struggle anymore.

"I promise." Icarus sends a dark and ominous aura around the sprite. I close my eyes, afraid of what's going to happen. All I hear now is a squirt of liquid and a faint sound of what I can make up—a scream.

I feel something warm on my left cheek trickling down to my jaw, dripping on the ground. I open my eyes. On the floor, wings dyed crimson and the creature's body standing, both parts detached.

"Okay." the sprite pronounces her last words with hands reaching out for the sky. "I'm done for." her body drops dead, pale as snow. The corpse coats itself with thick, pure blood.

My mind blanks for a moment. Regret of letting this happen seeps through my bones.

What have I done to deserve this?

What did she do to deserve this? All she ever did was help us.

Is it my fault this happened?

Why did I risk the lives of people and creatures around me by following the letter that was sent to me at home?

My life is falling apart slowly. I begin to see dews of tears appear in my eyes that refract light from gigantic waves that start forming in the waters around the ship.

Just knowing that I'm capable of doing so much damage makes me pant, "No. No!" I wipe my tears with my arm. "No. No. No."

"The Regales are far more ruthless than what I did, Damian." Icarus says expectant that I would look at him. "One day, I'll get to tell you what they've done. I think that's enough stories for one day."

Icarus doesn't know why I'm upset. I should really draw back some of the tears.

My hair casts a shadow on my forehead hiding my eyes. I look gloomier than I already am.

I wipe the tears away with my arm hoping I can wipe away the melancholy in me just as fast, but it just comes back every time I look at the tiny corpse on the floor.

I look at Icarus. "Hey Icarus, can you remove the corpse on the floor?" I force a smile, but I know I look horrible.

"Sure, but I think we need to honor her death. Without her we couldn't make it to the situation we are now." Icarus puts a finger on the blood of the sprite, lifts the finger and drags it across the palm of his hand.

"We wouldn't want her spirit to haunt us because we didn't give her the "RIP" she wanted, right?" Icarus says.

We couldn't make it to the situation we are now? The statement repeats itself in my head. It hits me harder than anything I could imagine. Does that mean that this—having to be trashed on the ground by monsters, having to survive in conditions where we put our lives at risk—all happened simply because of that little sprite and the leisurely realization of Icarus? That all of this could be avoided if we hadn't come across them?

I try to push the thought as far away from me to the farthest back of my head as possible knowing that if I erupt now some kind of argument will go down with it.

I'm squeezing my head with palms wanting to meet each other's ends.

The single touch of blood smeared on the palm of Icarus starts glowing for a second and then it's gone. No sight of blood on the palm. The floor starts cleaning itself up. The corpse glows and then it's gone.

A rush of shoe soles tap on the floor. "We just finished making the food!" Serenity says. I look to her. She's with Isis.

"God, I'm hungry." Ross says with his body inching up over the ground, eventually gets on his feet. Same goes with Violet, Shun, Connard, Icarus and I.

I feel lighter than few minutes ago, but now I'm consumed with anger and the anger just wells up in me. "What are we waiting for, let's eat!" Icarus sounds so optimistic. His optimism is infectious. He's so full of joy.

I dust off any dust from my jeans.

I wish I could let all the anger out.

Isis and Serenity lead us down to the kitchen area of the ship.

In front of us, the isle table holds pasta coated with a rich, red color that reminds me of blood spill, on a long, slender plate that looks could serve a family.

Little crescents of shrimp tops the pasta paired with rounds of scallions. Looks restaurant-class-expensive, but somehow it was believable that Isis did all of this with Serenity from every meal she's cooked for us in the past.

"So let's dig in!" Ross says.

"Do we need plates when eating or do we eat it as is with forks?" Isis slides open a drawer at the isle table and brings out forks with their four points glaring in our direction from the light atop us and looks at us with a cute look in her face. "We can just eat it as is." Violet who's beside me says. "Okay then." Isis hands out the forks.

The cold silver surface scrapes my hand to numbness but then becomes warmer each second.

Icarus jabs his fork into the pasta and twists it, forming a tornado on the fork. He lifts it and stuffs the food in his mouth. His eyes say it's delicious.

My stomach grumbles and Isis asks, trying to hold her laughter, "Damian, what are you waiting for?"

"Nothing." I smile. "I just want everybody to eat first."

"Fine." Isis smiles at me and it's as if there's no worry in the world.

* * *

It's already nightfall, almost two days in this unusual island—maybe—I don't know how we got here, but the last thing we saw before coming here—the barrier that encrypts a message in the air, everybody suddenly knocked down on the floor.

I'm still trying to figure out what's up with this place. It feels wrong just being here. It's like everything here is an experiment to begin with. Hopefully we'll be able to leave soon. Maybe I should ask Icarus to make wood again.

Isis is cradled in my arms reading a book. We're in a place people would least find us in the ship, a room that Isis called her "Private Study" from the numerous bookshelves and books in here. It isn't just a room; it's a mini library. Books from her past up to this point, all in perfect condition, stored in this one very room, all in alphabetical order. The room is filled with walls that look like mahogany to me, bookshelves covering two of four walls, a black leather couch shaped as an "L" enclosing a center table, homey lights that are controlled by one switch which also controls their brightness, I could get used to this. We're sitting on the couch and Isis always shifts her position, forming new shadows all over her body that interests me.

"What are you reading?" I ask.

She turns to the cover page long enough for me to read the title, *Hysteria.*

"What's it about?" I raise an eyebrow, but she doesn't look back.

She replies in a dull voice, "It's about an ordinary girl who gets haywire after falling in love with the hottest guy in her school. She gets friendzonned eventually by him, but then it's too late for the guy to take it back because he realizes he has feelings for her and they've created a crazy world in between each other with tears, laughter, joy, etc."

"Oh-kay" I say, astounded by the brief, yet informative summary of the whole book.

"Isis . . ." I start with the thought of the sprite's death present in my mind, making questions appear again in my head. "Were you the one who put the letter in front of my doorstep when we were in Seattle?"

"What are you talking about, Damian?" she looks at me, confused. "All I remember when I was in Seattle was me arriving to walk around the city, you, your sister and your friends showing up to my ship and asking me if we could go to your father's archaeologist camp—and we did. And that's how everything started." she says. "What was the letter about anyways?"

My mind spins. So Isis wasn't the one who put the letter at the doorstep with the round stone and the map around Mellous.

"It was a really strange letter supposedly from the boss of the archaeologist camp saying we can ride a boat to the camp to help look for our father because he went missing." I say.

"Well that's one weird, vivid, anonymous letter." Isis drops her head on my chest and closes her book. "Plus it had a circular stone wrapped around a leather parchment with the map of Mellous." I say. "When we got there the boss insisted that he didn't send us that letter and that our father was accurately missing. It makes no sense at all. At first I thought I was being set up or framed, but now that all of these things has happened it's like this was all on purpose."

The silence in the room teeters my eyelids to drop and bring me to sleep.

* * *

March 27, 2041

Pulsating sounds above us startle me. I'm awake. Isis—on my chest—wakes up too. "Are we expecting visitors?" I question with expressions on my face exploding.

I get to my feet and carry Isis. I'm alert. What's happening?

My feet tramp on the floor out the room and Icarus who's going down a flight of stairs sees us and says, "Get Up Here, Quick!"

"What's happening?" I ask. "Not the appropriate time for question and answer, Damian." he replies, worried "Serenity's been kidnapped!" and my legs start running by themselves.

My heart palpitating and trying to keep up with fast movement, we go up the flight of stairs and to the deck of the ship, my eyes quivering left, right, up, down, sideways, upward, downward, everywhere, looking in every possible direction and angle, looking for any sign of movement besides ours.

"The others are chasing down the kidnappers." Icarus leads us down the ship and to the ground of black obsidian. "Which way?" I'm shouting. The thought that Serenity was kidnapped makes me angry.

My arm where the tattoo of the upside down teardrop becomes warmer and it ignites in a white light.

I put down Isis and her right arm where the tattoo of the diamond is as same as mine. We're both lumens in the dark.

The ground is shaky under our feet and it starts disassembling itself. It starts breaking.

Isis looks at me with eyes in blue light.

"Guys, control your power. Please, you're going to destroy the place." Icarus says, scared.

Dawn takes over the land, the sun starts rising, it's warm, orange light showing cracks on the obsidian ground, only getting bigger from here.

"How are we going to control it? I don't even know if we can!" I reply.

"Too late for that, let's start running, they're so far." Icarus says and the ground shatters when we start running. Everything behind us breaks. "Don't stop running, Damian, Isis." Icarus shouts.

To be honest, I'm freaking out. My powers—our powers jolting out of us, spreading like a wildfire, adrenaline causes my legs to not feel tired in our run, and the air seems so heavy, it's a burden my chest keeps.

Up ahead we see the others—Shun, Cipher, Ross, Violet, Connard—with a pair of people in black ski masks. They must be the ones who got Serenity.

Too much emotion bombarding my mind with thoughts, I bite my lips to a bleed and every emotion gushes out with each drop of blood that falls

I run as fast as I can, disregarding Icarus and Isis, my heart racing to pump gallons of blood and tanks of air and nothing more. I feel like a cyclone, my hair flowing against the direction of the wind, destroying everything behind me, it doesn't feel like it matters that I destroy as long as Serenity's okay. I don't care if I look like a monster now; I just want to know if she's okay.

Fury twists my face, my forehead dotting with sweat, I'm angry, I'm infuriated, I'm irate, I'm mad, I'm outraged at the kidnappers who dare steal my sister away from me.

I'm running for Serenity. Serenity, I'm running for her and her only in this moment.

Serenity wait for me, I'm coming for you. Don't die on me. Not now. Not ever. You're my only relative in blood I have left.

* * *

Chapter 16

Severe Intentions

Anger persuades me to hurt the kidnappers. I get closer to them with fingers clasping to a fist full of resent.

Ross looks back and sees me, "Damian" he says.

"Get out of the way, Ross!" I shout. They give enough way for me to pass through and prepare a lethal blow on one of their heads.

My arm thrusts forward, aiming for one guy's jaw and I shout, "Give Back Serenity!"

One lethal fist served on a silver platter. He doesn't have enough time for an escape.

I deliver the blow. Hard, direct, arm pivots back to me, bones crackling, knuckle and teeth clench together in unison, his body flying and twirling then crashing on the ground, sent flying back one meter at most, stays on the ground. Permanently.

Nobody will ever be able to separate Serenity and I. I only destroy in this moment. The rush in my body, gushing like a waterfall, it feels like nature is inside me. I feel magnificent.

The guy's accomplice is now beside me. He tries to run, but I let my power out, I imagine a vine that constricts his leg and crushes it. It happens. "Who asked you to kidnap my sister?" I ask dully. He shouts and screams and wails and yelps and begs for the pain to stop. I don't have the mercy to stop. I continue crushing his leg until he'll cooperate. The noise just becomes louder and noisier, it's irritating, it's relentless, it's annoying. I want to kill him to make it stop, but I know his noise has a limit. He can't do it forever. I have the patience to wait for him.

I turn around and ask everyone, "Where's Serenity?" and realize that Isis and Icarus are here too.

"Damian, please stop. Let him go. He can't walk anymore so there's no chance for him to escape anyways." Isis slaps me to sanity. I can feel pain now. Pain on my knuckles, on my legs, anger's slowing down. I see the path we took to get here, it isn't broken. Maybe I was hallucinating.

"Well, bravo." someone says behind us, clapping at us like we're some kind of spectacle to be shown and to entertain.

I look behind. It's a guy wearing a crisp, black suit with a red tie, his hair black slicked back, his facial features sharp and no blemishes, his body frame is so still and smooth.

He smiles insipidly at us and says, "Where are you fine people going? And why are you here?"

"It isn't your business." Ross says.

"I have been feeling strange, powerful magic around the area—four to be exact, four strange, powerful—and yet so distinct—magical presences roaming around the area." he starts walking around us.

"Two having the essences of Nature and Frost themselves," he stares as if hungry. (Isis and I)

"one having a mixed elemental magic which is pretty rare," his eyes light up. (Icarus)

"and the rarest of them all and haven't seen or felt in the longest period of time, two with the power of the Soul-Sentinels, one of them having the essence of Nature, the other only their power." he licks the corner of his lip. (Me and Serenity, probably because we're both Grey's)

"What a glorious day! Meeting a handful of the most powerful magic-users of this generation." He continues.

He repulses me. His stare sickens me. The way he stands makes me want to puke. The way he walks just makes me want to commit suicide.

"Who are you?" I ask with a bitter taste in my mouth.

"You don't need to know that now . . ." he stops moving. "Right now you need to worry about your sister. She might be suffocating in that sack she's in right now."

I turn to Violet and ask her, "Where's Serenity?!" and I'm frantic. My voice shaky and unsteady. "She's been placed inside a trailer. The kidnappers that were here right now were just trying to stall us so that we couldn't catch up." Violet says.

I turn around and I find my feet sprinting forward.

I hear shouts from behind saying:

"Wait!"

"Stop, wait for us!"

"Come back here, it's impossible to get her back!"

but I don't stop. I won't stop for anyone. I need to get Serenity back. No matter what happens. I can't just let them escape with her.

* * *

Isis—

I wake up to a burning sensation on my arm.

My body lifts and I stand up.

It's warm here. Warmer than usual that is.

I try to recall the last thing that could've held my arm . . . Damian!

My hand quivers on his face and I get it off him from the immediate feel of fire on my skin.

Oh no, Damian. What's happening to him?

It's more than just a fever.

I push his chest to try to wake him up, but he's not. He's not waking up. This is terrible.

I try calling out his name, "Damian, Damian." and try to shake him out of his sleep cautiously by not touching his skin. "Damian, Damian."

His skin as if on fire, I need to get Icarus.

I run out the door barefooted, the floor giving off an icy sting to its touch. I shout out as loud as I can, "Icarus, Icarus!!!!!!!!!!!!!!!!"

I'm desperate for his help, most especially at this time.

My feet runs along the corridor and then up a flight of stairs, still calling out for his name.

I'm more desperate now. I call out for everybody, or anybody who would hear me.

I'm lucky. Ross, Violet, Shun, Serenity, Connard and my sister are at the deck. "Help!" I call out and they wake up. "Where's Icarus?" I ask.

"What's the fuss about?" Shun replies.

"All I remember about Icarus is that he went out to do something . . ." Serenity says. "I think he said he would be practicing his magic. But I don't know where he went."

"Thanks Serenity." I say. "We should look for him!"

"But why do we have to?" Shun asks.

"There's something wrong with Damian.

"What's happening to my brother?" Serenity gets to her feet.

"His skin is as hot as fire. Which is why we need to find Icarus. I don't know if this is some kind of effect from his magic." I say. "If you need to find him he's in the library downstairs." I turn around, "I need to look for Icarus." and start running.

"Icarus!" I shout.

"Yes?" I finally get a reply.

"Where are you?" I end up on the railings.

I hear shoes that tap going down to the floor below me.

"I'm outside of the ship. Wait for me inside!" he shouts back.

"Hurry . . . please! There's something wrong with Damian!" I look behind me to see if anybody was still on the deck. Nobody. Except. Me. Surrounded by darkness. Under a magnificent sky dotted with stars. I'm below the grandeur of the night, but the beautiful night conceals pain of others, like the pain I'm feeling because of Damian. I'm anxious with the fact that his condition could get worst. I'm scared.

"Isis!" I hear Icarus shout and his voice buries me in a blanket of hope.

"Icarus, thank God you're here." I try to navigate him in the darkness. "Go downstairs. And Quickly!"

I run towards the light that comes from the floor below us starting with the staircase. Finally, I'm free from the silhouette of the sky.

"Isis, where's Damian?" Icarus who's now behind me asks.

"Just follow me." my legs pounce and I'm running through the hall.

I get to the door at the end of the hall and open it. My Private Study.

I see everyone staying as close to Damian as possible either bent on one knee or standing.

Violet turns around and says, "This is beyond any medical case I have ever seen in my life."

Icarus gets a closer look at Damian. He tries to hold his hand that hangs on the edge of the couch and then lets free instantaneously, he turns around and looks at me with a vile look in between his eyes, "What happened to him?"

My hands clutch on my hair and I say, "I don't know." I walk closer to him and my fingers loosen on my hair avoiding myself to rip it off my scalp, "We were just sleeping together for one second and then all of a sudden he starts burning and I wake up realizing there must be something wrong with Damian for him to heat up like that, and probably it might be because of his magic, or even any kind of magic in general."

Sweat starts to build up on my face. Adrenaline makes my heart burst into fragments that run in my blood and my body feels heavier. My throat is dry and aching from shouting. I'm trying to catch my own breath.

"Sorry, Isis, we should push the furniture to the sides. We need more room for this." Icarus apologizes.

"Just do whatever you can to please bring him back or get him back to normal." I reply.

"Ross, please push any piece of furniture to the side." Icarus commands.

"Rodger that." he goes to the center table and pushes it to my direction, "Excuse me, Isis."

"To the rest, please help in bringing Damian to the center. But be careful." Icarus looks at me.

His stare is nerve wrecking. It beats my soul to the pulp.

I go to Damian and help the others lift him.

Connard lifts his head, Shun and Violet supports his arms and back, Icarus and I get his legs. We resemble a body carrying a body.

* * *

Damian—

My legs feel like they're getting heavier by the second, but it's all worth it.

I can see a pickup truck up ahead, peeking out on the horizon.

I keep running and it's close to my touch. My hand extends to its end. So Close.

Finally I get a grab on it.

I hop on the end and I let the pickup do the running for me.

I get in and I pull myself nearer and nearer to the base of the pickup.

Suddenly I see something I don't expect to see here in the island.

It transforms into a lush rainforest. The tall trees breaking and crushing the obsidian beneath me rises in front of my eyes. The obsidian up ahead rises and cracks and then water gushes out of the cracks forming a waterfall. The water makes the obsidian in its way sink to make way for the flow of the movement of water. The obsidian below the truck starts flourishing in green—grass and moss coating the black obsidian—and the air starts getting moist—no, it start's raining, tiny dews of water bombarding on my body, a war on my skin. My hair gets damp along with my clothes. The droplets of rain still keep sinking. They don't stop. It's relentless.

The truck stops in the middle of no civilization, what in the world is happening?

The drivers of the truck get out and are out of my sight.

"Hello, again." says someone behind me. I recognize the voice, the person in the suit that I despise so much.

"How are you able to get to me?" I ask.

He walks towards me with hands on his back, "You'll know more that you bargained for in the future. But right now, your priority is to get your sister out of captivation, I believe." his arms are pushed to the side and I see him holding someone on the elbow, trying to squirm its way off his grip, a sack on its head . . . Serenity!

"How did you end up getting her?" my voice deepens with anger in me.

He pushes Serenity to the ground, her knees scraping the floor of the forest. She screams.

He removes the sack on her head and she yells, "Damian, help me!"

"Oh my. It's simply to die for to see a family reunion come together like this." he says with his head held high.

"Damian." another familiar voice beckons. My Dad?!?! This is insane. He's alive?! Living?!

I turn around to see his face. He looks just like he did the last time I saw him. His forehead having five lines that crease whenever he's angry, eyes like mine, only mine turned green, a pointed nose that shapes a triangle with one side that curves down, his lips always forming a straight line when he smiles, his hair having white features, now fading in color and looks like they're turning clear as glass.

He opens up his arms to me, but I turn around and still see Serenity on her knees. I'm honestly confused on whom to pick.

The guy gets a knife from his pocket and then puts it against Serenity's neck ready to pierce through at any given moment.

The choice is now obvious. I'll save Serenity first.

I turn around and say to my Dad, "Wait here." and then start sprinting towards the mysterious guy. My fist launching itself to his face, but he grabs my arm almost instantly, "Too easy" he says and then launches me to the ground back first. My body is electrically charged, I'm persistent, and I keep going, trying to hit him, but always end up the same each time. The next try he grabs my finger and then tips me off balance.

"This is purely amusing!" he says.

I don't attack next time. I'll use my magic.

I summon a vine to appear under him and constrict his leg just like the kidnapper.

He has a sadistic smile on his face. His lips grimace and says, "This is too easy, Damian. You have to do better than this to get back your sister."

I'm thinking my brain out. It's too difficult to think of a strategy. I look around me, panicking that if I don't figure out a strategy soon he'll kill my sister.

My magic—the essence of nature based on the mysterious guy, but why is that so powerful? And then it hit me. Nature—meaning both living things and non-living things essential that to making life possible—makes my variety of magic comprehension wider. In short—it's the magic of life.

I shouldn't just focus my attention on vines—more so, any kind of plant.

I summon the moss around us to swirl in around us and then I start attacking again. My fist flinging itself to his face, but before he gets my arm I use the moss to get into his eyes. Finally, a hit, my first hit, his streak of defense as the best offense is over.

He tries to rub off the moss on his face, but there's so much moss to go around. He's shouting.

I kick his ankle and he collapses on the ground.

I let the moss rain on him and then look for Serenity and Dad.

Serenity is on her knees beside me and I extend a hand to her. She looks at me and grabs my whole arm, almost pulling me down with her.

I say to her, "We need to get Dad."

She looks at me weirdly, "Dad? He's here?"

I look back to the truck and he's yelling, "Damian! Serenity! Come over here!" and gets off the truck.

We're happy to see him again. We run to him and consciously hug him, hopefully not wasting our time because the moss turrets won't last forever.

I grab both of their hands and start running.

Dad detaches his hand and runs in front of us and says, "Where are we going?"

Serenity moans in pain and says, "Damian, my knees . . ."

It's difficult to run like this, our clothes damp and giving us extra weight.

"Serenity, jump on my back." I say to her. She does and I'm carrying her legs. She holds on to my neck. I'm getting strangled, but I don't mind.

I don't know where we're headed. I don't know what direction we're supposed to go to, there's no clear path to where we're going.

We pass through trees and stomps and obsidian and rocks and more moss and grass and vines and bushes and shrubs, we're passing through so many stuff, I'm unable to name them all.

I see something ahead of us, the waterfall.

"Prepare for a swim." I shout at both of them.

My legs are getting heavier and heavier.

My shoes too damp to be even called shoes

My clothes constricting my body and maybe making it smaller by the second.

I'm incredibly tired.

We reach the waterfall and I put Serenity to her feet.

I look back to see if the guy is there. He isn't. But an extra precaution, I timber some trees in on the path we used.

The falling trees create vibrations on the ground that could be considered an earthquake.

* * *

Chapter 17

Single Drop

I sit down and circumnavigate the place only through my vision. I'm confused at where we should go.

"Damian, where are we?" Serenity asks from behind me. The sound of the waterfall gushes into my ears. I don't bother replying to Serenity. I'm busy trying to find a way out of here, before you-know-who or don't-know-him gets here.

Across the waterfall is a pure obsidian road to nowhere. It's worth trying to see where it leads.

"Serenity, Dad, we better cross the waterfall." I say.

I plunge in the water. Let's see, I was wet because of the rain, but now I'm drenched because of this waterfall. This is going great.

The water hugs me in its freezing temperature. My body's warmly cold. My feet are touching the bedrock. My head is slightly sticking out on the water. I'm gasping for air. I end up swallowing some water. It takes me few seconds to get used to it . . . I start running in the water, but it's tough. It's as if I need eternity to cross this waterfall.

I look back to see if my sister and Dad are behind me. They are.

I'm trying my best to keep up to the movement of my feet. Not only is this tiring, but I'm barely drowning. My lungs compete for air, the other fighting the other for more air. And then I fall into a pit in the water. Now I'm drowning.

Outturning waves splash all over in raspy violence. It sparks me cold and I find myself under the turbulence of the blue that brings me trying to find any sign of oxygen—air. Breath felt short, I swim my way to the surface. It's as if the water gets deeper each second I swim. I'm being pushed and pulled in thousands of directions all at once.

* * *

Isis—

The others are asked to get some materials—Icarus' orders.

Icarus turns to me and says, "We need his blood to do this."

"Are you crazy?!" my words are filled with rage released by me. "You're going to hurt him!" I yell.

He faces my direction and says, "You didn't let me finish. I only need a drop."

A hand pats me at the back. I turn to see who it is—Ross. He says, "Relax. I think Damian will be fine . . . considering what we've been through these past few days? Yeah I think he'll be fine. He's stronger than you think." I stare at Damian's slowly impaling body. Ross continues, "When Damian and I were freshmen in our high school—we weren't exactly close that time—there was this one point where our finals were just around the corner and he fell ill to a sickness the doctors said would last a week and our finals was during the week of his sickness. Everybody insisted that he go home but that whole week he endured the sickness just to finish the finals and surprise, surprise, he became Valedictorian. He received praise and respect for what he did that year and the years that followed . . . point is that Damian's persistent. He's relentless and that's what I learned to like about him—so don't worry, he'll be fine."

I don't know why, but somehow Ross' speech about Damian made me feel assured he'll be okay.

I turn to look at Icarus and I say, "I'm trusting you on this." in a sympathetic tone.

He brings out a dagger from his pants and it sends my heart going berserk and uneasy. He positions the dagger on one finger of Damian and creates an incision in a gentle glide avoiding skin contact. A faint line on his flesh suddenly dots with blood that flashes light to my direction. There's a bowl Icarus gets beside him that he grabs.

Action after action brings uncertainty rippling all over my body creating a tidal wave of anxiousness. I try to stop myself from screaming. I'm biting my tongue.

Icarus wraps his hand in his shirt and gets Damian's hand and puts it on the bowl leaving blood to trickle down to the bottom of the bowl. Icarus dabs two fingers—his pinky and thumb—of his in the bowl of blood and then presses his pinky on his chin and his thumb on his chest.

I'm bewildered. I'm confused. I don't know what to feel.

Icarus calls out, "Violet." And she comes out with a small jar in her hands and Icarus takes it off her hands with his free hand. He releases the fingers on Damian's chest and chin. He closes his palm for a moment and then opens it. A strange aura colored purple floats into the air and into Damian through his mouth partially opened.

What comes out next: 3 colors, 3 different auras, green, red, and purple.

What happens next: 2 auras—green and purple—extinguish the red aura and then Icarus sends the green aura into the jar and the jar mystifies. Icarus gets a grab to his aura and squeezes his palm and then it's gone.

* * *

Damian—

I find a way to drift in the water. I've found my momentum. Suddenly someone is shouting, "Damian, where are you?! Come out, come out wherever you are, I need to end you . . . now!" And I recognize that morbid voice—that strange man. How is it possible that he can still see or get here?

End me now? Does he mean he needs to kill me?!

I panic and I start swimming—swimming like my life is hanging on a piece of string, which could happen to become reality few minutes from now! Pandemonium bleeds in my flesh. I'm getting too tired. Stamina hates me. It feels like my arms are paddling in mud. I'm too tired, but I keep swimming, hopefully he doesn't find me.

"There you are!" he shouts. Worst-case scenario happening right now, everything's going against me right now—stamina, hopes, strength, luck. I'm depleted, but I'm still moving. I turn around to see where he is . . . he's already meters near me. Is there anything to at least slow him down? Slight second decision—fish are my only option.

I visualize fish swarming the meters between him and me and close my eyes to see a more concrete image in my mind. I'm praying this works.

I don't dare to look back anymore and keep moving forward. I can't afford to make a mistake now. Not now.

I hear him shouting behind my back, clamoring in pain and grief and failure.

I'm near the end of the waterfall and I can feel the pavement of the waterfall under my feet. I use my last few ounces of strength to get out of the water and onto land. I'm lying down flat on the ground. I smell the earthy soil. Before I get the chance to stand up he steps on my arm. I'm in agonizing pain. Too much pain, my body feels like one big wound. I'm yelling at the top of my voice.

"Going somewhere?" he asks. I barely have enough energy to look him in the eyes. I'm panicking in tens of hundreds of tones in my voice. I feel confused and scared and angry and anxious all at the same time. I let it all out and violently remove my arm from his foot's wrath. I stand up without trouble; he doesn't stop me from standing. Big mistake.

"We're having so much fun, don't you agree?" he says unhesitant to get into violence. I say in a raspy voice, "Just please don't speak for a moment please." with my fist preparing for a fight.

He launches an all-out assault in one fist vaulting towards my direction. I swiftly step side wards dodging his punch. I thrust my fist and send it hurdling to his stomach and it tunnels deep, inching with pain, intensifying pain, but he's like a mannequin—unable to react to anything by voice or by facial expression. He coughs blood to the ground.

Each movement unleashed, crisp and fast, my punches are critical. Every fist dredges on his body so easily. This power is spiraling all over my body—but this isn't my power.

I'm too strong to be Damian.

I'm too swift to be Damian

I'm too critical to be Damian

I'm roaring inside, ferocity trying to get out, but caged, ferocity bounces off each corner of the cage as a desperate attempt to get out, claws get out and they're slashing the cage, angry, enraged, and relentless. I'm an animal with the instinct to eliminate those who try to get in my way. And then the cage breaks and my fullest potential is released into each of my fist's punch and yet he doesn't scream in pain.

Suddenly someone grabs my arms stopping me from landing a single punch and then power is almost drained from me again. My body fails to do whatever I try to let I do. I look behind me to see who stopped me—Isis. Of all people it had to be Isis. "Shhh . . ." she says. "I miss you." And then everything around me turns pitch black. All I see is Isis and only Isis. It feels like she's draining my energy every second she holds me and then her face gets sucked into the darkness and I'm all alone . . . again

* * *

Isis—

Everyone's left except Icarus and I.

Damian flinches and I'm terrified. I'm terrified to hold him because I know his skin is as if on fire but my body persists and I'm holding him and enduring the pain, but he isn't as hot as before, it's hot but bearable.

Icarus is beside me so calm and relaxed. He faces me and says, "Don't worry. He'll wake up tomorrow, but if he doesn't, just wake me up."

"I forgot to tell you," Icarus adds, "the others are staying in the rooms down here for the night."

"Okay" I say and I've never sounded so sure ever since Damian started heating up. I ask Icarus, "What happened anyways? Why did this happen to him?"

Icarus brings out a small jar from his pocket with a dark green liquid barely filling half of the whole jar and says, "It has something to do with his excess power in his body which caused his body to heat up. Just think of it like a computer—if you charge it too long it shuts down and starts overheating." he says.

"Then what's that strange, red aura?" I ask and his face is filled with anxiety.

"It's probably best if we don't talk about that now. All I know is that it sends people into a deep coma." Icarus stands, says goodnight to me, then leaves with his footsteps reverbing along the hall slowly diminishing each step he takes and I'm alone with Damian in this room again. I hope he wakes up soon.

* * *

Damian—

I'm lying down flat on darkness and I let myself sink into its eternal abyss.

My hair flocks in strands on the wind going against me.

Lights flicker all over almost like fireworks in every possible color and place thinkable and then it's plain white all over and I'm standing on firm pavement.

I start walking for no apparent reason to be walking. I'm looking on the ground and notice something in between my legs. Blood; Lots of blood; Blood pooling around me and slowly covering the whole ground; I turn around to see what could that blood be . . . the boss of the archaeologist camp, a guard, Dad, Serenity, Ross, Violet, Cipher, Connard, Icarus, Isis, Mom, Crissy, all of them having one similarity, dead, piled up on each other!

I'm freaking out and shouting, but nothing comes out of my mouth.

I close my eyes and brush my hands on my hair hoping that the image disappears. I'm terrified. Hoping that the next time I open my eyes the scene will be gone and will be replaced by something different.

I slowly let my eyelids part and I see Seattle in flames, in pandemonium again just like the time of the nuclear bombings. Cars ignited, the streets crinkled in ashes, buildings split into bits of pieces, corpse bodies lying on the streets impaled with a horrified look on their faces, the whole city casted by a spell of malevolence and maleficence, no sign of life to be found anywhere I look, and then I see balls of fire hurdling all over the place like meteors, 7 people fighting against one in the streets. Their auras illuminate the street in different colors. Suddenly a surge of auras mix and then a bright light blinds me.

I wake up . . . that's weird, I woke up. I'm glad it's all just a dream. It's a peculiar dream though.

My heart is racing and I breathe slowly.

I'm on the floor with Isis' head pressed on my chest and her hand holding mine. I don't move out avoiding her to wake up, but she does and says in a weak voice, "Damian." and my body lifts from the ground and Isis' head falls to my lap.

I ask her, "Why did we end up on the floor and how did we end up on the floor?" and she looks at me surprised.

"You don't know?"

"Was I supposed to know something before I woke up?"

"Yes!" she yells and gets up. "You were supposed to know. How could you not know that your skin was as if on fire and you wouldn't wake up no matter how many times we tried to wake you up? I was so worried last night—we were so worried last night! I had to call for everybody's attention just to get you all better!" she marches out of the room with tantrums and I get up as fast as I can. I get out of the door and notice she's half way across the corridor.

"I'm sorry!" I shout and she stops.

I run as fast as I can to get to her and she turns around. Adrenaline fades away and I get my voice to soften and say, "I'm sorry I didn't know."

"It's not that you didn't know . . ." she says. ". . . it's because you made me so scared. I actually thought you would die for a moment there. Because of everything we've been through it's like we've been dodging death so many times that it's so likely that one of us will die soon."

I feel flattered. Blood gushes on my cheeks and I'm hugging her so tightly.

*   *   *

CHAPTER 18

WHERE OUR CLOUDS MEET

"Isis, why can't we leave the island?" I ask Isis.

"Because there's a storm coming, and if there's one thing that sailors should be scared of, it's storms." Isis turns around and then back to me. "Here, I'll show you what I mean." she holds my hand and pulls us out of the empty hall to the deck of the ship, and then she's pulling me to the control room's building where a flight of stairs only go up to the last floor.

She points towards an area of the sea in a grave shade of blue below what I can pick up, gray clouds that flutter all over place, lighting up, dimming down and the sea is at its mercy, submissive to the clouds. The clouds are raging, and with its rage the sea starts its torrential burst of waves.

"That's the only reason why we haven't left yet, because if we did leave with that thing following us we could end up as corpses scattered in the sea." she turns to me and asks, "We probably have an hour to stock up our food, so can you help me?"

"Sure." I give her a smile.

"Great, we should go to the deck, that's all, because I want to test out my powers." she smiles back. "Race you down." she taps my shoulder and starts running. I start running too; she's already gone down one flight of stairs. I won't let her beat me that easily.

There are four flights of stairs; in between them is pavement to get your momentum back from running down.

I catch up to Isis, but then she goes 3 steps at a time. Last step to the way out and she trips, I hold onto her waist before her body slams to the ground. She gets back on her feet and we're laughing.

"Okay then." Isis runs to the railings with excitement. "Ready?" she asks.

"Yes, I think?" I walk to her, suddenly she's spiking water all over the place and freezing it at the same time and I'm left in awe. "How?" I'm lost in words, I'm breathless, I'm amazed, and I'm laughing in hysteria.

The frozen water—it's as if the water is trapped in time, unable to fall down, left to float midair, the solid water glinting and shining and light is splattered all over the place like paint flicked on an empty canvas, only, the paint is constantly moving, crisscrossing, moving sideways, moving up and down and in all directions.

"This is my power, Damian, I am the essence of Frost, I am the essence of all things non-living and cold, I give non-living life." Isis says with her eyes turning blue, like sapphires have been stabbed into them as a gift from the gods.

"Damian, we'll be fishing. The reason why I need you is because I can't sense the fish, only the water. Because you're the essence of living I think you can. Probably you could tell me where they are." Isis goes to me. "Lillend taught me these things if you were wondering. Do you remember that thing about ions that Elemental Spirits have that can be used to communicate through our minds?"

"Yeah, but why?" I'm astonished with how much Isis knows about our powers. I never bothered to try.

"Well I learned that those ions could be used as all of your senses; to hear, to touch, to smell, to taste, and to see. So basically it's like saying that magic is just an extension of us, and the only problem with that is that we can get tired when using magic. The effects of overusing it vary on how much of it you use." Isis says. "In my perspective, there's no such thing as magicians, or sorcerers, we're all just human, it's just that there are those that have capabilities that others don't have."

Isis' perspective on things are so much different from others, they are like eye-openers to so many different possibilities and dimensions.

She continues, "So what I want you to do is to use those ions to sense the fish in the ice and I'll just catch them and put them in the boat."

Suddenly we hear thunderstorms rolling towards our direction, getting louder each inch it takes nearer to us, and the ship is rocking side wards and back and fourth and the water melts and starts pouring on Isis and I.

"What's happening?" Isis is asking, tucking her hair behind her ears and her blue eyes turning green again.

Our legs are unsteady on the endlessly moving deck of the ship. A wave splashes to my right makes the ship get in motion with it, making Isis and I fall down and slam our backs against the railings.

The floor is slippery, the ship is always moving, a storm is coming—just a few symptoms that this isn't going to end well.

I grab tight on the top of the railings with one hand and I'm gripping as hard as I can, just hoping I won't fall down. With my other hand I help Isis up.

"Help me anchor the boat!" she says. "There are two anchors on the boat, so far we've only anchored one. The other one is at the tip of the boat . . ." it starts raining.

The raindrops feel like needles that don't get into your skin, but they melt on contact and make your body feel heavier and heavier.

Isis continues, "the only reason why I didn't anchor it yet was because I didn't think the storm would come soon."

My feet are standing on toes, trying to find stability in each action I take. My heart is throbbing tremors into my body.

"Just keep moving forward, Damian." Isis says. "Faster. I don't think we have much time left before it comes."

I'm dragging my feet across the floor just to make myself move.

The water is slamming itself to the ship and we're bouncing.

We finally reach the edge; only we can feel the boat tilting with us going up and the boat going down.

I'm rotating a wheel to get the anchor going down, and the ship slowly levels it. I'm still spinning it and then it just stops and creates recoil.

"Damian, let's get inside." Isis says.

We both run towards the entrance going downstairs and pass the flight of stairs. Isis turns on the lights located beside the fireplace. She goes just a few steps up the stairs to slide close the entrance. She looks back at me and says, "Don't worry, it's strong enough to endure the storm." she steps down and to the hallway with me, "All we have to do now is wait for the storm to calm down." she winks.

"We need to get dry first though. You might catch a cold." I say.

"What more if it's you? You might catch a fever." she replies coldly.

"Just get dry." I sigh.

Ross comes out of one of the rooms in the hallway and walks towards me asking me, "Are you okay, Damian?" he shakes me and says, "You scared the hell out of us. If it weren't for Isis who called for all of our attention I wouldn't know what would happen to you . . . and why are you wet?"

"There's a storm outside, so we just need to stay in the boat. By the way, have you seen my luggage?" I ask.

"They all just stuffed their things in my room last night . . . so . . . your luggage might be in my room." Ross replies.

"Thanks." I get into the room Ross went out of and I'm looking for my luggage for my towel and a change of clothes. I get it and open it to get the things I need and then zip it lock and tight.

I step out of the door and put the towel on top of my head to stop my hair from dripping torrent water infused with rainwater.

"Where do I change?" I ask Isis.

She points at the room beside her private study, "Possibly there?"

"Okay then." I walk slowly there and open its door. It's dark and my hands are scouring the walls for a switch, and my hand ticks something upwards. The light blinks open and I'm amazed to see, a bed, not just a bed, a king-sized bed. Beside the bed is a closet, a closet made of mahogany. Under the bed, a red carpet. Lights above that resemble sunlight. I'm amazed with how big the ship is. The ship resembles a house made for the luxurious that travel by sea.

I close the door behind me and start by struggling to remove my shoes. I unbutton my jeans and remove it. I lift my shirt up and have it removed—I'm basically having all my clothing removed, and then I'm wiping myself into the towel's fibers before I get into the change of clothes I got in my suitcase.

I leave the room and I'm shocked to see, in thunder roaring in the sky, Isis at the entrance of the room.

"Oh crap, you scared me!" I say.

"Really?" she scans my body.

"Yeah." I say reciprocating the scanning process to find out she has a change of clothes with her along with her own towel, "You need to get in now?"

"Yup."

I open the door for her and gesture her in. She enters and I close the door.

What now? There's nothing to do but wait for the storm to subside and disappear, and I can't believe everybody slept through the way the waves stirred the ship round and round.

The door opens behind me and I see Isis, wearing girlier clothes than usual. A long-sleeve with round collars dotted with black tucked in extremely small shorts that covers an eighth of her legs. I'm nodding, trying to take it all in. "You don't like it?" Isis asks.

"It's not that I don't like it . . ." I'm being direct, "It's just that . . . I didn't know you were into these stuff."

"Well, I'm a girl you know, every girl wants to feel beautiful some point of her life." she says.

Isis stares at the floor flatly, her lips are moving, but I can't hear what she's trying to say.

"What's that?" I ask.

She stares at me openly with eyes gently staring and softly asks the question, "Do you think we could lie down together in the bed until the rain stops?"

"Of course, whatever you say." I reply.

She opens the door and gets herself inside the bedcovers, waiting for me. I close the door from the inside and get in the bed with her.

"Are you okay?" I put her in my arms and she snuggles closer to the center of my chest.

"I just can't get over what happened last night."

"Was it that scary?"

"I got so scared."

"I think you're just lacking sleep. C'mon, be the strong Isis I know and love, please, I don't like seeing you hurt and vulnerable."

We both get drowsy in the bed. I miss the nice, soft, cotton mattress under my skin and the warm, wool blankets all over. We're sinking into the fabric in the movement of the boat and the silence of being under the sea.

I plant a soft, lingering kiss on her cheek and our hearts are colliding in reciprocated admiration. I feel her heartbeat on my body that pulsates. Her skin is so warm and soft on mine, coarse and cold. It's weird how two exact opposites can be together and feel so great together, she's the essence of all things non-living and I'm the essence of all things living, she's a princess and I'm a citizen.

She falls asleep and I'm feeling her breath puff warmth on my fingertips.

My eyes flutter shut and my mind gets light. I don't think of anything, I don't feel anything except Isis on my body. We're under the silence of the sea. I'm breathing slowly and casually nimble. I fall asleep

* * *

I wake to the ship as if struck by a grenade. The storm is too much for me to sleep on.

I sit down on the bed and Isis asks, "What was that."

"Hypothetically, it could be a huge wave." I reply.

Suddenly it happens again and again, repeating in rounds, getting stronger each hit. The ship is bouncing and shaking and moving too much, I feel nauseous.

"That's it." Isis sits down and sends her hands circling in the air and the ship stops moving.

"What did you do?" I ask.

"I froze the water surrounding the boat." she puts her hands down. But even with that, the strongest waves I have ever felt keep striking the boat.

Isis gets out of the bed and requests me to get out of the ship with her to investigate what's happening. I do.

Isis drags me out the door, through the hall and to the staircase. She motions her hands to create an imaginary dome on top of her and opens the door going to the deck.

We're outside and it doesn't rain on us. Repeatedly the wave hits . . . no, it isn't a wave.

Smoke comes out of nowhere, and now I know for sure that it must be some kind of explosive.

We're looking all over the place, scanning with our heads tilting and turning and eyes focusing on so many different things just to find out what/who is causing this and suddenly a fireball starts hurdling towards us. We have no way to dodge it; it's gaining speed too quickly for us to escape.

We're pushed backwards because of the force field, but we feel its impact to the force field.

Isis swirls her arms in the air and drops them forcefully.

Clouds fall down from the sky to Isis' command and they disperse around the area.

"Run!" Isis says.

That one word brings so much meaning to me. It tells me to be careful and cautious. It tells me to move on, sprint. It tells my feet to move quickly. It tells me to simply run. It tells me my life is in danger. It tells my mind to panic.

Adrenaline rushes in at the right moment.

I don't know where I'm running to, all I know is that we're dodging the fireballs that threaten to burn us at stake.

I visualize plants growing somewhere out of the ship that grows quickly to have its everything defend me.

I'm stopped by someone in front of my, and that someone is someone I don't know, I don't recognize him in the mist that Isis decided to bring down. What happened to Isis?

I run the opposite direction and I'm stopped again.

Anytime now, those plants need to come out quickly, but they don't appear anywhere, what's happening? It's as if my magic isn't working.

I run backwards and then to the left, hoping nobody's there, but someone is.

I think I'm surrounded.

"Damian, help!" I hear Isis scream, and then the scream diminishes.

All at once someone behind me puts is hand forcefully around my mouth and I'm trying to remove it and I end up biting it and I'm transported to an unusual place, and I'm with Isis.

The person that placed his hand on my mouth gets his hand off and transports somewhere and Isis and I are left alone, in this unusual place.

Everything is surrounded by white, nothing but white extending to unfathomable lengths. I look up and it's the same, all white.

"Welcome, Elemental Guardians." someone behind us says. It's a voice I recognize, eerily.

Isis and I turn around to see who it is.

It's him. The same guy in my dreams, still the same the last time I saw him, wearing a crisp, black suit with a red tie, his hair slicked back, his facial features sharp and no blemishes, his body frame is so still and smooth, only this isn't a dream.

"My name's Chance. Chance Sautter." he says.

Coincidentally his last name sounds like "slaughter."

"Are these them, Chance?" someone behind us asks, a voice belonging to a girl, another voice that sounds so familiar. We hear her heels walk her way to Chance, and before we know it she's in front of us.

"Cathy Abrahams, is that you?" I feel and sound shocked.

There's something different and off about her now. Her skin is as pale as glue, her eyes stare sharply with her eyelashes dipped in thick mascara, her lips are as red as blood and her hair is put down.

"I'm shocked you remember me." Cathy says.

"Damian, who are they?" Isis looks at me.

"Cathy Abrahams is a classmate in my school." I pause. "And Chance Sautter . . . last night when I was in a deep trance, I was fighting him."

"You remember us too well!" Chance says.

"I don't go by the name Cathy in these premises. I go by Verona, Verona Abrahams." Cathy—no, Verona says.

And I have this weird feeling in my chest that something bad is going to go down soon enough.

* * *

CHAPTER 19

SHADES OF DISMAY

The room's silence is too much for me to handle, the silence is like noise to my ears, noisy silence is all over the room, I'm scared of the silence.

"Why are we here?" Isis demands an answer.

Verona and Chance walk away slowly.

Before Verona gets out of the room I say the name she doesn't use in this place like profanity, "Cathy." I stop, and she looks back to me. "What happened to you, why are you here?" I ask pleadingly.

"Want me to show you why I'm here?" she's asking a question back to me and points a finger pointing directly at me.

I try to open my mouth, but I can't. I try to move my hands, but they don't move. I'm paralyzed. I can only look at the floor and nothing else; I'm not controlling my actions. My knees collapse on the floor, I'm not controlling this. My arms put their weight on my hands and my hands clasp onto the floor, I'm not controlling this, and suddenly I'm feeling pain, pain that intensifies and becomes more and more painful by the second. It hurts too much, I can't close my eyes to try to shut the pain out, I'm left to suffer.

"What's happening to Damian?" Isis asks agitated.

My eyes go teary from the excruciating pain I've endured for seconds now. It hurts too much.

I know that Isis is watching me, but doesn't know that I'm suffering, only knowing that I'm tearing.

My tears get off me and I know that Isis is the one who's controlling it.

I hear Isis scream and I hear a whistling in the wind, and I hear Verona silently moan. I'm out of the paralysis and the first thing I do is inhale deeply.

I look at Verona and her leg is bleeding, but her face tells a different story. It's like she doesn't feel anything. "What was that?" I'm scanning her body, and she isn't flinching in pain.

"This is my magic. I have cognitive influence over the body." Verona says.

"Come on, Verona, we still have a lot to do." Chance says.

Verona turns around and goes to Chance immediately.

Chance turns around and our eyes meet, "Be aware, Damian, Isis, be ready for anything."

Chance and Verona disappear.

"Damian, is that really you?" someone behind us asks to me. The voice is so warm and familiar. I stand up and turn around immediately.

"Mom?" I ask. I'm ecstatic right now. I'm lost with words. I'm laughing hysterically happy. I cover my mouth in excitement.

Her hair shines pearl-like and curles down to her shoulders. Her cheeks are draped calmly over her face and she smiles with both corners of her lips meeting the ends of her face. She looks at me with azure eyes slightly squinted with her smile. Her frail body wears a short yellow dress and she looks like a stolen piece of sunlight stripped from the sun itself.

I run to her so quickly and her arms open up to me. We're holding each other in each other's arms. I can't believe that it's really her. I hug her so tight, "Serenity and I missed you so much, Mom, we thought we lost you forever." and I'm crying. I'm so vulnerable right now.

"How's Serenity? How's everybody? How are you?" she asks so many questions. By the tone of her voice I can tell she's as hysterical as I am.

"Serenity's fine. She's doing well. Crissy, she's been an amazing governess after all of these years." I say.

"How's your Father?" she asks a grave question.

We keep hugging, hoping that she gets the message. I don't want to tell her.

"I'm so sorry, Mom." I say. She starts crying.

Our emotions are all over the place.

"I miss you so much. We miss you so much." I say with tears slitting my soul apart.

"I know, I know, I know, I know." she says repeatedly.

We meet eye to eye and she says, "Damian, you grew up to be such a handsome man, you grew taller since I last saw you, right?"

I can't explain how much I miss her right now. I can't bare it. I start crying again. We start crying again.

"I love you, Damian."

"I love you, Mom."

There's a slight pause to our overflowing conversation, and there's this tension of seriousness I feel.

"Damian, I'm not supposed to tell you this, but Verona and Chance are going to test out your powers, I already know you have the essence of Nature. Please be careful." she says wiping her tears.

I almost forgot about Isis. I wipe my tears before turning around to see how she's doing.

"I almost forgot to ask, but who's the girl? All I know is that she has the essence of Frost." my Mom says, but I don't know where she's getting this information.

I ask her where and she says that she's been eavesdropping on Verona and Chance.

"How long have you been staying here?" I ask.

"Ever since I was reported to be missing in Seattle." she replies. "Now, who's the girl?" she raises an eyebrow.

I turn around and see Isis and tell my Mom, "Her name's Isis." and my Mom's eyes widen.

"Isis? Her mother is my co-prisoner."

"Isis' Mom?" and my eyes widen too. "Where is she?" I ask.

"She should be arriving here any time now. Wait a moment, why do you— . . ."

I run to Isis and tell her instantaneously, "Your mom, she's here!"

"Really?" Isis sounds shocked. She jumps to give me a hug and I hug her back and I'm spinning her around. She's so happy.

I stop because someone appears in front of me, she says out loud, "Isis!" and Isis gets off me to look at her.

She has light brown hair that runs smoothly to her elbows and eyes greener than any I have seen and stares calmly on Isis. Her face is long and elegant with cheekbones sharp as flint, she stands up, ceremonial with a dress just like my Mom's. Isis has a lot of resemblance. Her mother looks like a kind person, and yet an industrious one, and also a well-educated woman.

"Mom!" and they're running towards each other. "I thought you were dead."

Her mom explains how she was cursed to have cancer and then woken up and kidnapped by Chance.

I'm happy for all of us, but why did they have to kidnap our mothers? Why did they have to keep us in here, here of all places? And then I remember what my Mom told me moments ago: . . . *Verona and Chance are going to test out your powers . . .*

I go to Mom and tell her, "I love you" and kiss her forehead.

Chance comes out of nowhere and says, "That's all the time we have to get sentimental."

He snaps a finger and my Mom collapses into my arms. He laughs uncontrollably.

I try to wake her up, I'm shaking her and she isn't waking.

"What did you do to her?" I'm staring daggers into his soul—only if he did have a soul that is.

"I did nothing whatsoever, except put her into a deep sleep."

"I wasn't done talking to her . . ." I look at my mother's eyes, roofed by eyelids that symbolize as doors that she can close shut that just stops all feelings of reality.

Her skin became paler the last time I saw her which was few years ago. I was eleven years old when she was reported missing. I can remember and feel and see and smell and hear the city like it was yesterday; it's an unblemished scene that's scarred my mind forever. Everywhere, everything, having a slight scent of smoke, screams and shouts found on our street every minute that passes, the city's torn apart from the window I look out to the world, that one square window I would look out at only to find out the city gets shattered more and more each day until rescue teams appeared and saved us and the government decided to send damage funds to each city affected by the nuclear bombing.

I let my Mom slowly on the ground and my feet jolt towards him and I punch him all in one swift movement. He doesn't feel anything . . . just like Verona . . . just like in the dream . . . his body doesn't feel pain, it only reacts the way it's supposed to react, except feel. If I punch him at the nose, he's supposed to scream in pain and bleed both at the same time, but he'll only bleed.

"Why can't you feel anything, why can't you feel pain, why can't you be inflicted in pain?" I'm punching him repeatedly, angrily, endlessly, and still no painful reaction.

"That's enough!" he gets my fist and tosses my body in the air. I slam my waist on the cold, white floor. Why can I not feel pain just like him? This is so painful.

"Damian!" Isis shouts and heads towards me, leaving her mother, but her mother runs with Isis. "Your mother, she's with Chance."

"Where's Chance?" I'm looking around the room.

"Your mother and Chance disappeared." Isis' mom says.

I sit down and look around. They must be here somewhere.

I still keep in mind what my Mom said about Chance and Verona going to test our powers.

I tell Isis and her mom about it and Isis' mom replies smartly, "I think they're planning to use your mother and I to force you guys to use your powers in such a way that your powers are the only things capable of freeing us."

"Now I know where Isis get's her IQ from." I say aloud, not meaning to say it to anyone else.

"I'm sorry?" Isis' mom says.

"Oh, I didn't mean to say it out loud." I say.

My eyelids flutter as I keep looking around. I stand up this time, hoping I get a better view of the room that exists endless and I'm finding blindness in the sallowness of the pure white.

"Damian, your mom, look there!" Isis points at a corner of the room, so far away from us.

I to the corner and I find my Mom's legs tied and hands behind her also tied with knots of rope, mouth taped with duct tape, looks like she's screaming at the top of her voice, but we don't hear it.

Suddenly I hear wolves roar behind me. They're running towards all of us, we're running away from them, my adrenaline should be depleted but it isn't, we're running in speeds that intimidate the wolves. The wolves are white with black hair peeking out, they seem too big to be wolves. I think I know what to do now. I have to tame them.

I try to tame them with my magic, I stare into their eyes and imagine them in my total control but it doesn't work. I guess taming them wasn't the right answer.

"Run towards my Mom." I shout.

"Is not that doing the opposite of saving her?" Isis' mother shouts with her voice trembling with fear. "You're going to bring her closer to death."

"Please just trust me." I start running towards my Mom's direction, and as expected the wolves follow.

Isis and her mom follow my lead.

My hypothesis to the problem . . . Verona and Chance obviously hid the answer in the least expected places, and bingo, I find a small brown pouch beside my Mom with small plant glancing at us.

I hope my magic works. I visualize it growing and turning the whole room into a whole forest of thorns. When we get to my Mom.

We reach my Mom and we turn back, I'm surprised we outran those gigantic wolves, and I look immediately at the plant. My imagination and reality is in sync. I close my eyes and imagine the plant distributing its roots all across the floor and then immediately thorns come out starting from the plant, the wolves don't bother chasing us anymore because they're running for their lives before they get swallowed by the forest of thorns, but they're too slow and get slaughtered by the thorns. I open my eyes, and everything in my mind is a reality.

I instantaneously try to get my Mom free. I get the wootz dagger out of the scabbard and use it to cut the ropes that bound her hands behind her back. While I cut the rope on her legs she removes the duct tape from her face and the forest of thorns withdraw to the plant. Who knew that the little plant could cause so much destruction? The room is all white again . . . except for the center filled with blood and corpses of the wolves. I look back to my Mom, all unbounded, but then she screams, "Damian!" with her finger pointing at the center of the room.

Those aren't wolves . . . they're living humans. I press my hands on my mouth with force and my feet are pushing me to the edge of the room.

"The-the-e-e-the-they . . . a-a-a-are . . . h-h-h-u-m-m-an" my lips shudder under the palm of my hand under my other palm of my hand.

I just keep staring into the eyes of one of the corpses, teary, black-pitted, naked, bleeding, screaming, shouting, scarring.

Someone claps at this . . . it's already recognizable that it's Chance. "Amazing." he says with his lips forming an appalling smile on his face, still clapping. "Honestly, I didn't think you could save your Mom when they started chasing you." he stops to breathe heavily under his skin, "I knew it would be difficult for you to kill those werewolves if they were in human form, so I asked them to transform for you. I must say, I feel very considerate right now, so in the future, you should know that . . . you cannot control humans."

I don't dare to look at him.

"It's such a pity that we treat animals and humans differently, isn't it?" and he snaps his fingers again. Oh no. Isis' mother!

"Your turn, Isis." Chance says, and now I'm looking at him. "Don't worry, Damian, your girlfriend here will have the same, equal treatment like you did, only the scenario will have to involve inanimate objects." Chance picks up Isis' mother and disappears.

Isis latches onto me and says, "Please help me."

"I'll try my best, Isis. Let's get your mother back." I reply and suddenly the whole room floor except the edges is on fire, a fire taller than any of us.

It gets humid in the room; I'm sweating all over. The inferno is too hot. Even if we're far away from the inferno itself, it's still hot. The room is like an oven ready to explode.

I look at the ceiling, as white as everything inside the room and at its center—a woman with her life dangling on a rope, literally, her whole body balanced out like she's lying down . . . Isis' mom!

The rope is descending fast, but has to cover a lot of ground before Isis' mom reaches the tip of the inferno, but I don't think we have much time before Isis' mother is burned at stake.

I ask Isis, "Can you remove the fire?"

"I've been trying for few seconds now, but it can't."

I don't see any way of removing the fire.

Thoughts in my mind collide with each other in the making of an idea. I can't find any.

We're panicking, we don't know what to do, and Isis' mother already reaches half of the journey before she scratches the surface of the fire.

Not much time left until . . .

I have an idea.

"Isis, remember what you told me about those ions we use for communicating with our minds? Maybe you can use them to look for hidden inanimate objects that can extinguish the fire.

We're feeling the heat and the pressure both at the same time.

Isis closes her eyes and focuses. I know in my heart that she can save her mother. I just know it. This can't be the end of her mother's life, again. I don't want to see that side of Isis where she has to go through a lot of emotional trauma, again. I just can't let that happen.

We're using all that we've learned with out new, found powers and they're putting them to the test.

"I found water!" Isis says.

"Bring it out!" I shout. We're panicking more and more.

"They're found at the ceiling. There are disabled sprinklers." Isis says with her arms lifted up and her hands open wide. She squeezes her hands and parts of the ceiling break just enough for the sprinklers to break with it. Water comes out just the right time. Isis controls it and then sends them to the edge of the room and to the base of the fire. Just at the right time, before Isis' mom touches the inferno, the fire weakens and steam is all over the room, and now the fire is gone and the water keeps sprinkling all over the place.

Isis goes into my arms as we wait for Isis' mother to reach the ground.

The steam mystifies the place. We've grown tired of the color white. I want to see more that just white. I'm exhausted seeing white.

In the middle of the steam we see someone carrying a body going here, and unbelievably it's Chance.

The last few minutes here were insane and intense, a trot revolving the word "emotional". I'm relieved for Isis and I, we were able to save our Moms . . . and that was something we never expected to do because we thought they died.

Chance stops walking towards us when we can see our faces in the mist. "Isis, your mother, I assume." he puts her down, lying on the floor. Isis jolts to get to her as fast as possible.

I stand up and I ask, "What happens to us now?"

Chance says, "If you didn't know, we're the Regales . . ." and I'm hit by a hammer in the head. He's part of the Regales.

"Is Cathy—Verona part too?" I cut his sentence.

"Yes, she is, in fact, she's even one of the five Elite that rule the Regales." he says.

All I'm wondering now is how Cathy turned into Verona, or how Verona turned into Cathy, but I'm afraid they might end me if I ask too much questions and get on their nerves.

I can't believe that these people are part of the infamous Regales. I never expected to find Cathy here, or our Moms. This is too weird.

I have this one question that will make all the questions I've asked seem pointless, "Why did you abduct our mothers?"

He sighs at me and says, "You'll find out the whole story in the future, but one of the reasons why we did was because we were afraid you wouldn't cooperate with us" he walks around us and says, "Anyways, you four will be staying here for two nights, three days." Chance says. "Today is the first day, later is the first night, tomorrow will be the second day where you'll prepare to retrieve the Motion Gem, or as you would probably call from its appearance and power—a circular opal stone with the essence of Movement, the night of that day will be your second night, the day after that day will be the day you retrieve the Motion Gem."

"And if you try to kill me, your mothers are going to die with me." he smiles at us and his hands clasp and we're transported somewhere else.

We're at a corridor carpeted with brown and walls grayish in color, lighted with a warm orange light. It has that feel of home, but still feels foreign at the same time. With every room there's a desk beside each door.

Chance walks to the nearest room and opens it, "Come on now, this is your room." and we follow him to the room. "Sorry for the inconvenience, but this is the only room available right now." he gestures us in.

* * *

Chapter 20

Cleithrophobia

When entering Chance shuts the door on us.

I just notice now—we're finally alone with our mothers, safe, no sign of danger.

The room has more silence; more noise to my ears, and the room looks vaguely familiar.

My footsteps are the only noise in the room. I'm scanning the place.

The bed looks familiar, the desk beside it looks familiar, the closet looks familiar, the window at the corner of the room, opened, looks familiar.

The wind coming from the window makes my clothes rustle, I remember opening a window and feeling of wind ripping through my body and I now realize—this is my room.

The bed, the desk, the closet, the window, all mine.

I turn back to them and I'm asking out loud, "Why are we in my room?"

My room looks as empty as I left it. I remember hiding my stuff in the closet. I open it and . . . my things are there.

On top of the pile of stuff—my laptop, I get it an open it. I press a button at the upper right corner and the screen is white, then the laptop's applications and icons appear. I'm dragging the cursor pad to the "signal" icon to do as it says—to determine and/or find signal. "NO SIGNAL" it reads.

My room . . . who would have guessed . . . but why my room?

I look around and it's the exact same replica of my room.

I open the door and peep out of the entrance and we're still in the Regales hideout.

Why would they make a duplication of my room?

Chills spike down my back with the way all of this is creeping me out.

I close the door slowly.

My Mom lets her fingers roll on the walls and says, "This room," she inhales the words. "I don't recognize it."

"We moved to another home after the nuclear bombing." I say and her expression is a mix of shock and melancholy.

Her lips quiver, unable to say another word, her body frozen, paralyzed and her feet planted deep into the ground. Her eyes blink slowly and tears start making their way out of her. I hug her as tight as possible, only hoping that it helps.

We all sit down on the bed talking about who will sleep where.

I end up staying on the floor—because I offered—and Isis beckons to sleep with me, she does even if our mothers say otherwise.

Isis and I lie down on the floor and I put my arms around her. She looks into my eyes so deeply and I do with hers. The stars will be jealous of her eyes that sparkle brighter than any crystal or comet or star out there. Her whole body is a universe full of possibilities.

Our lips gently press on each other. Our hearts beat in one rhythm. Our hands clutch onto each other in one movement and we're sharing the same heat. We breathe into each other, each lung filled with each other. Our hair twists onto each other. Our noses lie down on each other. Our skin feeling each cell as if it were its own. Our eyelashes tickle one another. Our two completely different worlds broken apart and we're free at the moment.

The cool air in the room makes everything seem lighter; it makes my body feel like it's floating.

Isis falls asleep with our lips locked on each other.

I close my eyes to the last sight of Isis' skin. I fall asleep.

* * *

I wake up to a knocking on the door and my head pounding. I let go of Isis' body slow enough that she doesn't feel a difference and get to my feet carefully and discretely as possible.

I wobble trying to find balance. I walk towards the door and casually open it.

Surprisingly Cathy—Verona's here in a thin, white fabric draping on her body, a bed dress.

"Damian, can I talk to you?" she asks sweetly, with no hint of Verona running in her body. This is Cathy asking. Verona isn't able to feel compassion.

"Cathy, what is it?" I reply by asking another question.

Her feet tiptoe and her fingers fumble on her palms.

"I'm incredibly sorry for earlier. They don't want me to be kind . . . the Regales don't want me to be kind. I'm Cathy, but my name to them is Verona." she says nervously.

"It's fine," I pause. "but why and how did you end up with the Regales?"

"My magic, they say it's rare to find someone like mine. I can control the whole nervous system, and the rarest part—I can control as much nervous systems without bringing myself to exhaustion or death." Cathy says honestly, breathing deeply.

"But I though all magic-users have limits to how much they can use magic." I'm shouting softly.

"Normally yes, but that isn't my case." she replies.

"How?" I ask another question.

"I don't know. Nobody knows . . . I've been brought here few years ago and the Regales were trying to figure out how so that they could have unlimited magic power. Unfortunately for them they couldn't find out how and all of a sudden I'm part of the Elite in the Regales . . . I'm their youngest Elite, being recruited at the age of nine. They think that observing me at a closer level can make them figure out how . . . in my opinion, I don't think anyone has the knowledge and wisdom to figure out." she explains.

"That's a good thing, right?" I say.

"They kept my parents captive and they're still keeping my parents captive, just like what they're doing with yours . . . it isn't a good thing." she says. "You and me, we're alike, along with Isis. We are just puppets and tools for the Regales until they get the information they need from us. The Regales don't tell me any of their plans so I don't know why you guys are here." she explains.

A hushing wind fills the halls. The place is empty.

"So what are Chance's powers?" I ask.

"Spatial magic A.K.A magic that controls emptiness. Spatial magic's rare . . . those that are part of the Elite in the Regales have a unique power or characteristic." Cathy says.

It's weird how Cathy knows the answers to my questions, but I'm glad she knows. I hate unsatisfied curiosity; the question slowly eats you alive only until you've figured out the answer.

"The other three in the Regales' Elite are: Adeline, Haynes, and Phillip."

"Adeline having the powers of Fission and Fusion or to put it simply, the power to separate and/or combine. She has hair as red as fire."

"Haynes has the powers of Waves. It's self-explanatory. He can control all kinds of waves. He carries a violin with him because he's fond of controlling sound waves."

"And finally, Phillip, he has the power of Combustion, or you could call him the bomber of the Regales. He's devilishly gorgeous. One characteristic that makes him look different from everybody is his heterochromia—his right eye's blue and his left eye's dark brown." Cathy tells me so eagerly.

"Thanks so much for the info, Cathy." I smile at her.

"Be careful when you're around them." she warns. "They can be sadistic at times."

"Tell me about it. I've seen a glimpse of them on Chance already." I sigh.

"Is that the only reason why you're here?" I ask.

She takes a step backwards and says, "No. I still need you to give you something to Isis' mother." she opens her hand and there's a small white pill. "Isis' mother needs the medication. I've been asked to give it to her ever since she's been here. She's told me it's her medication. I guess the Regales need her alive."

I take the pill and tell her, "Thank you for everything. It's fine for you to hurt me to prove your worth to the Regales. The Regales are unexpected so I think it's best to do as they say."

Cathy walks away with her bed dress making her look like an angel descending from heaven.

I get inside the room and they're all still sleeping.

I tiptoe cautiously to Isis' mom and wake her up. She sits down and asks, "What is it?"

I hand her the pill and says, "This is from Cathy."

She gets it and replies politely, "Thank you, Damian."

"No problem." I say.

She tosses it into her mouth and she forcefully swallows it.

She lies down again.

I lie down beside Isis and wrap my arms around her.

The night.

I'm both scared and amazed with it.

I'm scared of the way that moonlight pierces through the darkness as cold and sharp as a silver sword and how it might be capable of stabbing me.

I'm scared of what might lurk in the crevices of the dark, hoping nothing will harm me.

I'm scared of the way people talk about it like the night is cursed, like how vampires and werewolves are active at the time and ghost exclusively appear and magic-users are more powerful—I highly doubt the rumors are real.

I'm scared of the fact that the night hides danger and we don't see them happen.

Otherwise . . .

I love the way the night is so serene and calm and everybody's pacified in their beds anticipating sunlight to strike any moment.

I love the way everybody rests in peace, not having to worry about anything from reality and dreams float above lethargic heads.

I love the way city lights illuminate the night and make the city look like art.

The night reminds me that everything has a fair share of good and bad; positive and negative; pros and cons; optimism and pessimism, yin and yang, black and white.

I twist and play with Isis' hair and fall into a deep chasm of darkness that lives under my eyelids.

* * *

Serenity—

The storm's gone and finally the sky is at peace.

I get out of bed, out to the corridor and onto the deck. Everybody is all up and walking around in fast motion.

"What's happening?" I ask.

"We can't find Damian and Isis!" Violet says.

I eyes prop open and my feet start moving around the ship.

I go into the control tower, search every staircase, my heart thumping oceans into my bloodstream, end up in the control room—not here.

I get out of the control tower and back to into the corridor. I open up all the doors and search each room as fast as possible, analyzing, wondering where they could've gone, my head turning left and right and left and right and left and then right, only to find that their neither in my left nor my right. I'm breathing heavy on stale air.

Not in the kitchen.

Not in the furnace room.

Not in any of the bedrooms.

Not in the library.

Not in the bathroom.

They're nowhere to be found.

I get back to the deck and Icarus shouts, "I can find their magic presence! Get your weapons. We might need them."

I run back into the room I slept in and find Isis' bow on the tabletop beside the bed and the quiver loaded with arrows leaning on the table leg. I grab both, run into the corridor yet again, simultaneously fastening the quiver lace on my shoulder and running up the stairs.

Downstairs is a flood of sounds coming from footsteps. I get to the center of the deck and everybody bursts out of the stairs.

I load my arrow and Icarus yells, "They could be in danger! They're surrounded my powerful magic users!"

I run into the railings and jump over it, I land feet first on the dark ground and start running and sprinting.

Wait for me, Damian, I'm coming for you!

* * *

Chapter 21

Precision

Damian—
March 28, 2041

Sunlight passes through the window, the light scattering around the room and glistening

I blink a few times before I get up, and when I do nobody's awake.

What are we supposed to be doing today?

I take the opportunity to look around the Regales hideout.

I step outside the door and close it creaking.

I'm looking right and left and up and sown, scanning and analyzing and memorizing the walls and the floor and the ceiling. I move forward to two staircases, one leading up and the other leading down.

Each distance, each breath, only for me to memorize and learn the place.

I move forward to the staircase that goes up and find an arsenal of weapons—apparently—and a library beside the arsenal. I don't think ordinary librarians would approve to have their libraries filled with objects that obliterate other objects like books and bookshelves.

I draw closer to the library. The books are so old and they've been kept in such condition that they're not destroyed or torn.

I let my fingertips glide across the bookshelf full of books and get deeper into the library with the bookshelf's color getting darker in brown.

I reach the end of the bookshelf and see numerous bookshelves in front of me that resemble a maze . . . and a statue at the center of the isle that separates the books from my side and the books at the other. I walk to the statue, carved on stone, with six pillars. I see an ancient writing written on the bottom of the statue. The message deciphers in front of my eyes. It says:

> "SIX ELEMENTS, SIX POWERS, SIX ESSENCES BROUGHT THE WORLD, TRANCEND THE WORLD, AND WILL INEVITABLY BRING CATACLYSM TO THE WORLD"

and suddenly the griffin comes out of me. I smile and say to him, "Long time, no see."

He looks at me in horror and says, "Not now, Damian. I sense the Essence of Void so strongly. It must be coming from the statue." he walks around the statue. "The Void gem is a dark purple amethyst in a shape of a prism."

In griffin's command I walk around the statue and look for it. I can't find it. I'm touching the statue and looking for some kind of button or secret compartment. Still nothing. It must be infused with the statue, or I really can't find it . . . but I haven't checked the pillars yet. The pillars have gaps shaped as the gemstones. I find the upside-down tear-shaped hole on one pillar and a message saying,

"NATURE"

and another with a diamond-shaped hole on another pillar and another message saying,

"FROST"

and another with a triangle-shaped hole on another pillar and another message saying,

"INFERNAL"

and another with a disk-shaped hole on another pillar and another message saying,

"MOTION"

and another with a square-shaped hole on another pillar and another message saying,

"LUMEN"

and another with a hole filled with the prism amethyst on another pillar and another message saying,

"VOID"

I get the amethyst and keep it in my pocket. "Nice one!" the griffin says and suddenly I hear Chance's voice behind me asking, "Looking for something?"

I turn around to see him and I say nervously, "Nope, nothing, I'm just very interested in sculptures."

"Hmmmm, I see."

I sigh.

"What kind of sculptures are you interested in." he asks and that's when I start sweating.

I'm thinking of different kinds of sculptures and their sculptors and think of different kinds of words that are appropriate when talking about statues and I organize the thoughts in my head and come up with, "I'm very interested in abstract sculptures that show a variety of contemporary, like the ones in EMP Museum back in Seattle, and each sculpture a different attitude, showing the attitude of the sculptor himself, making the sculpture less 'abstract' if you know what I mean."

"You have such an artistic sense." he says. *Yeah, right, not really* my mind babbles. "Do you want to walk around with me? It gets very lonely in the library sometimes. It's as if the Regales want to be uneducated baboons. Yes, the Regales has its scientists, but what if they suddenly died, who would replace them?" Chance says and his watch suddenly beeps, "TEET TEET TEET TEET, TEET TEET TEET TEET, TEET TEET TEET TEET!"

"Come with me." Chance says while a siren roars in the background and red lights flash and turn in the room.

"But I need to get Isis, her mom and my Mom!" I shout.

"Don't worry, everybody will go to the same place. Our hideout has been breached." Chance says.

"I don't care. I have to get them. Where are we going anyways?" I yell.

"In the basement, while our defense and offense units neutralize the threat/s" Chance shouts back, surprisingly helping me with directions.

I start running against Chance, and he doesn't try to stop me.

I run passed the bookshelves and the arsenal of weapons, going down the stairs and sprinting towards the room. They're all getting out of bed. There's a red light here in the room too with the siren yelling at the top of its voice.

I'm just wondering who would attack the place at a time like this . . . Icarus and the others? No. How can they be able to find us? Considering how talented Icarus is with magic, possibly. I should just go with the flow of things and follow Chance's orders just to be safe.

"Faster, we need to get to the basement as quick as possible!" I get in the room and grab Isis' hand.

"What's going on?" she sounds clueless.

"Chance says that someone's breached the hideout." I tell her.

Her eyes widen and she says, "Don't you think it's Serenity and the others?" as if she's read my mind.

My head is spinning, trying to come up with a decision—to go to Chance and Cathy, or to go to, possibly, Icarus and the others by chance? I look at each one of them, slowly swift and Isis says, "Just think about it. Do you think anyone would go here in the middle of nowhere for nothing but to try to attack the place?"

All of a sudden the ground starts shuddering under our feet.

I hear a sharp whistling in the wind and then an explosion comes to life, shattering eardrums that are in its way. All the explosions are coming from the hall.

The room is filled with smoke, my lungs filled with clouds dyed in fire and gunpowder, my eyes grow squelchy, I'm still holding Isis.

The smoke gets out through the opened window and we can see again.

"Faster, Isis!" I squeal.

Isis gets to her feet, along with our mom's.

We start running outside, the corridor still filled with smoke.

"Damian, let's get out of here!" I hear a familiar voice, one that's deep and succulent and crisp—Ross.

I'm looking around for him but I can't. Someone grabs me by the arm, gripping me on his tough hand. It's Ross. I look at Isis and she's holding onto her mom and her mom's holding onto mine. We're a chain.

Ross starts running and we start running. "Slow down!" I shout.

He looks back and asks, "Why?"

"Because our Mom's might not catch up!" I say.

"I thought your Mom's dead."

"Let's get back to that sooner, but right now we have to go out of here." I reply.

Ross leads us down the stairs and into a hall clear of smoke. I can breathe again.

Blood courses around my body, warm and spiked with adrenaline and oxygen.

At the end of the hall there's a hole going out of the Regales hideout.

Ross keeps running, and he goes running towards it.

The light of the outside is blinding, but I already see what's ahead—freedom.

We're finally out and we're in the obsidian Island, and surrounded by Regales troops, wearing a threatening shade of red armor, sadly.

The Regales troops point their magic at us—they must be the offense unit.

I have my own offense, but before I attack them Ross turns around to give me a small jar filled with almost half, dark green liquid and tells me, "Icarus told me to make you drink it. He said something about it giving you more power."

I twist open the cover and let go of Isis to hold the cover with one hand and I use the other to put the jar into my mouth. I let the liquid sink into me, it tastes as stale as water. I seal the jar and keep the jar in my pocket.

I don't need to visualize my powers, my powers already know what I want, the ground shakes and small holes burrow under the Regales offense unit. Gigantic worms come out of them and scare the life out of the Regales troops. They run away, this is our time to escape.

I grab Isis' hand and start running with Ross on the lead.

"Where are the others?" I shout into the wind.

"They still must be inside, but Icarus' orders was to go directly to the ship after retrieving you guys." Ross replies.

I let go of Isis' hand and tell her, "I'll just communicate with you through telepathy, I'll find the others."

I run back and I hear Ross shout behind, "Damian, get back here!" but I don't stop running.

I'm inside again, I run to a staircase going down and I find Icarus and the others in a corridor, surrounded by Regales troops.

I let plants penetrate the building and let them constrict the Regales troops by ones and twos and threes like gigantic snakes.

Icarus looks back and he recognizes me, "Damian!" he shouts with a smile on his face and the others turn around too to the shout of Icarus.

"Let's get out of here!" I shout back.

I run going up the stairs and back to the corridor where they infiltrated the building, and the others are behind me.

"Faster!" Icarus shouts.

I get my telepathy ready and tell Isis, "I'm with Icarus and the others already."

She replies quick, saying, "Okay, get out quick, there are more Regales troops heading to the hole."

"Thanks." I say and start running again.

"Isis says that there are more Regales troops going to the hole." I say to Icarus.

"No problem." he says with a fireball radiating with heat forming in his palms.

We get out and, not a surprise—more Regales troops.

Icarus launches the fireball forward, only getting bigger and bigger. It hits a few Regales troops and makes a way for us to escape. We sprint into the path, avoiding the Regales troops, but they follow us.

Isis and our Moms and Ross are few meters ahead of us. Using our telepathic prowess I command Isis, "Isis, please block the Regales that are behind us. Use the obsidian to create a barrier."

"Got it!" she replies.

The obsidian plates start shaking and we're running against the quake.

I look behind and find the obsidian plates shattering and getting into the Regales' way. They stop to try to fend off the shards of obsidian. Some of the Regales get stabbed by it, some are wounded by it, just enough to buy us time to escape . . . but Isis is hurting them. Why didn't she listen?

We gain speed and we're with Isis and our Moms and Ross.

"Why didn't you make a barrier?" I ask.

"Because . . . I don't know, Damian. My powers are going berserk." she replies.

I see the coastline up ahead. We keep running.

"Damian, please slow down, I don't have the stamina." my Mom catches her breath.

We start slowing down, and Serenity notices and says, "Mom?"

So does Cipher with their mom, "Mom?"

We stop walking.

Serenity hugs Mom and says, "I miss you." and starts crying. "I miss you too." Mom replies quickly, stroking Serenity's hair.

Cipher's hugging their mom so tight.

The wind of the coastline is crisp and refreshing. Every breathful I take rejuvenates my body, and my soul feels renewed. I'm breathing at ease and for the first time I feel my breaths.

I feel safe now, with Icarus and Isis and Serenity and our Moms and Cipher and Ross and Violet and Connard and Shun—everybody with me . . . I feel more than safe, I feel like I'm home.

"I hate to break it to you now, but we need to get out of here as fast as we can because the Regales will be looking for us once they realize we're gone." Icarus says. He looks at me and he tells me, "You need to make trees grow here. We need the wood for the ship . . . not unless . . ." he turns to Isis and asks her to try to find or make an oil deposit so that we can use the oil for the ship. She nods then closes her eyes, either visualizing herself bringing out an oil deposit out of nowhere, or finding one.

She opens her eyes and says immediately, "There's an oil deposit near the ship!"

She starts running forward with Icarus to the ship. I shout, "Slow down! The obsidian's slippery from the storm!"

I start running too, leaving those behind me alone to catch up.

I jolt, catching up to Icarus and Isis, with legs spreading into the wind, covering so much land.

Blood pounds in my head and all over my body. Sweat dots around my forehead.

I catch up to Icarus and Isis and I slow down and I tell Icarus, "The Regales wanted us to retrieve the Motion Gem, Stone thingy today." and suddenly his eyes open, eclectic and scared.

He replies harshly, “We Need To Get That Gem Before They Do.”

“Why?” I ask.

“Long story short, their goal is for humanity and magic to live “harmoniously”, and their intentions are completely wrong because just thinking about it, if everybody had powers there will be those that will use them to harm, and magic was intended neither for good, nor bad so they don’t have any restrictions.” Icarus makes a fair statement, but how does he know what they’re going to do? I don’t bother asking now because we finally reach the ship.

I look back and the others are catching up.

* * *

Chapter 22

Moonlight Sonata

Isis plants her hands on the obsidian and closes her eyes.

"Damian, do you know where the Motion Gem is?" Icarus asks.

"I have no idea . . . don't we need the stone thing to open a pillar or something to get the Gale Gem?" I ask.

"Yes, we do . . . shucks, I forgot that that mysterious guy got it when we were in the temple" Icarus presses his hands on his chin. "What does that guy look like?"

I try my best to remember . . . his hair is slicked back behind his ears is all I remember . . . and I realize, Chance also has his hair slicked back . . . and he told us to retrieve the Gale Gemstone which hypothetically means he was the one who got the Gale Stone from us.

"Icarus, I think I know who it is." I say.

Suddenly oil the ground shakes and black, smooth oil gushes out of it

Icarus and Isis wave their arms around in the air in a flamboyant motion, controlling the torrential oil. The gushing of the oil stops and all the dark oil is midair.

The others appear at the scene, right on time.

My Mom walks up to me and asks me, "What are you doing?

"We're just filling up the ship's talk with oil." I reply as politely as possible, even if we're in the midst of rushing.

Ross awes behind me, like he's never seen us do things like this, ever.

Isis stops waving her arms around and runs towards the ship, getting into it with a knotted rope dangling from the side. She runs across the railings and stops to a small, silver-like circle just below where she's standing. She twists it and detaches it from the ship . . . not there's a small hole on the ship.

Icarus gets the oil levitating into it, and Isis helps by directing the oil into the hole.

The sea looks like shards of glass ready to rip the ship apart, twisting and turning and jumping and descending all over itself.

All the oil is in and Icarus looks at me, "Who is it?"

"It's Chance. One of the Elite in the Regales." I say and Icarus smiles.

"If only we knew it was him when he threatened us." Icarus laughs.

Icarus makes me more curious. Why does he know so much about the Regales?

I ask him the question and he stares at me with a hysterical grin and answers, "I was one of the Regales Elite"

At that moment everything is mute to me, Icarus and I are staring at each other and the space between us expands, but I still see him so clearly. I'm looking right into his irises and he's looking into mine too. My mind is whirling and I feel like I'm going to hurl.

Icarus' grin diminishes and he tells me, "Don't worry. I'm not one of them anymore."

"What is you power?" I ask, confused. I've seen him throw fireballs and control water and create a glass pane box we used to escape the water metropolis. "What are you?" I ask.

He looks down to his feet and replies, "I'm a magic mimic aka Icarus . . . my magic is artificial." looking disappointed. I don't know why.

I don't know how to reply. I leave my mouth open. "Okay." is all I can say.

Icarus further explains, "An Icarus is the lowest class of Magic, having to copy magic from an original source, they call us 'scavengers'. The reason why I became one of the Regales Elite was because I mimicked magic from some of the strongest sources, and I can mimic as much magic as I can—which normally, Icaruses can only have one at a time. I'm the best of the worst, you could say."

In the midst of all the action there's a melodious sound of the violin playing, I can almost feel the bow sliding on the violin, my ears are obsessed with its sound.

Darkness starts spilling onto the bright, yoke-like sun and the sea looks like a dark beast slowly getting its way here.

The song is still playing, and I don't know where it's coming from.

"Icarus, do you hear that?" I look at him.

I start searching around the place, turning around trying to find it, where the sound is coming from. I can't find it.

"If you mean the violin then yes, I can definitely hear it." Icarus replies.

Isis runs towards us and shouts, "Where is that sound coming from?!"

We hear a scream and a shout, and thunder rolling while the song plays, I'm feeling delirious. I'm thwarting my ears to hear the sounds, but even with that I can hear it loud and clear in my ears . . . the same goes with Icarus and Isis and Violet and Ross and Connard and Serenity and Cipher and our Moms. We're terrified of the sounds we hear. What is that?! I'm going insane, I'm bashing the temples of my head with fists, only to find out that the sounds keep playing.

"BRING DAMIAN AND ISIS TO THE REGALES HIDEOUT, NOW, BEFORE WE OBLITERATE SEATTLE IN AN HOUR" Chance's voice trembles in anger, and we don't know where it's coming from and the noises end and the song ends in a sharp. I'm scared. Why Seattle? Why my home? Why our home?

I look at Isis and then Icarus and then I tell Icarus, "Keep everyone safe, I need to go to the Regales Hideout. We might not have enough time to get back to Seattle and save it. Don't worry, I know how to save myself," And then I look back at Isis and tell her, "please come with me. I need to save Seattle." and she nods as agreement to same Seattle.

I start running towards the direction of the hideout with Isis' hand clasped on mine.

My arm starts burning—just like when I got the Nature Gem, only I feel dark, mellow, negative emotions swirl in me and I don't faint. I gasp in pain and Isis hears me. "Are you okay?" she asks.

I turn my head to her and say, "Yeah. I think I am."

I don't see much of Isis' face in the dark but I know that with her expression that something's wrong. We stop in the middle of the track going to the Regales Hideout

I ask her and she replies, "Look in a mirror."

"Isis, just tell me, please! They might be on the verge of destroying my home, just like the nuclear bombings and I don't want that to happen!"

"There's something wrong with your eyes," she says. I face her properly and she continues, "not only are they glowing, but one is green and one is purple." As soon as Isis says that I'm looking for a mirror, searching my body for a mirror, and then I look into Isis' eyes and I see myself.

My right eye—brilliant emerald green.

My left eye—magnificent amethyst purple.

I'm trembling, my hands, my knees, my head are trembling.

I'm turning into a monster, slowly, physically, painfully . . . only, I don't think of those things right now. I try not to think of those things because I have a task—to save Seattle from being obliterated, not by nuclear power, but by magic, unexpectedly magic. Nobody will see it coming, not to mention that those who are going to destroy it are the best of the best in terms of magic.

"Isis, we should keep going," I tell her. "we need to keep going because we have less than an hour to get there."

Isis nods.

I start running.

She starts running by my side.

The obsidian terrain starts getting coarse with obsidian chips and shards—they must be from when Isis attacked the Regales offense unit, meaning we're going the right direction.

We see the Regales Hideout, lights scattered around the building . . . the lights more focused on the gaping hole Icarus and the others created and used to free Isis and our Mothers and I, and the hole is surrounded by what I can make out: Regales defense unit behind the Regales offense unit based on their formation.

Isis and I keep running towards them and they notice us.

Instead of running towards us they change into a formation that welcomes us into the gigantic hole, which I now realize is a door with a huge hole on it.

We stop running when we come face-to-face with one of the Regales units with a slightly different uniform having both the colors of offense and defense units. He must be the commander of the unit. He looks at me and tells me, "Elite Chance is anticipating both of your arrivals in his office. We are assigned to escort both of you from here on out. Do you dare try to attack we are also assigned to put you two to an immediate end."

Isis and I walk passed the guards and I hear footsteps walk from behind us to in front of us and they say in chorus, "Follow us."

We enter the premises and we're in the hall. The guards walk to the right to another corridor and then left and then left again. I'm about to feel dizzy. I'm trying to work my mind through the maze.

We finally stop to a double door entrance and Chance's eyes meet mine. I'm nauseated and a spike of adrenaline kicks in.

Before Isis and I enter I look around and see four other people.

One of them is Cathy.

Another is playing the same song we've heard when filling up the ship with oil with his violin. His skin is pale and stale and he smiles devilishly kind and his eyes squinting, feeling the music he plays. His hair kept short, wavy, and put back. His body structure is firm and muscular, yet supple and careful not to be able to break the violin into splinters . . . he carries a violin with him, he must be Haynes.

Another is looking at Haynes stroke the violin with the bow. She has hair made to look like fire and her face igniting with passion and feeling from hearing the violin. She smiles mildly with rosy cheeks . . . which makes me suspect she must adore Haynes . . . hair as red as fire, she must be Adeline.

The last one holds one hand in the air with a ball of light in it. He looks at me and my heart is strangely magnetized to him it scares me. His eyes are lustful and calm, one eye color blue and the other dark brown his hair is smitten with silver and gold strokes, pale skin and red, ruby-like lips, his frame I can only describe as made by demons to be absolutely traumatizing . . . heterochromia, his right eye's blue and his left eye's dark brown, he must be Philip.

What surprises me about this bunch of Elites is that they're beautiful and they're stronger than any pack of lions and jaguars and cheetahs combined.

When stepping in I immediately notice the red plush carpet under my shoes, so pure and warming like blood.

"We're Here, Don't Destroy Seattle!" I'm shouting.

Chance looks into my soul that begs not to be noticed.

"All I Want Is That You Don't Destroy Seattle. Please. It's Been Destroyed Once And I Definitely Don't Want To Relive That Dreadful Series Of Events When We Go Back. I'm Begging." I'm pleading and shouting and feeling and caring and upsetting and throwing emotion around. I have never looked so dead serious in my life. The doors shut behind us and the room is silent and mute that I believe I'm not capable of hearing.

Chance smiles . . . unexpectedly, he smiles, he also starts laughing silently and all eyes drop on him. "We're safe here." he says and everybody is in shock.

"What?" I'm asking, only realizing I'm not talking to anybody and then exchange looks with all the people in here. To Isis, to Cathy, to Philip, to Haynes, to Adeline who all seem to be shocked, and then back to Chance.

"We're all here," he says. "and now I can tell my side of the story now that nobody from the outside can hear." His voice is so free and calm.

He looks at each and every one of us carefully and says straightforwardly, "We're all victims of the Regales Monarchy." And we're all dumbstruck. "We won't harm you. We won't destroy Seattle." Chance says.

*   *   *

CHAPTER 23

MINUTE

I

CANNOT

BELIEVE

WHAT

I'M

HEARING.

AM I GOING C R A Z Y?

I FEEL LIKE ALL BAD BECAME GOOD . . . WHICH IS EXACTLY WHAT I'M HEARING.

ARE ANGELS DISGUISED AS DEVILS AND DEVILS DISGUISED AS ANGELS?

IS LIFE DEATH AND DEATH LIFE?

DID DARKNESS TRANSFORM INTO LIGHT AND LIGHT TRANSFORM INTO DARKNESS?

AM I DYING?

A minute passes and we're still shocked.

Chapter 24

Flight and Magma

"Are you joking?" Haynes asks followed by a laugh.

Chance looks at Haynes with splintering eyes and a placid expression. Haynes stops laughing. Chance says, "I'm not joking."

He looks at me and then Isis and says, "Both of you, I'm truly sorry for keeping your mothers captive over the years and instinctively attacking you and forcing you to do as the Supreme Commander pleased. I did everything so that I could survive. I wrote that letter to you stating it was from your father's boss, Damian." And I'm shocked.

Chance looks at Isis and continues, "The Supreme Commander took advantage of you, Isis, leaving Archaea when you had your annual ball. The Supreme Commander disguised himself as your Father and kicked you out of Archaea. He knows that you dreamed to go to what was known as the United States of America so he practically knew that you would go to the nearest state of America which was Seattle and that's where both of you, Damian and Isis meet.

"You and Damian went to Damian's father's archaeologist camp and it was unsuccessful. The Supreme Commander knowing your good will, Damian, you convinced your friends to go with you to get Isis' locket in Archaea.

"You rested at the other side of Archaea—which was the beach and the next morning you found yourselves being chased by a dark figure which was the Supreme Commander.

"He shifted the currents to get your ship to go to the Nature Island and end up with Icarus and then you find the Nature Stone and he sent a sprite to lead you to get the Nature Gemstone. He asks me to steal the Motion Stone from you by threatening to kill one of your friends so that he could get an idea of who he's up against."

He looks at me, pauses to catch a breath and continues, "He puts you, Damian to sickness to give himself time to recover his magic.

"He then again shifts currents to lead you to Mermaid Territory to get you to retrieve the Ice Stone and Gemstone.

"On your way to Seattle the Supreme Commander placed a barrier which stops you from going to Seattle, not unless you retrieve all the Elemental Gemstones, he became tired eventually from exerting too much magic so he used the tranquilizers to put you all to sleep while he drives you all to this island also known as the Stability Island—the island of the Motion Stone and Gemstone.

"He tells us to put matters in our hands and make you retrieve the Motion Gemstone. This is the whole story. This is what's happening. This is the truth of what's happening right now."

I'm devastated. I'm confused. I'm torn. I'm hurt. I know part of the truth of what's happening right now. I feel dizzy and nauseous, I want to throw-up on the red carpet and have the carpet brought to the dry cleaners which will give me time to look through Chance's files and find out who the Supreme Commander is and where I can find him so I can make his blood splatter all over his living room.

He also looks at each and every member of the Elite and apologizes, "To you all, I'm irrevocably sorry for allowing the Supreme Commander to control me in such a way that I could have brought you harm. Adeline, Haynes, Philip, and Cathy," he says. He called Cathy "Cathy"! ", Please forgive me."

Adeline doesn't seem to mind and lets him go easy.

Haynes says, "No sweat. If it weren't for you I could've died out there!"

Philip grins. Weird.

Cathy looks angry and shouts, "Why only tell us now?!"

Chance looks at Cathy in a deep, intense way and replies, "Because the Supreme Commander's powers don't monitor me when something disrupts Regales hideouts and headquarters." And Cathy looks at Chance in a different light.

"Who's the 'Supreme Commander' and what does he have to do with all of this?" I ask. I forgive him over the sincerity of his voice, but it still shocks me.

The Regales Elites, including Cathy, look at me.

"The Supreme Commander is the highest position in the monarchy." Chance explains. He brings out a piece of paper and a pen from his desk then makes an illustration.

He points at the top of the illustration stating, "Commander" and says, "The commander is the only one who has complete control over the Regales."

He drags his finger down to five sections labeled, "Elite" and continues, "The five under the Commander is us."

He again drags his finger down to multiple sectors labeled, "Intel," "Defense," "Offense," "Pacify," and "Neutral" He continues, "Each of us Elite are assigned to one major sector. The sectors are scattered around the globe and the reason why us Elite are not in our sectors is because of safety precautions." And the illustration ends there with the edge of the paper crumpled and torn and folded.

"The Supreme Commander has the ability to kill us within seconds because we're part of the Regales." Haynes says.

"Is there even a way to stop the all-knowing, all-powerful Supreme Commander?" Isis asks.

I look at their faces, clueless . . . except Chance.

Chance corrects Isis, "He didn't expect the Regales hideout to be infiltrated."

Chance stands and looks at Isis with dilated eyes. He replies, "None of us can do it. We can't, or else he would kill us." Looks at me. "But you can. You can destroy him, Damian, Isis, you can destroy him, along with your friends."

"Then how?" I'm asking. "How do we 'destroy' him?"

All eyes fall on Chance, again. He opens his mouth and his lips bobble up and down creating words that will change everything. I nod in reply.

All of a sudden someone knocks on the door and says, "Sir Chance, The Supreme Commander will be here in an hour to personally set up his magic on the property. He would also like to remind you that the Motion Gemstone is in the hands of Damian. Time is of the essence, sir. Please hurry."

Everybody is standing tall, stiff, and alert. I feel the adrenaline coursing through our bloodstreams and the oxygen in the room is tense.

Chance walks up to the door, opens it, and asks the guards, "Is it still dark outside?"

One word, one meaning, one chance, "Yes!"

"Then please step aside." Chance turns around. "We need to retrieve that Motion Gemstone and bring Damian and Isis back to their boat before the Supreme Commander gets here all in one hour, we need all the help we can get." He stares at me. "Hold my hand." I do as told and Isis holds my hand and Cathy holds her hand and Haynes holds her hand and Adeline holds his hand and Philip holds her hand, we are chained by a common enemy—The Supreme Commander. "Hold on tight." Chance says and we're moving at the speed of darkness. We get out of the hideout in a matter of seconds. We're circling around the island and we stop . . . at the foot of a volcano . . . at the foot of a volcano?

We take our first steps and Chance instantaneously says, "Run." pointing at the entrance into the volcano. Automatically we start running as if running was the only thing we had ever done in our lives. We reach the entrance and here is where the obsidian is as black as ebony and as smooth as powder.

Chance runs up a few rocks and into a whole different world. We follow him and we're at the base of the volcano. A bubbling magma pit full of rock stilettoes at the center, igniting colors of orange and red, radiating with scorching and singeing heat. Immediately my face starts dotting with sweat.

"Adeline, freeze all particles in the area." Chance orders.

"Got it!" she says, putting her hands on the magma and closing her eyes. She shouts briefly and a blue aura circles around her and starts beating all the way up to the volcanoes roof. Suddenly the ground starts shaking and from the magma a black creature ascends from the frozen particles. It's covered with magma and slowly the magma drops to the ground and hardens. It roars and starts spewing fire all over the ground.

Teeth gritting forward and eyes glowing extreme red, it has white horns that erect up. Its neck waves down with a white, round stone at the epicenter of an golden amulet—the Motion Gemstone—lacing a loop to its body covered in scales and wings that spread outward, it's gigantic, it's an obnoxiously huge creature that I can describe as a dragon. This isn't good.

In between the golden amulet of the beast that locks the amulet in place is a gaping hole that fits the Motion Stone.

I shout at Chance, "Where's the Motion Stone?"

He replies, "It's with me!"

"Toss it to me! I know where the Motion Gemstone is!"

"Okay" he replies.

He flings it towards me and my arms jump up to grab it.

I can't use my magic so I can't do anything to help except get the Motion Gemstone.

Adrenaline courses in my veins and I'm sweating pools.

I start running towards the dragon only to realize he's coming after me. I run back and around and I have no clue where I'm going.

I see everyone surrounded by colored auras spinning pinwheels all over the place, the auras spiking the walls and everything it touches. The dragon is still after me. I'm running for my life. Fire is being shot at me, ricocheting all over the ground. The fire touches one of the pins of aura and it bombards. Boom.

Smoke fills the base of the volcano and the dragon is pushed back.

Haynes grabs my arm and drags me out of the base of the volcano. The place starts booming in so many different directions. Lights puncture the smoke in different ways. My eyes can't keep up with the lights and smoke and action going on. I'm breathing heavily and my heart's racing.

"What's going on, Haynes?" I ask as he drops me at the foot of the volcano, outside, exposed to the darkness. I see everybody outside too.

"We need that dragon dead." he replies.

My eyes widen and I reply as quick as possible, "We shouldn't! The Motion Gemstone is attached to the amulet it was wearing!"

His eyes widen too and he lets go of me.

I stand as quick as possible and get in one more time. Suddenly the inside of the volcano is brattling and then crumbling. I get out as quick as possible, embracing the darkness.

We're outside and watching the volcano self-destruct. Boom! The dragon is back for another fight.

Out here I can use my magic.

I visualize walls and walls of plant growing out of the ground. The ground under me crushing each other and comes out the plant walls, elevating me to meet with the dragon's face, the plant wall as firm as concrete.

We're looking at each other in the eye and I throw a punch into it.

It growls and its slobber is all over me.

I let the plants slowly descend me to the firm ground and then go after the dragon. It's useless. The dragon burns my plants in hellfire.

"Distract him for me!" I'm yelling for help.

I'm running again, with the Motion Stone at my grasp. I'm clutching onto it so tight, I forget the wound I got from the

Mermaid Territory on my palm, it starts opening again and it bleeds.

My hand is thumping, but I can't let go of the stone, not now, not when this is the most important task I've ever had so far!

I'm gripping onto the stone so hard it's like it's working its way into my flesh. I shout in pain and terror.

The dragon is shooting fireballs at me, it's relentless. I'm guessing he wants the Motion Stone, but I can't let him have it.

I hear music . . . from the violin, throwing high-pitched sounds in the air almost like a thousand birds chirping at the same time.

I look back and the dragon is retreating from the sound and not chasing me.

I see them spinning auras around and coating the dragon as it tries to run away. It then starts flying. Ascending and descending, clueless on where to go, just wanting the noise to stop.

They try coating the dragon again with the auras, the mixed auras. It's so beautiful, just like a personal aurora show, shifting with colors of red and purple and pink and blue and indigo and yellow and then it detonates with the dragon in the blanket of colors. It's mesmerizing.

The dragon falls down headfirst and it feels like experiencing the nuclear bombing again.

The wind of the fall incursions our bodies and the impact of it on our bodies are like being pushed by a car. I naturally put my arm in front of my face to stop crumbs of obsidian from getting into my eyes and close my eyes. The sonic winds push me far enough to catch me off balance with my back bound to the ground and the winds stop.

"Let's hurry!" I shout.

We all stand up slowly.

We walk towards the dragon slowly, letting our shoes drag on the obsidian and the sound of it is the only thing we hear in the darkness, in the emptiness, after the fear and suffering, after all we've done to get this far.

I'm breathing air into the deepest parts of my body, slowly, carefully, abundantly, and orderly.

The atmosphere around me is tense and it feels wrong breathing in it.

Gradually we meet and the atmosphere changes when Philip laughs.

"We did it." Haynes says like he's never accomplished anything, ever, he laughs too.

Isis sighs in gratitude.

"Thank you, all of you." I say with appreciativeness. I smile.

"We didn't do anything yet. We still have to bring you to your ship." Philip's eyes glitter with moonlight

We lean nearer to the dragon, affix the bloody Motion Stone on the hole and push it into the amulet.

* * *

Chapter 25

UNTOLD

The amulet dismantles to the sound of a click, releasing the white gemstone that Chance insists is called the "Motion Gemstone"

Chance gets it and tells me, "Keep it. The Supreme Commander will think you got it."

He hands it to me and I ask, "What happens to all of you after the Supreme Commander gets here?"

"He'll keep us captive again and force us to be unkind, so you can't talk to us formally like this after he's here so better ask us and tell us whatever you need and can before he's here." He looks at his watch. "We still have five minutes so spill whatever questions and side comments you have."

I ask, "Where do we go from here?"

"If you remember there's a map of Mellous that was part of the things you received when you were still in Seattle. I attached it just in case you probably got lost.

"Mellous was personally put together by the Supreme Commander himself so the Elemental Gemstones are around Mellous.

"Ask Icarus to cast a reveal spell on the map and the map will reveal the places you need to go." Chance starts running and shouts, "We better get going now. I don't have enough stamina to pull-off another transportation from here to your ship and then back to our hideout."

My legs jolt forward with the others.

Chance shouts again, "Cathy, Haynes, Philip, Adeline, get back to the hideout. I'll catch up, but I have to escort Damian and Isis back to their ship."

"Rodger that!" Haynes shouts back at Chance and we separate ways. "See you someday, Damian, Isis!"

I look back at them and Haynes waves at us. We wave back.

The Elite are surprisingly not what I thought they were; sadistic, sociopathic, egotistical—in fact, they're the opposite of what I thought about them. They're as human as we are. They're wired with the same human emotions as we do. I need to free them.

"What will happen after we gather all the Elemental Gemstones and why does the Supreme Commander want them so much?" I throw another question to Chance while sprinting.

"After you gather the Elemental Gemstones the Supreme Commander himself will get it from you. I don't know how he will, but he will." Chance takes substantial breaths to continue running and talking. "This is just my hypothesis, but I think by gathering all the Elemental Gemstones he has the power to give magic to everybody, accomplishing the goal of the Regales, 'To make humanity and magic live harmoniously'" he took the words out of Icarus' mouth. ". . . which is a belief that will cause more destruction than harmony. Icarus opened my eyes to realizing that the Regales goal is risky. He . . ." I cut him and ask another question, "Why couldn't you quit the Regales like Icarus did?"

The wind flocks and brings our hair to life. The temperature suddenly drops dead cold.

Chance replies, "Because by the time Icarus quit the Supreme Commander realized that it would be risky for a Regales member, most especially an Elite, to quit because those who quit have the ability to leak important and classified information to anyone, thus threatening the existence of the Regales.

"Icarus' head is worth more than you think. Bounty hunters are looking for him and trying to kill him for the bounty he's worth. From what I hear his bounty is worth literally a ton of silver." he says.

I swear I'm going to bring down the Supreme Commander and force him to let go of all the Regales, even if it's the last thing I do. Getting the Elemental Gemstones now serve as a double purpose—to bring us home and free the Regales members.

I ask one last question, "Why can't the Supreme Commander gather the Elemental Gemstones himself?"

Chance's eyes light up with fire and replies after a long pause, "Because your father, Damian, died to put a curse on the Regales members, past, present, and future, who are willing to do anything in their power to get hold of the Elemental Gemstones' powers."

Those words impale my heart. My Father's dead.

Finally after all the running and questions and answers we can see the ship with lights I've never known turning on and the ship looks as if darkness never existed on it.

I look eye-to-eye with Chance and tell him, "I thought you were a bad person when I first met you . . ." and we both laugh our hearts out. ". . . but now I see that you're totally different from what I thought you really were. Thank you for everything."

Chance looks forward and says, "I will never forget you, Damian, Isis, even if I have wronged and hurt you two, both of you still have the compassion to forgive me. I am obliged to have both of you forgive me." and he says.

The thought that Chance, Cathy, all the Elite, all the Regales members have to stay in the Regales hideout, stay in bastille, stay being imprisoned, flocking like birds in a cage desperate for freedom, is sickening.

"Damian, Isis, I have one more thing I need to tell both of you." Chance says slowly. "I need to keep your mothers in the Regales hideout so that the Supreme Commander will not suspect anything."

I clench onto Isis' hand and tell her, "We need to free them," with tears dwindling down and off my face, "and letting them keep our mothers in there for a while will help free all of them."

The untold secrets are now told.

Secrets are like the way we're running now: eager.

Eager to get out.

Eager to be heard.

Eager to be kept.

Eager to be told and untold again and again, now and forevermore.

* * *

Acknowledgements

To God, firstly, this book is embedded on His words because He's given me the perseverance and the wisdom to write this book through all the post-dramatic stress from schooling and oodles of school works and basically just being in high school.

To my parents, for their unfathomable support, this book wouldn't be made possible if it weren't for them. I'm forever indebted to them.

To Partridge for their perseverance, for turning my words into something incredible. To Shelly, for sticking with me throughout this journey and informing me about everything. To Marlene who has encouraged me with her kind and heartwarming words.

To my friends who have stuck by me and encouraged me all throughout.

To my readers for choosing this book out of all the books out there. For whatever reason you chose my book, thank you. I hope you enjoyed the experience as much as I did writing it. I can't thank you enough. This book is just the start, so until the next book.

Hugs and goodbyes, best regards

-David

THE FATALITY OF THE SITUATION CONTINUES
IN THE ENCHANTING SEQUEL:
CATACLYSM

Chapter 1

Darkness Tears

Isis cries.

Serenity cries.

Cipher cries.

I'm bound to cry any moment now, but before I do I stay strong for Serenity because staying strong is the only choice I have left.

Our mothers are gone.

Chance is gone with them.

Cathy is stuck with them yet again.

The Regales Elite are stuck under the reign of the Supreme Commander.

The Regales themselves are stuck under the reign of the Supreme Commander.

I remember Chance's last words before getting our mothers beckon to me loudly and devastatingly, "I will never forget you, Damian, Isis, even if I have wronged and hurt you two, both of you still have the compassion to forgive me. I am obliged to have both of you forgive me. This is where we part ways. Until we are free, we will unite again."

Until we are free, we will unite again.

We will free them, we will unite again.

My tears dangle from a string. The string snaps.

Tears stream down my face like raindrops desperate to touch virgin ground in the desert.

I plant my face in Serenity's shoulder and shout a gentle sob.

The darkness conceals feelings, but the light reveals it, the ship's lights reveal my emotions. My emotions have nowhere to hide. My emotions are bare and raw to the light, but clothed in darkness. My emotions put on a strip-tease to the light and the light seems evil now.

I can't stop crying, it's too unbearable.

My father died protecting the Elemental Gems.

My once-dead-to-us mother has to go back to a cage also known as the Regales Hideout.

All I feel now is tragedy.

Love is a tragedy just inevitable to escape.

Serenity watches my lips quiver with grief, nothing more, nothing less, just grief, all grief, pure grief.

I feel the tears sink into the deepest parts of my skin and ripping my soul apart like acid.

There's a fire inside me flourishing darkness. Instead of it radiating with heat, it radiates darkness and frost.

Everybody around me is scared. Scared of me crying? No. Scared that they don't know how to make it stop? Yes. I don't know how to stop myself. They don't know how to stop me.

My hands are numb with the cold.

The ocean under me rush and rock me and I can hear it telling me, "Hush, hush."

I try stopping myself, I try my best, I hold back some tears.

I lift my face and stare into Isis, her eyes drowned with tears, I tell her, "I'm fine."

She looks at me and her face is shrouded with reality, reality that all of this is real and we're not dreaming.

The tears that stream down and the pain I feel remind me that all of these things are real.

Magic.

Elemental Gems.

Mythical creatures.

The Regales Monarchy.

Another soul besides ours inside us.

A mortal enemy—the Supreme Commander.

Mothers taken hostage.

Fathers dying.

Regales members forced to do things they unwillingly do.

All of it—as real as air.

Even if we don't see the magic we feel it—just like air.

Isis, Icarus, Serenity, Cipher, Violet, Connnard, Shun, and Ross now know everything. We all have something to fight for and we're all willing to do whatever it takes to get it.

"Okay." Isis says halfhearted.

I remind her, "We need to free them."

We need to free our mothers.

We need to free Chance.

We need to free Cathy.

We need to free Haynes, Philip, and Adeline.

We need to free the Regales.

We need to free Mellous.

We need to free the world.

We need to put an end to the Supreme Commander and we know his weakness.

* * *

DAVID PADDIT

Is a 14-year old student, currently residing in Baguio City, a small city overpopulated with people and pine trees that has a fair share of sunshine and rainfall, studying in the prestigious University of Baguio Science High School, who started writing at the age of 11 as a diversion from all the post-dramatic stress of school. He tries his best to juggle homework, reading, and writing. *Enigma* is his first book.